# THE
# DARLING DAHLIAS
## AND THE
# RED HOT POKER

# THE
# DARLING DAHLIAS
## AND THE
# RED HOT POKER

*Susan Wittig Albert*

PERSEVERO PRESS

Publisher's Cataloging-in-Publication data

Names: Albert, Susan Wittig, author.
Title: The Darling Dahlias and the Red Hot Poker / Susan Wittig Albert.
Series: Darling Dahlias
Description: Bertram, TX: Persevero Press, 2022.
Identifiers: ISBN 978-1-952558-17-7 (hardcover) | 978-1-952558-18-4
(paperback) | 978-1-952558-19-1 (ebook)
Subjects: LCSH Women gardeners--Fiction. | Gardening--Societies,
etc.--Fiction. | Long, Huey Pierce, 1893-1935--Fiction. | Depressions-
-1929--United States--Fiction. | Nineteen thirties--Fiction. | Murder--
Investigation--Fiction. | Alabama--Fiction. | Historical fiction. | Mystery
fiction. | BISAC FICTION / Mystery & Detective / General | FICTION /
Mystery & Detective / Women Sleuths | FICTION / Mystery & Detective /
Historical | FICTION / Mystery & Detective / Cozy
Classification: LCC PS3551.L2637 D37 2022 | DDC 813.54--dc23

Each of us is born with a box of matches inside us.

Laura Esquivel
*Like Water for Chocolate*

We have organized a society, and we call it "Share Our Wealth Society," a society with the motto "every man a king." Every man a king, so there would be no such thing as a man or woman who did not have the necessities of life. Every man to eat when there is something to eat; all to wear something when there is something to wear. That makes us all a sovereign.

Huey P. Long
Radio Address
February 23, 1934

October 1935
The Darling Dahlias Clubhouse and Gardens
302 Camellia Street
Darling, Alabama

Dear Reader,

We realize that this book comes hot on the heels of our latest book about the Voodoo Lily. But things have been a little heated around Darling in the past few months and it seems like there's a lot to tell. Mrs. Albert invited us to sit down, take deep breaths, and try to put it all together for you so we wouldn't forget what happened, which was altogether quite remarkable and which got connected to an even more remarkable happening over in Baton Rouge, Louisiana.

It started with a little bonfire and went on to bigger and more spectacular blazes, while the citizens of our little town slept with one eye open and kept glancing over their shoulders and got more and more scared and suspicious as the weeks went by. Of course, it didn't help that the Hot Dog fire chief election went off the rails the way it did, and that somebody got elected who didn't have the least idea in his head of how to put out a fire and didn't care to learn. There was an arsonist in our little town, bound, bent, and determined to burn us down to the ground. It was the only thing we talked about. It was the only thing we thought about.

Well, except for the exciting news about Senator Huey P. Long making a campaign stop in Darling, which isn't something that happens every day of the week.

Or the heartwarming news that the Magnolia ladies' corner garden of red hot pokers, sunny orange dahlias, hot pink cosmos, fire-red salvia, and artemisia won the August garden prize.

*Or—when we found out about it later—the shocking news about Mr. Ryan Nichols. But the least said about that, the better, for even though he was a Yankee, one or two of us were really quite smitten.*

*And then, of course, there was . . . but Mrs. Albert thinks we should save that for our story, so we'll just leave it there.*

*As you may know, we like to name our books after a plant that seems to . . . well, carry the message, so to speak. Sometimes that's a challenge, but with this book, we knew right away that we wanted to call it* The Darling Dahlias and the Red Hot Poker. *Of course, Miss Rogers (our Darling librarian) strongly suggested* The Darling Dahlias and the Kniphofia Uvaria, *but we were afraid it missed the point. We're told that red hot pokers come from South Africa, but they're right at home in Darling gardens. We're sure they'll be at home in yours, too—as long as their feet don't get wet, which puts their fire out, so to speak.*

*As you know if you've been reading our books, the Dahlias are a garden club and our members believe in the power of gardens to keep us steady and give us hope in difficult times. Times like now, for instance, when this Great Depression—like the War to End All Wars and the terrible flu pandemic of 1918, which killed so many people—is still causing so much trouble for so many. Our big vegetable garden feeds lots of Darling folk who are down on their luck, and the flower gardens we tend around town remind us that natural beauty is a balm for the spirit. We're sure you'll agree that without these, life would be pretty ugly and grim, especially when somebody you know decides to start burning down your town.*

*Thank you for reading our book. Thank you, too, for the cards and letters and the packets of garden seed and the recipes you've been sending. We share them with our Darling friends, who appreciate them as much as we do.*

*Sincerely,*
*The Darling Dahlias*

# THE DARLING DAHLIAS
# CLUB ROSTER

## Fall 1935

THE CLUB TAKES ITS NAME FROM MRS. DAHLIA BLACKSTONE, founder and chief benefactress. Mrs. Blackstone, who died in 1930, gave the club her house at 302 Camellia Street, one block west and one block south of Darling's courthouse square. Now renovated and used as the Dahlias' clubhouse, the Blackstone house has a flower garden in the back and a large vegetable garden in the adjoining lot. The flowers brighten the lives of Darling shut-ins, and the vegetables help feed Darling's needy.

CLUB OFFICERS

**Elizabeth Lacy**, president. Garden columnist for the *Darling Dispatch*, author of a just-published novel and assistant in the law office of attorney Benton Moseley.

**Ophelia Snow**, vice president and secretary. Works for the Federal Writers' Project. Wife of Darling's mayor, Jed Snow, owner of Snow's Farm Supply. Teenage children: Sam and Sarah.

**Verna Tidwell**, treasurer. Cypress County clerk and treasurer. A widow, Verna lives with her beloved Scotty, Clyde. She goes out with Alvin Duffy, the president of the Darling Savings and Trust. Her passion: reading mysteries.

**Myra May Mosswell**, communications secretary. Co-owner of the Darling Telephone Exchange and the Darling Diner with her partner, Violet Sims. Myra May and Violet live in the flat over the diner with their adopted daughter, Cupcake.

CLUB MEMBERS

**Earlynne Biddle**, co-owner (with Mildred Kilgore) of The Flour Shop, a bakery on the Courthouse Square, and current president of the local Share Our Wealth Club. Married to Henry Biddle, the manager at the Coca-Cola bottling plant. One son, Benny, comanager of radio station WDAR.

**Bessie Bloodworth**, owner of Magnolia Manor, a boardinghouse for genteel elderly ladies. Bessie is Darling's local historian and knows whose skeletons are hidden in whose closets.

**Fannie Champaign**, noted milliner and proprietor of Champaign's Darling Chapeaux. Married to Charlie Dickens, editor, publisher, and owner of the *Darling Dispatch*. Fannie's son Jason, a polio survivor, is in rehabilitation at Warm Springs, Georgia.

**Zelda Clemens**, new member. Head bread baker at The Flour Shop. Zelda is unmarried. She lives just down the street from Liz Lacy and grows berries in her backyard.

**Voleen Johnson**, widow of the late George E. Pickett Johnson, the former president of the Darling Savings and Trust Bank. Mrs. Johnson is very proud of her greenhouse, the only one in town.

**Mildred Kilgore**, co-owner (with Earlynne Biddle) of The Flour Shop, also an active member of the Share Our Wealth Club. Married to Roger Kilgore of Kilgore Motors. They live in a big house near the ninth green of the Cypress Country Club, where Mildred grows camellias.

**Aunt Hetty Little**, senior member of the Dahlias and Darling matriarch. Practitioner of traditional crafts and (occasionally) natural magic, Aunt Hetty is a good listener with friends in all corners of the community. She knows a great many Darling secrets.

**Lucy Murphy** supervises the kitchen at the CCC Camp outside of town and grows vegetables and fruit on a small market farm on the Jericho Road. Her husband (Ralph Murphy) works on the railroad and is gone much of the time, so she's developed a strong independent spirit.

**Raylene Riggs**, Myra May Mosswell's mother. Cooks at the Darling Diner, manages the garden behind it, and lives at the Marigold Motor Court. Her friends and family recognize and accept her as a clairvoyant.

**Dorothy Rogers**, Darling's librarian. Miss Rogers knows the Latin names of all the plants in the Dahlias' garden and insists that everyone else does, too. Longtime resident of Magnolia Manor.

**Beulah Trivette**, owner of Beulah's Beauty Bower on Dauphin Street, where the Dahlias go to get beautiful. Artistically gifted, Beulah loves cabbage roses and other exuberant flowers.

**Alice Ann Walker**, secretary to Mr. Duffy at the Darling Savings and Trust Bank. Alice Ann, her disabled husband Arnold, and their three grandchildren have just moved into a new house with a bigger garden, where Arnold grows enough zucchini to supply all of Cypress County.

# FIRESTARTER

THE FLAME HAS A DOZEN BRIGHT, THROBBING TONGUES, LICK-ing hungrily at the tinder-dry grass, knee-high and brown after a summer's growing. The firestarter stares at the flame, mesmerized, torn between the desire to do right and stamp it out and the even more urgent need to let it go and do what it does best.

He lets it go. It isn't his now, anyway. It's its own self, with its own appetites, its own greediness, its own freedoms. As with so many things in his sad and sorry life, once he starts something, events always take over. Like this fire, everything has to run its course, however it ends up. All he can do is watch.

He sighs a long sigh. It's too bad that things have come to such a miserable pass. But as Huey always says, this is through no fault of his own. He is just another of the downtrodden victims of the banks and the big corporations, doing whatever he has to do to hang onto what had come down to him through his daddy's and his granddaddy's hard work. The powermongers in Wall Street and Washington control the markets and manage the prices so nobody else can turn an honest dollar unless he's already a millionaire. And the millionaires are all as crooked as a dog's hind leg, anyway. Until Huey P. Long gets to the White House and takes over the government, nobody is ever going to be anybody, let alone a king. Huey is right when he says that only he can make America *work* again.

Fierce with resentment, the man squints through the shimmering heat that rises above the flames. The fire is snapping like a whip. In a few minutes, old Miz Murchison up the road—this is her pasture, this little patch along the creek—will see the smoke and run to the telephone. These days, Darling has a new fire truck and a new alarm that gets the Hot Dogs moving faster. They'll be here before the fire can burn as far as the trees along the creek, so there won't be any serious damage.

Damage? The firestarter chuckles grimly. He's actually doing old lady Murchison a favor. High time this little pasture got burned off. Come spring, the grass will be thicker and greener and the weed seed will be burned up, which is all good, isn't it? The old lady oughtta thank him, that's what she oughtta do. But will she? Of course not. Nobody's grateful these days. He shakes his head disgustedly. Everybody's out to get whatever they want and the devil take the hindmost.

He turns back toward his car, parked along the road. He's done what he came for, and the fire boys will be here pretty quick.

Time to be on his way.

# CHAPTER ONE

## THAT'S POLITICS FOR YOU

*Saturday, August 31, 1935*

THE THICK GREEN VINES OF THE POLE BEANS IN THE GARDEN next to the Darling Dahlias' clubhouse were heavily loaded with bright green Kentucky Wonder string beans. Which was a very good thing, Bessie Bloodworth thought, since it was the Dahlias' turn to feed the crowd at the annual supper for the men and boys of the Volunteer Fire Department, collectively known as the Hot Dogs. Bessie's Cajun green bean casserole (a recipe borrowed from a Louisiana cousin) was on the menu. So she, Aunt Hetty Little, and Ophelia Snow were picking beans—early, to avoid the heat of what promised to be another simmering late-summer day. While they worked, they discussed the plans for tonight's dinner, which featured (what else?) hot dogs.

"Liz is managing the hot dogs and buns," Bessie reported, stretching up to snag a bean hanging at the top of the tall cane-pole teepee. This year, she had been the one to organize the food, a job she always enjoyed. "Beulah is bringing all the stuff that goes with hot dogs," she added. "Mustard, catsup, relish, onions—and cheese, of course. She's also offered to fry a couple of chickens if we need them. She says she has an extra rooster."

"I don't think we'll need Beulah's rooster." Ophelia tossed a handful of beans into the bucket at her feet. "I'm making a pot of potato salad and three dozen deviled eggs. And Mildred and Earlynne are each bringing a big bag of roasting ears."

"And I'm bringing a bucket of coleslaw. Everybody likes that." Aunt Hetty straightened up with a hand on her aching hip. She was eighty-something, sometimes walked with a cane, and always tried to snatch a little nap in the afternoon. But she never let age or temporary infirmities keep her out of the garden. "And Myra May and Violet are bringing a kettle of pulled pork and sandwich buns. That ought to be enough to feed the thirty who have signed up for the supper."

"Plus my green bean casserole and Alice Ann's stewed okra," Bessie reminded them. "Oh, and Lucy says she's got more ripe tomatoes than she's got time to fool with. She said she'd slice them up with some red onions and dill."

Ophelia swatted a mosquito. "Don't forget pie. Raylene said that she and Euphoria will bring as many as we want from the diner."

"Plus the five or six gallons of iced tea that Mildred is brewing, and that should just about do it," Aunt Hetty said. "Sounds like a feast, girls. Let's hope the Hot Dogs bring big appetites."

"Oh, they'll be hungry, all right," Ophelia said. She held up the lard pail she was using to collect her beans. "I've got three quarts here. How are you doing, Bessie?"

Bessie looked down at her basket, which was gratifyingly full. "Almost a gallon. You, Hetty?"

"Three quarts," Aunt Hetty said. "That gives us close to three gallons, which ought to be enough for your casserole, with some left over for your Magnolia ladies' supper." She dusted her hands on her rickrack-trimmed red print apron and regarded a leafy green teepee still studded with beans. "Don't you just love these Kentucky Wonders? Best pole bean ever. We've picked enough for the supper and there are still plenty left."

"Which is good," Ophelia replied, "because the First Baptists are coming this afternoon to pick for their Labor Day canning party. Liz told them they could take beans and okra, plus all the cucumbers they want. Mrs. Rothbottom said they were getting together to put up dill pickles."

The long, hot Alabama summer still wasn't over, but the Darling churches were already starting to stock the town's free food shelf—the big pantry closet in the courthouse base-ment—against the coming winter. Now in its fifth year, the Depression had hit everybody hard. There were too many people with empty cupboards and hungry children to feed. The Dahlias helped by putting in a garden big enough to share, free of charge, with those who wanted to come and pick for themselves and others.

Well, not exactly *free*, Bessie knew. There was a sheet on the back door where people could sign up to trade a few hours of weed-pulling and row-hoeing for a bucket of vegetables. Most did, and as a consequence, the garden was well tended. It looked very pretty, especially considering that there hadn't been any rain at all in the month of August and it was hot enough to fry an egg on the courthouse step—as Earlynne Biddle's boy, Benny, had demonstrated last week. He had even broadcast this sizzling event on WDAR, Darling's recently launched radio sta-tion, which he helped to manage. A remote broadcast, he said it was. Which Bessie wondered about because the courthouse was not a bit remote. It was smack-dab in the middle of town.

"Let's call it quits and get these beans snapped," Bessie said, holding out her basket for Aunt Hetty's and Ophelia's beans. "With three of us on the job, we'll be done in a jiffy."

A few minutes later, the ladies had divvied up the beans and settled down to work in the shade of the big pecan tree behind the Dahlias' little white frame clubhouse. It had needed a new roof and some major repairs when they inherited it, but they had rolled up their sleeves and gotten to work. They were still at it, too. Just the week before, Violet Sims and Myra May Mosswell had teamed up to paint the kitchen a bright, sunny shade of yellow—a great improvement, everybody agreed.

It wasn't ten o'clock yet, but Bessie could feel the perspiration beading on her forehead. It was going to be another blister of a day, maybe the hottest yet this summer, which was one of the hottest anybody could remember. She was sick and tired of the sweltering heat but there was nothing you could do about it—just as there was nothing you could do about the Depression except smile and act like you meant it, even when you didn't. What was the name of that song she'd heard on the radio the other day? Something about letting a smile be your umbrella on a really rainy day? But it wasn't an umbrella or even a smile she needed right now, Bessie told herself. What she needed was for Mr. Hawkins to fix the switch on the electric fan so the residents of the Magnolia Manor—her home for genteel older ladies, right next door to the clubhouse—could enjoy a cooling breeze while they played bridge or worked on their jigsaw puzzles after supper.

This morning's breeze wasn't exactly cool, but it carried the fragrance of the Dahlias' flower garden, over an acre of lovely plants and lush green grass, all the way down to a little wooded area and the clear spring that was surrounded by bog iris, ferns, and pitcher plants. The garden had been designed and lovingly tended by Mrs. Dahlia Blackstone, who had bequeathed it and her little frame cottage to the garden club that had taken her name.

In its heyday, the garden had been written up in the *Selma Times-Journal*, the *Montgomery Advertiser*, and in newspapers as far away as Tennessee and North Carolina. In Mrs. Blackstone's later years, however, the garden had gotten away from her—which happens to every garden when the gardener gets busy or gets old or just stops paying attention. Even the most mannerly and well-disciplined plants, left to their own devices, grow unkempt and disorderly. They wander off in whatever direction suits them, putting out a stray bud here and an unruly branch there and dropping seeds or poking roots and tubers into their neighbors' beds. By the time Mrs. Blackstone's estate was settled and the cottage and gardens turned over to the Dahlias, her backyard was more like a subtropical jungle than a garden.

"I wouldn't be a bit surprised to see a tiger in there," Violet Sims had said, surveying the tangles.

"Or an anaconda or two," muttered her partner Myra May Mosswell. "There's bound to be snakes, girls. Watch where you step."

But nothing daunted, the Dahlias pulled on boots and gloves, got their garden tools out of the old shed by the fence, armed themselves with Flit guns to fend off the mosquitos, and went to work. They snipped the overgrown clematis, mandevilla, and wisteria. They trimmed the trumpet vine and the untrammeled Confederate jasmine. They divided and replanted the orange ditch lilies that Mrs. Blackwell had loved, and the oxblood and crinum and spider lilies, as well as daffodils and narcissus. They cleared the curving perennial borders of weeds and invaders, giving the larkspur, phlox, Shasta daisies, iris, alliums, and asters more room to relax and spread out. They pruned the gardenias and roses—the climbers, the teas, the ramblers, the shrubs, and the boisterous Lady Banks, whose gorgeous yellow blooms in spring were a sight for sore eyes.

And even at the height of a sultry summer, something was bound to be blooming. Today, it was (fittingly) the August lily, which Miss Rogers, the Darling librarian, insisted on calling by its Latin name, *Lilium formosanum*. Its massive white trumpets hung heavy on five-foot stems, their delicate, delicious fragrance filling the air.

It was the August lily that Bessie smelled now, as she, Aunt

Hetty, and Opie pulled up chairs and settled down under the pecan tree. The quiet of the Camellia Street neighborhood was broken only by the distant *hoot* of the railroad train on other side of town, a dove's melodic *who-cooks-for-you*, and the distinctly unmelodic disharmonies produced by the student who was taking a piano lesson from Ruth Annie Perkins across the street. "The Moonlight Sonata," Bessie thought it sounded like—when it sounded like anything at all.

The ladies could share the latest news as they worked, for all three had been snapping beans since they were girls in pinafores and knew just how to do it. Kentucky Wonders weren't just any old green beans, however. They were *string* beans. That is, a thick strand of vegetable fiber ran the length of every bean and had to be pulled out before the bean was cooked—a job worth doing because Kentucky Wonders were so flavorful. An experienced bean-snapper could flick off the tip ends with a thumbnail, zip out the string, and snap the bean into three or four crisp pieces without looking—and without dropping a syllable.

"I had a visit from Voodoo Lil last night," Aunt Hetty said. "She brought me some cane syrup—and a warning about the weather."

Big Lil Boudreaux, also known as Voodoo Lily, was a special friend of Aunt Hetty's and the most respected of Cypress County's half-dozen conjure queens. Big Lil lived in a wood-frame tin-roofed cottage in Briar Swamp, where Darling folk, white and colored, consulted her regularly on matters having to do with their pocketbooks, their hearts, their health, and the weather. When Lil predicted that something was going to happen, people listened.*

---

* For Lil's story, read *The Darling Dahlias and the Voodoo Lily.*

Ophelia looked concerned. "What kind of a warning? Not more of this heat, I hope."

"A hurricane warning. Lil says it's going to be a bad one and kill a lot of people. It'll hit the Florida Keys first, on Labor Day. She doesn't know where it's headed after that. It could turn into another one of those bad Gulf storms, though. She says she's got a feeling. We should get ready for anything."

Bessie made a mental note to ask Mr. Dalby to come over and check her storm shutters. Darling was only about seventy miles inland. Some years before, a hurricane had blown up in the Gulf, crossed the coast west of Mobile, ripped the roof off Jake Pritchard's Standard Oil station, plucked up fine old trees all over town, and sent Pine Mill Creek out of its banks, drowning Tate Haggard's cow. And late August, early September was prime hurricane season.

She had a different piece of news to share, though. "Have you heard that Rufus Radley has decided to run for fire chief?"

"But Archie Mann has been fire chief for *years*." Aunt Hetty was surprised. "And everybody says he's a genius at his job. That man knows fires."

"Rufus might know how to repair cars, but what does he know about being fire chief?" Ophelia wondered. "Is he *qualified*?"

The Hot Dogs always elected their officers at the meeting they held after the August hot dog supper. Archie Mann, the owner of Mann's Mercantile, had been chief of the Darling VFD for the past six or seven years. Nobody had expected any opposition to his candidacy—least of all from Rufus Radley, who owned Radley's Auto Repair two miles out on the Monroeville Highway and had joined the VFD only a few months before.

"Rufus thinks he's qualified to do anything," Bessie said with a dark chuckle. "But he's probably running for chief because he wants to drive that fancy new fire truck Miss Tallulah donated to the Hot Dogs."

"And blast that truck siren, to make everybody jump out of his way," Aunt Hetty said. She had been a schoolteacher when she was a young woman. "Rufus was a pushy little boy. I had him for third and fourth grades. When there were goodies being handed out, Rufus Radley always managed to get himself to the front of the line."

The chief was the one who got to drive the shiny new fire engine that the civic-minded Miss Tallulah LaBelle (a plantation owner whose family fortune mysteriously survived the 1929 Crash) had recently bought and donated to the fire department. Respectfully called Big Red, Miss Tallulah's truck had been the star of this year's Fourth of July parade, eclipsing the VFD's old truck, a rusty, banged-up 1925 Model T Ford stakebed that was weighed down with fire hoses, fire buckets, and a 100-gallon water barrel. Archie Mann had looked pretty fine at the wheel of Big Red, wearing the chief's shiny helmet (bright red, of course, with a gold No. 1 on the front), and running the siren while people cheered. Everybody was proud of the Darling VFD.

But Rufus Radley always got what he went after, and Bessie knew that if he wanted the fire chief's job, he was going to get it—one way or the other. It didn't matter that Archie Mann was the more experienced candidate and knew what it took to do the job. She hoped the Hot Dogs would reelect him. But Rufus always had a trick or two up his sleeve. If he wanted to get his hands on the wheel of that new truck, there wasn't much that was going to stop him.

It had been the kind of summer when fire departments all over the country were keeping busy. Everywhere, it seemed, temperatures had been in the nineties with no rain. In the Plains states, drought conditions had become so dire that the newspapers were calling it the "Dust Bowl." The land was literally drying up and blowing away—blowing as far east as Washington, DC, where the days were turned to nights by dust carried on the "black blizzards" all the way from Kansas, Oklahoma, and Texas.

Big Red and the Darling Hot Dogs had been in great demand in the last few weeks. July and August were spectacularly hot and dry, and a rash of fires had blazed up around town—a bad burn at the north end of the railroad trestle, another in Mrs. Murchison's pasture on the Jericho Road, still another across from the Academy's baseball field, plus one or two more that Bessie couldn't remember. And just the previous day, in town, when Reverend Peters had made the mistake of burning the Presbyterian parsonage trash in a rusty metal drum when the wind was blowing hard from the south. Sparks got away from the reverend and landed on the roof of Doc Roberts' garage, catching the shingles on fire. But Chief Mann, Big Red, and the Hot Dogs were johnny-on-the-spot. They had a hose on the blaze in nothing flat. The only serious casualty was the parsonage fence and Reverend Peters' reputation. He had been heard to use a bad word or two, and then to excuse himself by muttering that the devil made him do it.

"But there's more," Bessie said, now getting to the point of her story and dropping her voice to indicate that this was really confidential. "I heard that Rufus Radley has been calling each of the Hot Dogs to tell them that he will *personally* see that they receive a five-dollar bonus if he gets elected fire chief." She had heard this just yesterday from Myra May, at the Darling Diner. Myra May almost never passed along newsy bits she picked up from overheard conversations, but she had been so angry when she realized what Rufus Radley was doing that she repeated what she had heard to Bessie.

Aunt Hetty was incensed, too. "But that's . . . that's just the same as buying votes!" she spluttered. "Rufus Radley knows he's not supposed to do that!"

"Who's going to stop him?" Ophelia asked cynically, dropping a handful of snapped beans into the bowl in her lap. "That's politics, isn't it? That seems to be the way the game is played these days. Everybody knows that Rufus Radley is a bully. If he wants to win, he won't let anything stop him."

Round and bouncy, Opie had flyaway brown hair, freckles scattered across her nose, and a sweet smile that made dimples appear in her cheeks. She also had a sunny and optimistic disposition, so when she said "That's politics" with such fierce skepticism, both Bessie and Aunt Hetty noticed.

Aunt Hetty sighed. "Rufus Radley gets away with a lot of shenanigans, but that don't make it right." She snapped a bean. "Politics," she muttered. "Seems like that's what's on everybody's mind these days. That's all that's on their tongues, anyway. Folks can't stop talking about it. About Huey Long, for instance. You can't turn on the radio without hearing about him." She sniffed. "Some of us prefer to have nothing at all to do with politicians. No offense intended, dear," she added, with a slantwise glance at Bessie.

Bessie didn't take offense. She didn't share her friend's view, either. Politics might not be a pretty subject, but she believed that everybody who had the right to vote ought to have an informed opinion about whether or not the country was going to the dogs. And since women had had the vote since the 1924 election, she also believed they shouldn't ought to be shy about sharing their opinions just the way the men did. The 1936 presidential election might be fifteen months away, but it was already a hot topic—in the newspaper, on the radio, at the diner, after church. Whenever Darling folk got tired of talking about the weather, they could talk about who was going to throw his hat into which ring.

On the Republican side, there were a whole flock of potential candidates. Former president Herbert Hoover, soundly defeated for a second term in 1928, was said to be eager for a chance to get even with now-President Roosevelt. But the newspapers were also mentioning Charles Lindbergh and Henry Ford, as well as Theodore Roosevelt's oldest son, Ted, who happened to be FDR's fifth cousin—"fifth cousin *far* removed," as both Roosevelts liked to joke. (There wasn't a lot of love lost between the Republican Oyster Bay Roosevelts and the Democrat Hyde Park Roosevelts.) At this point, the GOP nomination was anybody's guess.

The Democratic ticket was still a mystery, too. Most people thought Franklin Roosevelt would run for a second term, but the man preferred to play his cards close to his vest, like a gambler who refused to tip his hand until the last minute—the week of the convention, likely. Nobody knew whether he intended to be a candidate in '36, unless maybe it was Mrs. Roosevelt, although she claimed that even she didn't know. "My husband never tells me *anything*," she said, in that funny, warbly voice of hers.

But Huey P. Long—the former Democratic governor of Louisiana, now a United States senator with presidential ambitions—was already blazing like a meteor up and down the campaign trail. He hadn't officially declared, but he was making it plenty clear that he intended to challenge FDR for the nomination. And his progressive platform, "every man a king" and "share our wealth," was getting plenty of attention.

In fact, anytime, anywhere folks picked up a newspaper, they could see a headline about him splashed across the front page. The *Tuscaloosa News* announced "I AM THE CONSTITUTION!" LONG CLAIMS. The *Anniston Star* declared that HUEY THREATENS TO FIRE HIS CRITICS. The *Birmingham News* posed the question, CAN THE KU KLUX KLAN UNHORSE HUEY P. LONG?

And *TIME* magazine featured him on the cover—picturing him with a clownish grin and an outstretched hand, as if he were reaching for something and aimed to grab it before it got away.

The story wasn't very complimentary, either. *TIME* described Huey as "loud, rough, and profane" and warned that if he didn't get the nomination, he was likely to run as an independent and split the Democrats. In that case, the only winner would be the Republican candidate, whoever he was, and Huey P. would be in an excellent position to take the White House in 1940. The Kingfish, as he liked to be called, was "obviously thinking ahead," the magazine remarked sourly.

*TIME* wasn't alone in its disdain. Most newspapers and magazines didn't like Huey P. Long. He didn't like them, either, and he wasn't shy about saying so. "Enemies of the people," he called the media. "Fake news." A couple of years ago, he had persuaded the Louisiana legislature to levy a two-percent tax on newspapers' advertising profits. "That's two cents a lie," he said, "and they tell millions of them." His own newspaper, *American Progress*, was of course an exception.

Bessie wasn't sure how she felt about Senator Long. But she had liked his ideas well enough to join Darling's Share Our Wealth Club—especially the part about the thirty dollars a month Huey wanted to give to everybody over sixty-five. She knew how much her Magnolia ladies needed the money, so she was especially grateful when Huey's share-the-wealth proposals had prodded FDR into proposing the Social Security Act, although the payments would probably only be about twenty dollars and nobody would get any money until 1940, by which time several of the Magnolias would probably be dead.

Bessie was also (and this was perhaps more relevant to matters of the moment) a cousin on her father's side to Roger Bloodworth, who managed publicity for Senator Long's campaign. She had read that the senator was scheduled to make a speech to the Birmingham Chamber of Commerce. So she had written to Roger, telling him about the Darling club and asking if there was a chance—any chance at all—of the senator's stopping off in Darling.

She didn't expect an answer. After all, she hadn't seen Roger since the summer she was sixteen, when the two of them had shared a few—well, somewhat more than a few—uncousinly kisses in her grandfather's hayloft just outside of Shreveport. But to her enormous surprise, Roger had answered her letter with a telephone call (long distance, all the way from Baton Rouge!) and the news that he had arranged for the senator's motorcade to stop in Darling on the way back to Louisiana. The Kingfish would give a short speech and spend a few minutes shaking hands and posing for photos with members of the club.

Bessie's heart was pounding and her breath was coming short and fast when she put down the phone. Little Darling was going to host the most talked-about politician in America! Why, the visit would attract people from all across this part of the state! It could put their town on the map! So the minute she could breathe again, she called Earlynne Biddle (the current Share Our Wealth Club president), who was just as thrilled as she was by the news.

"Senator Long, right here in Darling!" Earlynne cried. "How in heaven's name did you manage *that*, Bessie? I can hardly believe it!"

"Neither can I," Bessie confessed, and blushed when she thought about those kisses. When she hung up, she sat down at her writing desk and began making a list of the ways the club could spread the word about this momentous event. At the top, of course, was the new radio station WDAR, which could be counted on to include a bulletin in every local newscast and might even agree to carry the senator's speech live. Charlie

Dickens could run a front-page story in the next *Dispatch*. The club could get flyers printed with Senator Long's picture and the words EVERY MAN A KING as well as make signs that could be put up in businesses around the courthouse square—The Flour Shop, the bank, the Palace Theater, Hancock's Grocery, Musgrove's Hardware, the Darling Diner, Mann's Mercantile, Kilgore Motors, the Five and Dime, and Lima's Drugs. However they felt about the man, they'd all be glad to cooperate. They knew that farmers would flock from miles around for a chance to shake the hand of a man who might be the next president of the United States of America—and do a little shopping before and after.

But Bessie knew that Aunt Hetty and Ophelia were *not* Long supporters, so she hadn't mentioned any of this to them just now. They would find out soon enough. Instead, she cast a sympathetic look at Ophelia.

"You must be getting a big dose of politics too, Opie," she said. "How's your Jed holding up these days? Is he going to make it through the election?"

Ophelia's husband was Darling's mayor. Popular and friends with just about everybody, he had held the position for several terms but was now involved in a heated runoff against Marvin Musgrove, the owner of Musgrove's Hardware. The election was in November.

"Oh, Jed's all right." Ophelia spoke with a careless toss of her head and a tone that suggested that he really wasn't, and neither was she. "Of course," she added, "he's not just real happy about some of the things Mr. Musgrove has been saying about him. He thought they were friends. And because the oldest Musgrove boy manages WDAR, his dad gets all the advertising he wants, free. We have to pay for it." WDAR had started broadcasting in the spring and was already going great guns. Since the station covered all the local news (new babies, funerals, visits from relatives, local crops, and the weather), Darling folk listened all day long. And even if they weren't actually *listening*, they had the radio on, in case something serious happened.

"You have to pay for advertising and he gets his free?" Bessie gave a disapproving cluck. "Mr. Musgrove knows better. Why, he's a deacon in the Baptist church!"

"Politics," Aunt Hetty observed wryly, "has a bad way of getting between good people."

"I'm afraid you're right, Aunt Hetty," Ophelia said. "I don't think Jed will ever feel the same about Mr. Musgrove. It's a pity, too. They were great friends." She sighed. "He also knows he's got to make a few more speeches, which he really hates to do. He always says that mayoring would be a darned good job if it weren't for the speech-making. And if it paid a salary, which it doesn't."

Ophelia's voice was resigned. Snow's Farm Supply, which her husband had inherited from his daddy when he and Ophelia were first married, was no longer the money-making proposition it had been in the days before the Great War. Between the boll weevil and the rock-bottom farm commodity prices, farmers had been in serious trouble all through the 1920s, and the stock market crash and subsequent Depression had just about finished them off. Things had gotten worse every year, and now the federal government was paying folks *not* to plant cotton or soybeans or corn and raise fewer cows and pigs and chickens. And if farmers couldn't farm, farm businesses were in trouble. Snow's Farm Supply was between a rock and a hard place. It could barely pay its bills, let alone pay the owner a decent salary.

So in spite of Jed's publicly stated belief that a wife's place was in the home, Ophelia had gathered her courage and found a job. She had started out at the *Darling Dispatch* as a cub reporter, ad saleswoman, and Linotype operator. Then she was offered a better-paying secretarial job at Camp Briarwood—the Civilian Conservation Corps camp. That position had come to an end when the new commandant brought in his own secretary and Ophelia got her walking papers. She had hoped to get on at the recently opened Vanity Fair lingerie factory in Monroeville, but they weren't hiring. Charlie Dickens at the *Dispatch* had already found her replacement. And nobody in Darling needed a secretary.

Bessie knew that it had been a scary time in the Snow family. For several months, Opie and Jed had no idea where their next dollar was coming from. They persuaded Mr. Duffy at the bank to let them skip a mortgage payment, ate out of the garden and the chicken coop ("At least the hens are laying," Ophelia said), and sent their two kids to school in last year's clothes with the collars turned and the hems and sleeves let out.

But that spring, the WPA—the government's Works Progress Administration, which employed millions of unskilled men on public works projects—had opened the brand-new Federal Writers' Project. The program aimed to create a guidebook for each of the forty-eight states in the union, books that would include economic development, scenic areas, and places of interest, all aimed to encourage travel and tourism and boost local businesses. There was a focus on local history and folklore as well, documenting the stories of older folk, especially those who had settled the area.

Mr. Ryan Nichols, the director of the FWP's Southern Division, had hoped to hire Elizabeth Lacy—legal assistant to Mr. Moseley and the Dahlias' club president—as one of Alabama's project coordinators. But Liz hadn't wanted to leave her job with Mr. Moseley. Plus, her very first novel was being published and she had no idea what her life would be like after that. Not knowing what lay ahead, Liz had turned down the Writers' Project and recommended Ophelia for the job. At the interview, Mr. Nichols liked what he heard. Now, Ophelia was responsible for producing a large section of the new Alabama guidebook. And Bessie, who prided herself on her reputation as Darling's local history expert, had agreed to work as one of the writers for the project.

Thinking of that, Bessie snapped another bean and said, "Oh, by the way, Opie, I'm up to 1864 in the Darling history I'm writing for your Federal Writer's Project. That's when the telegraph came to town and changed everything."

It did, too. After the telegraph arrived, Darling was no longer the last town in Alabama to get the news. It had brought word that General James H. Wilson and his Yankee boys had just taken the city of Selma and were on their way to Darling; that the battleship Maine ("Remember the Maine; to hell with Spain!") had blown up in Havana Harbor; and that Galveston had been wiped out by a monster hurricane that had blown ashore without warning. The next big event in Bessie's history would be the arrival of the telephone, which happened about the same time Woodrow Wilson took office. (For the first enlightening and entertaining year, all two dozen subscribers had been on a single party line.) After that would come the Great War and the Spanish flu epidemic that killed half the town and put the other half in bed for weeks. But Bessie hadn't got that far yet.

Ophelia gave her a grateful look. "Thank you," she said. "Mr. Nichols will be here on Monday. If you'll let me have a copy of what you've done so far, I'll show it to him."

"Your boss seems like a likable enough young fellow," Aunt Hetty remarked. "Not handsome, but with a certain magnetism." She did not look at Ophelia. "Seems like a snappy dresser, too. Easy to work with, is he?"

"Oh, yes," Ophelia replied, with studied nonchalance. "He knows what our research is all about and where we are with the actual writing. Any little problem I have, he's always willing to talk about it. I can even call him, long-distance collect."

Bessie was not terribly surprised to see Ophelia's quick little smile and the sudden blush that rose in her cheek. She considered herself an astute judge of people and had already noticed that whenever Ryan Nichols made one of his periodic visits to Darling, Ophelia rushed right over to Beulah Trivette's Beauty Bower and got her hair done, put on her prettiest frock, and smiled as if she knew a special secret. Bessie didn't have to be Miss Marple to suspect that Ophelia had developed a crush on Mr. Nichols.

Her suspicions made Bessie uneasy, for this kind of thing was like playing with fire—you never knew when it might flare up and get out of control. But she was only a little worried, for she had known Ophelia for a long time and had a great deal of faith in her friend's basic common sense. And a crush . . . well, everybody had at least one of those somewhere in her history. It was all just a part of growing up, wasn't it?

Bessie certainly understood that, for she remembered the ill-advised attraction she had developed for the handsome, fine-figured fire-and-brimstone preacher who had come to Darling the summer she was seventeen. She had sat on the front row every single night of the revival, clutching her Bible, her eyes riveted on his sweating face and the tantalizing muscles under his white shirt, her heart pounding so loud she was sure he could hear it all the way up there in the pulpit. When he left Darling for the next town on his circuit, she packed her little cardboard suitcase, got on the Greyhound, and took a front-row seat for his next sermon. She had been heartbroken when he told her, pleasantly but firmly, to go home. She had cried for a week and moped for a month, until the boy across the street had asked her out and that was the end of *that*.

Bessie thought that Opie's crush might be the same sort of

thing, if maybe a little more . . . well, unfortunate. It was one thing for a teenager to go mooning after a revival preacher. It was quite another for a married woman to moon after her boss. To make things worse, Jed Snow was as fiercely territorial as a banty rooster, and he had always been a bit of a hothead. He had only agreed that Ophelia could go to work because it was either that or go on relief, which a Snow would *never* do. Mr. Nichols was surely no threat to their marriage, but Jed wouldn't take kindly to the suggestion that his wife might be . . . well, sweet on her boss.

And Jed wasn't very imaginative, either, Bessie thought. He would never, ever guess that Ophelia might be hungry for more than the humdrum dailiness of marriage, which had a way of wearing down to a jagged sawtooth edge over time—especially in the hard times they were all living through. A girl likes a little special attention now and then, and while Jed was a good man, he was not very good at demonstrating his affection.

What's more, Bessie suspected that Mr. Nichols himself had no idea that he might have ignited a little fire in Ophelia's romance-starved heart. Likely he didn't, for he seemed to have his eye on Elizabeth Lacy, which in Bessie's considered opinion was a very good thing. It might mean some temporary unhappiness for Opie but much less disturbance in the Snow family.

But it appeared that Bessie wasn't the only one who had tuned into this complicated state of affairs, for Aunt Hetty chimed in again. "Well, Mr. Nichols seems to have more reasons than one to come to Darling," she said in a knowing tone. "I saw him and Liz on their way to supper at the Old Alabama Hotel a couple of weeks ago. They were a good-looking pair, I thought. And Liz was all starry-eyed."

She gave Ophelia an innocent-looking smile. "Grady Alexander nearly broke Liz's heart, if you will remember. I'm sure all her friends are glad to see her enjoying a little romantic fling, even if the fellow is a damn Yankee."

Ophelia seemed to get the message. Her cheek turned from blush to pale and she ducked her head, "Oh, of course," she murmured, her gaze fixed on the bowl of snapped string beans in her lap. "I hope it works out for Liz, especially after all she's been through."

Aunt Hetty raised her eyes to Bessie's. She gave a quick, conspiratorial wink, and Bessie could see that she, too, knew Opie's little secret.

To rescue Ophelia from the uncomfortable conversation, Bessie took it in a different direction.

"Oh, by the way, Opie," she said, "Miss Rogers asked me to tell you that the library just got the two books your Sarah was asking for."

Housed in a ramshackle frame building behind Fannie Champaign's hat shop, the Darling Library didn't have a lot of extra money for new books. In fact, the library board sometimes couldn't find the money to pay Miss Rogers, even though she only worked there part-time and for practically pennies. But the Dahlias had donated the proceeds from their latest bake sale to the library board, which had given Miss Rogers a five-cent-an-hour raise and fifty dollars to spend on books. She always made a special effort to order titles that the young people were asking for.

"That's wonderful!" Obviously relieved for the change in topic, Ophelia added brightly, "Sarah will be so pleased. She's an avid reader—has her nose in a book *all* the time. Do you remember the titles?"

Bessie did. "Two books by Carolyn Keene. One in the Dana Girls series—number four, I think Miss Rogers said. The other is a Nancy Drew mystery, *The Clue of the Broken Locket.*"

"Oh, good." Ophelia smiled. "Sarah will run right over to

the library and check them out. She's crazy about Carolyn Keene." She snapped a bean. "And when she's done, I'll read them myself. I like the Dana Girls but I *adore* Nancy."

Aunt Hetty dropped a handful of snapped beans into the bowl in her lap. "That does it for me," she announced cheerfully. "I'm finished. Are you girls just about done?"

But their answers to her question were interrupted by an earsplitting shriek that broke the quiet morning air. It was the siren that the city council had recently installed on top of the courthouse bell tower. Before, when there was a fire, Hezekiah Potts, the courthouse custodian, rang the courthouse bell to summon the volunteer firemen. Hezekiah was not as nimble as he used to be, and if there was a fire at night or when he was in church, the bell might not get rung at all. The siren was a lot more reliable—more efficient, too. It went on blasting for over a minute, just to make sure it got everybody's attention.

Jolted by the noise, Ophelia had to juggle her bowl of beans. "*Another* fire? That's . . . what? Two this week?"

"A grass fire, likely," Aunt Hetty said. She stood and brushed off her apron. "Everything's awf'lly dry right now. If'n we don't get some rain soon, the trees are gonna start suffering."

"I swear," Ophelia said grimly, "every time that siren goes off, I jump right out of my skin."

"Between the fires and the hot weather, everybody's on edge," Bessie said in a comforting tone. She held out her basket. "Thanks for helping with the beans, girls. If you'll dump your snaps in here, I'll take them home and get started on the casserole."

Aunt Hetty dumped her beans. "Oh, and Bessie," she said, "I meant to congratulate you on winning this month's garden prize. Keeping a flower bed looking good is always hard in August, but you and your Magnolia ladies pulled it off. Those red hot pokers are spectacular." The Manor's corner garden also included orange dahlias (of course), orange and yellow daylilies, some hot pink cosmos, and spiky red salvia—all of it softened by a silvery border of Powis Castle artemisia.

"The pokers are like firebrands," Ophelia agreed. "And I love the way the pale gray artemisia cools all those hot colors." Her beans went into the basket, too.

Bessie smiled modestly. The Magnolia ladies worked hard on their garden, hoping to win the Dahlias' monthly garden contest at least once during the year. "Thanks." She settled her basket on her hip. "See you at the hot dog supper tonight."

"Looking forward to it," Aunt Hetty said with a wide smile. "Those volunteers do a great job for Darling, especially in weather like this. It's only right that we serve them supper. It'll be *fun*."

But Ophelia just nodded, and Bessie saw that she didn't look very happy. In fact, she had been glum all morning, not at all her usual smiling, chipper self. Jumpy, too. Bessie had a pretty good idea what was bothering her, but of course she didn't say anything. Instead, she gave Opie an extra-warm hug—just to show her that a friend cared.

# CHAPTER TWO

# FIRE IN THE HEART, SMOKE IN THE HEAD

OPHELIA SAID GOODBYE TO BESSIE AND AUNT HETTY AND started home on Rosemont, walking fast, hands in the pockets of her red cotton print dress. She was sorry about being so out of sorts with Bessie and Aunt Hetty that morning. It certainly wasn't *their* fault, and she knew they would have offered to help if she had asked. Aunt Hetty was sympathetic and Bessie (who as Darling's historian was pretty good at discovering the skeletons in a person's closet) might try to guess. But if they really knew what was bothering her, it would scandalize both of them.

No, this . . . this discontent (if that's what it was) was *her* problem, and she had to deal with it herself.

The Snows' house wasn't more than a block from the Dahlias' clubhouse. The small, citrus-yellow frame cottage had a green roof and bright purple shutters—an eye-popping color combination, but the paint had been on sale for half-price at Musgrove Hardware and those were the only colors Mr. Musgrove had left. Opie shuddered every time she looked at it, but a penny saved was a penny earned, as her father used to say, and every penny counted when it came to the Snows' puny little budget. It was a minor miracle that the house had been painted at all, so she wasn't going to fuss with Jed about the colors.

In fact, there was no point in fussing with Jed at all. Fussing never changed things, it just made everybody even more unhappy. If Opie had a philosophy of life, that was it. Don't fuss. Paste on your brightest smile and pretend that everything was just fine, and sooner or later, it *would* be. Or near enough. That's how she had managed to get through the first six years of this gawd-awful Depression. That's how she would get through the next six, although she wasn't going to allow herself to think that far ahead. What good did thinking ahead do, anyway? Something unexpected—like the Spanish flu or the boll weevil or the Wall Street Crash of '29—was bound to pop up and change everything. It always did.

Opie was stepping up on the porch when she heard the wail of a siren and turned to see the new Darling fire engine barreling down Rosemont. Chief Mann was at the wheel and didn't see her when she waved, but one of the young Hot Dogs hanging onto the back of the truck—wasn't that Benny Biddle, Earlynne Biddle's boy?—waved back as they flew past. Wherever that truck was going, it was going to get there *fast*. She shivered apprehensively, wondering where it was headed and hoping that Aunt Hetty was right and it was just another grass fire—not somebody's house burning down.

Few people in Darling locked their houses, so Opie didn't have to bother with a key. She opened the door and went inside—slowly, for the early-morning energy she had borrowed from Bessie and Aunt Hetty was already draining away. She felt as limp as the laundry in the ironing basket, and even though she had left the windows open all night, yesterday's leftover heat hit her in the face like a smothery hot towel.

Rudy Vallée, the family's tabby cat, came out from under a chair and purred loudly around her ankles. Jed was at the feed store and the kids were out and about this morning, so she could have the place to herself. Sarah was sleeping over at

Mary Lou Kramer's and Sam had ridden his bicycle out to the Marigold Motor Court, where he did a few handyman jobs for Pauline DuBerry when his father didn't need him. He'd be starting his last year of high school after Labor Day and he was trying to save something for college.

But Jed wasn't big on that idea. He thought Sam should come to work full time at the feed store and save his dad the salary he was paying Harold Matthews, who was looking to retire, anyway. This wasn't what Opie wanted, of course. Sam was bright and good at his books—Sarah, too. As their mother, she felt that both of them deserved a chance to get out of Darling and live a life that wasn't defined by the narrow limits of their little town—a life that gave them some real opportunities. She was vague about this, though. What did she know about opportunities outside of Darling? She'd never had any herself. But she was fairly certain that there must be *some*.

Opie opened the icebox (they couldn't afford an electric refrigerator—even a used one) and took out a dozen brown eggs, laid by the mixed flock of Barred Rocks and Rhode Island Reds she kept in the backyard. It had been hot all week and there was only a small chunk of ice left. She closed the door hurriedly, remembering that Monday was Labor Day, which meant that Mr. Griffiths wouldn't be around with another twenty pounds until Tuesday. She'd have to put a note on the icebox door, reminding the kids and Jed not to open it unless it was absolutely necessary.

She put the eggs in a large pan, covered them with water, set the pan on the stove, and turned on the burner. Then she dumped half a bag of potatoes into her dishpan. For tonight's VFD supper, she had promised to make potato salad and deviled eggs, since both were cheap and cheap was what she could afford. Potatoes were just eighteen cents for a ten-pound bag at Hancock's grocery, and the eggs were free. Well, not *really* free, since the wholesale price of the Purina laying pellets Jed brought home from the feed store had to come out of her skimpy grocery budget.

Feeling even more discontent, Opie carried the dishpan full of potatoes and a paring knife into the front parlor, where she turned on the radio, sat down in the rocking chair, and got started on the potatoes. It was a pretty room with ivory criss-cross curtains, the upright Kimball piano that had belonged to Jed's aunt, her rocking chair, and the floor-model Philco. There was also a coffee table in front of the sofa, where the family had left the Finance and Fortune game they'd been playing the night before. Looking at the board, Opie saw that she owned Broadway, Park Avenue, *and* Fifth Avenue, which was probably as close as she would ever come to actually owning a valuable piece of property.

But the real star of the room was a cozy pairing of davenport and chair in a rosy Jacquard velour. Opie had fallen in love with that davenport when she saw it on the back page of the Sears and Roebuck catalogue and—on impulse—had ordered it on the easy monthly payment plan. Then, aghast at her extravagance (it had cost twelve-fifty down and ten dollars a month for practically forever!), she had fibbed to Jed about the price, which was one of the things that had driven her to get her first job at the *Darling Dispatch*. Long before she finished paying for the furniture, she discovered that she loved "working out," as Jed's mother said with a disapproving sniff. And while Jed grumped and growled, he had to accept the fact that her paycheck covered the grocery bill. It still did.

She attacked her second potato. But while she had enjoyed reporting and selling advertising and operating the Linotype for Charlie Dickens at the *Dispatch* and doing secretarial work for Captain Campbell out at Camp Briarwood, the CCC camp, she absolutely *adored* working for the Federal Writers'

Project. She was sure that the Alabama guidebook was going to be a bestseller when it was finished. And the local history project—which included Bessie's history of Darling as well as interviews Opie planned with the oldest settlers, with the veterans of the War Between the States, and with former slaves and the children of former slaves—was already well under way.

In fact, just last night, old Cal Boomer had brought over his short piece about life in the early days of Cypress County. In his sloppy script, on a page of his grandson's yellow school tablet, he had written:

Pretty soon after the Creek War, around 1814, many settlers were terrorized by a ferocious outlaw named Savannah Jack, who claimed to be avenging the conquered Indians. Jack and a desperado band of renegade malcontents raided settlements, burning cabins, rustling horses, and robbing and tomahawking anybody who couldn't get away fast enough. But the Creeks said Jack wasn't one of theirs and helped the militiamen drive him down into the Florida swamps, where he bragged to the Seminoles that he had scalped and killed enough women and children to swim in a river of their blood.

Reading this, Opie had shuddered, thinking of Savannah Jack and his outlaws running wild in the streets of Darling. This was pretty exciting stuff and supposedly true, although she would have to check it against the big book on Alabama history that Miss Rogers kept on the reference shelf behind her desk in the Darling Library. But was this the kind of thing Mr. Nichols—her supervisor—would want her to include in the government's guidebook? She would have to put it on her list of things to talk to him about.

She reached for another potato. Then, just at that moment, the radio began playing a recording by Ethel Waters singing an old New Orleans blues song, "Hotter and Hotter." Appropriate to the outdoor temperature, yes, but also to the person—*that* person—who had been nibbling away at the edges of Opie's conscience for weeks.

The subterranean source of her discontent. Mr. Nichols.

It was true. Whenever she thought of him—of *Ryan*, when she dared—she began feeling all warm and fiery inside, as if she were filled with something like . . . what? She didn't suppose it was love, and anyway it couldn't be love, because she knew she loved her husband and loving Jed was nothing like this.

No, not love. It was more like . . . well, like longing. A yearning, burning secret desire, the way Joan Crawford felt about Gary Cooper in *Today We Live*, when Joan was supposed to be marrying Robert Young, the quintessential nice guy, but was sorely tempted by Gary, who was extremely . . . well, let's face it. Extremely sexy. Opie had cried when Robert's airplane was tragically shot down in the war, but if that was the price of two lovers' happiness, so be it. Anyway, Joan Crawford hadn't actually been married to Robert Young, just engaged, which made it only a little wrong. And it was only a movie.

But Opie wasn't in a movie. She was married to Jed. Really married. Which made it a *lot* wrong, she knew. Her father had been a Methodist preacher, and as a girl she had sat through innumerable sermons on the sin of lust, which was the same as desire, only cranked up louder and stronger. She also knew what First Corinthians said about the consequences of lusting after somebody in your heart. Even if you didn't *do* anything, even if you only imagined what it would be like if somebody like Gary Cooper or Ryan Nichols swept you into his arms and smothered your face with kisses, it was still a sin. And you had to stop.

Fire in the heart sends smoke into the head, her mother had always said, and her mother was right. Right now, her head was so full of smoke that she couldn't even begin to think where this might be going. But what did you do when just thinking about doing something was every bit as bad as doing it? And when you didn't want to *stop* thinking about doing it, whatever it was? And especially when thinking and doing were so mixed up in your mind that you almost couldn't tell them apart?

Still ensnared in the tentacles of this guilty conundrum, Opie finished peeling the third potato and then the fourth and the fifth. She was reaching for the sixth when the bell on the hand-crank wall telephone rang, startling her. It rang once, brashly, and then again, instead of the friendly two-shorts-and-a-long party-line ring they'd had until the new switchboard was installed at the telephone exchange. She set her dishpan on the floor and got up to answer it.

"Mrs. Snow?" A man's deep voice, clipped, with a Yankee twang, but personal and . . . yes, thrilling. "Ryan Nichols here. I hope I'm not interrupting anything."

Opie felt the man's physical presence with such a sudden force that she couldn't catch her breath. Over six feet, broad-shouldered, with athletic movements and a confident masculine energy. Blond hair, sun-bleached, with pale blue eyes in a darkly tanned face. Craggy features, not handsome but so compelling that you couldn't stop looking at him—or remembering how he looked.

"Mr. Nichols, oh, hello." She took a deep breath, trying to calm the flutters in her stomach. "What a surprise! I wasn't expecting . . . How very nice to hear from you." She was blabbering. She made herself slow down. "No, no interruption, really. I was just peeling potatoes. I'm taking deviled eggs and potato salad to the VFD dinner tonight and—"

She bit it off. Silly her. He was calling *long distance*. He didn't want to hear the mundane details of her day, especially when they had nothing to do with the job she was supposed to be doing for the federal government. For him. Her stomach muscles clenched and she felt that . . . warmth. The *hotter and hotter* Ethel Waters had been singing about. Could he feel it, too, through the phone? Could he feel the way she was feeling? No, of course not. That was ridiculous.

"VFD dinner?" He chuckled, teasing a little. "The Very Free Dissidents? The Viewers of Fabled Domains?"

"The Volunteer Fire Department," she explained. "They're called Hot Dogs, so it's a hot dog supper and it's the Dahlias' turn to serve and of course I want to do my part. It's been awfully hot and dry and there've been an awful lot of fires around town lately and this is our way of saying thank you. Of course, it's not enough, but—"

She bit her lip. Shut *up*, Ophelia!

Another chuckle. "Sounds like great fun. I've peeled a few potatoes in my time—I wish I could be there to help. I'm sure the Hot Dogs appreciate your support." His voice became businesslike. "Unfortunately, I'm stuck in Birmingham for the Labor Day weekend. I'm calling to say that it will be Tuesday before I can get to Darling. I hope that won't inconvenience you too much. And that you're planning to do something pleasant over the holiday."

Opie suddenly realized that she was holding her breath and she let it out. "No, no, of course not. I mean, of course, it won't inconvenience me. And actually, it's probably good. It'll give me another day to get a few more things together so you can see what I've put together before we get together."

Fire in the heart, smoke in the head. What an idiot she was. "Before you get here," she amended lamely, feeling the heat rise in her face.

"Right, then. Thank you. Tuesday it is. It'll likely be the middle of the afternoon before I get there, so I'll be staying over Wednesday to give us plenty of time to work. There are some new ideas floating around the Project office—I'd like to share them with you. I think you'll find them very interesting."

Hearing the smile in his voice, she closed her eyes and swallowed.

And then he cleared his throat. In a slightly lower and more intimate tone, he said, "I'm looking forward to seeing you again, Mrs. Snow. On Tuesday."

Before she could respond, before she could even *think* what to say, let alone get the words out, there was a click. He was gone.

And from the kitchen, the sound of a sharp *pop* and the smell of something scorching. The eggs had boiled dry.

# CHAPTER THREE

# RECKON WE GOT US A FIREBUG

IT WASN'T A GRASS FIRE, OR SOMEBODY'S TRASH FIRE THAT GOT out of hand. It was a fire in a pile of old boards and discarded shingles stacked right up next to a storage shed that leaned up against the back wall of the Coca-Cola bottling plant south of town.

The fire might have been a whole lot worse if Henry Biddle, the plant manager, hadn't arrived when he did and parked his 1929 Chevy where he did—that is, behind the plant instead of in front of the plant, so he could use the back door. It was Saturday and they were closed for the weekend, but he had some paperwork to do and he'd planned to get at it while nobody was around to distract him.

Henry had almost changed his mind about working on Saturday, though. He and Al Duffy and Tate Haggard had played poker the night before, late, in the back room of Pete's Pool Parlor. Because Henry was winning (he went home with an extra buck-fifty in his pocket), he stayed for an additional hand or two. He had overslept, and when he got up, he wasn't very eager to spend the morning at the plant. But he felt better after Earlynne stirred up a batch of buttermilk pancakes. He decided to make the effort.

He was glad he did, for when he pulled the car around

behind the plant, he saw the flames licking up the back wall of the shed. He sprinted into his office, telephoned the Darling Exchange, and reported the fire to Violet Sims, who was on the switchboard that morning. After that, things happened the way they were supposed to.

Violet called the fire chief—Archie Mann—catching him just as he was finishing one of Twyla Sue's big Saturday breakfasts: bacon, eggs, buttermilk grits, and biscuits.

Chief Mann told Violet to push the red button that sounded the siren at the top of the courthouse bell tower. He stuffed a couple of slices of bacon into a hot biscuit before he dashed out the door and ran the two blocks to Blackjack Frazier's barn, where the VFD's fire truck lived when it wasn't out on a job. By the time he got Big Red started, a couple of Hot Dogs had climbed on the back and were ready to go. Just fifteen minutes later, they were pulling up at the fire, flasher flashing and siren wailing.

The chief managed the pump on the truck while the Hot Dogs began pulling hose and unloading equipment. Three more Hot Dogs arrived in somebody's jalopy and began extinguishing the pile of flaming lumber.

Meanwhile, back in Darling, Violet had called the sheriff's office after she got off the phone with Chief Mann and pushed the red button to sound the siren, which was still blaring when Sheriff Buddy Norris picked up the phone. Violet told him where the fire was. He grabbed his cap and ran for his car.

When Buddy was a deputy working for Sheriff Roy Burns, he rode an Indian Ace motorcycle that took him pretty much anywhere he wanted to go, fast. After his predecessor had met his maker (in the person of a rattlesnake with a short temper and a long and lightning-fast strike), Buddy inherited the sheriff's old four-door Ford, which kept him out of the rain and looked official but wasn't nearly as fast as his Indian Ace. He converted the Ford into something resembling a squad car by fastening hog wire to the back of the front seat so he could haul a prisoner without worrying whether the fellow was going to grab him around the neck and snatch his gun—if he was wearing it. Buddy didn't wear his gun very often. He didn't feel it added a lot to the conversation.

This morning, Buddy was delayed when he saw that the Ford's right rear tire was nearly flat. No big surprise, since the tires were worn slick and he'd patched all four inner tubes so often that they looked like crazy quilts. Luckily, he kept a tire pump in the battered tin box mounted on the rear bumper. But the old pump had leaks of its own, so it took him ten minutes to wheeze enough air into the tire so he could drive off. He got to the fire just as the Hot Dogs were packing up the hose.

He walked over to Archie Mann, who was leaning against the fire engine, watching the boys finish the job. The fire was out, the shed looked to be safe, and several of the younger Hot Dogs were shoveling dirt on the smoldering woodpile, making sure there wouldn't be any flare-ups.

"Mornin', Chief," Buddy said. "Hotter'n the devil this morning."

"You said it, Sheriff," returned the chief, whose sweaty face wore a smear of dark ash across one cheek.

Buddy surveyed the scene. "Any idea how it started?"

The chief took off his helmet and wiped his face with his sleeve. "Henry said he got a good whiff of kerosene when he first came up on it. Said to tell you he's in the plant office if you want to talk to him." He paused. "And one of the boys found this." He produced a book of matches and a three-inch white cardboard tube, stuffed with cotton fiber and heavily charred on one end. "Same as those other two we found."

Buddy studied the device. No question, then. He tipped

back the bill of his sheriff's cap. "This makes how many? Five, is it? I'm losing track."

"Yeah. Five fires, counting this'un. But not counting the good reverend's trash fire yesterday. We know how *that* got started." The chief chuckled. "The devil got into the old boy and told him to go in the house and forget what he was doin'. Wind took care of the rest."

The chief was right about the fire at the parsonage, Buddy knew. And yes, there had been five all together: the fire across from the Academy, another at the foot of the railroad trestle, plus two in town: number one in the trash bin behind the Peerless Laundry, number two just outside the town dump, way out on Dauphin Street. And now this.

Buddy frowned down at the cardboard tube. "Five fires of undetermined origin in the space of . . . what? Three weeks, is it? Reckon we got us a firebug."

Actually, they *had* determined the origins of all five fires. Somebody had set them using kerosene and a thing like what Buddy held in his hand. They just didn't know *who*. Or why. Or what might be next. Which qualified the origins of the fires as "undetermined," according to the National Board of Fire Underwriters, which had the last word when it came to describing fires.

"An *arsonist*," Buddy added gloomily, not liking the taste of that word. Arson wasn't an easy crime to solve unless the firestarter hung around to share in the excitement. That didn't seem to be happening with these fires. Most of them had been in out-of-the-way places that didn't attract an audience. They were more like hit-and-runs. Set the fire and scram.

"Yeah." The chief pulled off a leather glove. "Kids, maybe, I'm thinkin'. Could be they just like the smell of smoke. Or the sound of the fire siren." He took off the other glove. "Or the idea of making everybody jump and run." He tossed the pair onto Big Red's seat. "At least there ain't been nobody hurt. And no insurance claims."

"So far," Buddy said. "I'm thinking, though, that it's time to notify the state fire marshal's office." He gestured toward the shed. "Henry tell you what's in there?"

"If this had gone up, there would've been a claim," the chief said. "Henry says they've got three, maybe four thousand dollars' worth of new bottling equipment stacked in there. Coca-Cola shipped it from Atlanta a week ago. It'll be a couple of weeks before the installation crew finishes another job and gets over here to set it up. Just luck that Henry decided on comin' out here this morning. And luck that he got here before the fire took off. Otherwise, we'd've lost the bottling plant." He grabbed Big Red's steering wheel and swung up into the truck. "You coming to the hot dog supper at the church tonight?"

"Oh, you bet." Buddy grinned. "Wouldn't miss it."

Cypress County had no fire marshal, so either he or his deputy sheriff, Wayne Springer, made it a point to show up at all the fires. They had even been known to grab the hose or a fire shovel or pickaxe when an extra hand was called for. He and Wayne considered themselves part of the crew, so they had both signed up to go to the supper.

Plus, it was a free meal, and since Buddy was saving his money, he ate free whenever he could. He had decided to ask Bettina Higgens to marry him—not right away (Buddy was a cautious man) but when he could afford his share of the groceries and half of Bettina's rent. He didn't mind so much that his wife would likely want to keep her job at Beulah's Beauty Bower, where she was a beauty associate and loved what she did. What he minded was not being able to carry at least half of the bills. Being the Cypress County sheriff might be long on status, but it was pretty damned short on salary. And the county was usually so strapped for money that it paid late. It was nearly the end of August and he hadn't yet been paid for the first two weeks. It was no time to get married.

"Hey, you two." Archie Mann turned on the fire truck's seat and waved at a pair of sweaty-looking Hot Dogs. "I'm taking Big Red back to the barn. If you're coming with me, load that hose and hop on. The rest of the crew can mop up." The chief turned back to Buddy, his soot-smudged face serious. "Listen, Sheriff, I would mightily appreciate it if you'd cast your vote for me tonight. For fire chief, I mean. Wayne, too. You tell him I said so, will you? I hate to be pushy about this, but I want your votes."

Buddy raised an eyebrow. "I don't think we're Hot Dogs, not officially, anyway. We just act like it when it comes to free meals. We probably won't vote."

"I am hereby declaring that the two of you are honorary Hot Dogs," Archie growled, "and honorary Hot Dogs can vote just like everybody else. I need all the help I can get. I gotta beat him."

"Beat who?" Buddy hadn't heard that anybody else was fool enough to want the fire chief's job. It took a lot of time, sometimes dragged you out of bed in the middle of the night in bad weather, and it didn't pay a plugged nickel. All Archie got out of it was the badge he was wearing and the fun of driving that shiny new truck.

"Beat that no-good Rufus Radley." Disgusted, Archie spit in the dirt. "He's decided he wants the job, so he's buying himself a big bunch of votes. He's promising everybody a five-dollar bonus if they vote for him. Five dollars!" He turned and looked back at the Hot Dogs, raising his voice. "Benny and Junior, you get that hose loaded and hop on, pronto. Them other boys is gonna stay and clean up. I'm getting' ready to roll."

"A five-dollar bonus? That don't seem right," Buddy said. It also didn't seem legal, which wasn't always the same. "I'll have to ask Mr. Moseley what he thinks about it." Mr. Moseley was the county attorney and Buddy's source of reliable information about the law, which was full of nooks and crannies and crevasses deep enough to trap an unwary sheriff who didn't watch where he put his feet.

"Don't seem right to me, neither." The chief turned the key in the ignition, raising his voice over the noise of the engine. "So tonight, both you and Wayne gotta vote. For me." He gave Buddy a hard, straight-on look. "And on Monday, you stop by the Mercantile and pick out one of them Gene Autry hats you've been droolin' over. Not Wayne, though. Just you. No charge—just tell Twyla Sue that I said you should have it."

"That's a joke, isn't it?" Buddy asked. He hoped so, anyway. He was a longtime fan of the Singing Cowboy and his horse, Champion. He knew that those big white hats, which he had long admired, went for a whole ten bucks apiece. He frowned. A ten-dollar Gene Autry hat wasn't any different than a five-dollar bonus—except it was maybe twice as bad.

"Ain't no joke," Archie said grimly. "That hat'll look swell on you, Sheriff. Make Bettina's sweet little heart go pitty-pat." He pushed down on the clutch and shifted the fire truck into first gear. "If you're fixin' on driving back to town, though, you better pump up your right rear. It's flat."

"Oh, *hell*," Buddy muttered. As the fire engine roared off in a cloud of dust, he went for the tire pump.

He was still pumping when Wilber Casey, the eager-beaver young reporter from the *Dispatch*, showed up with his camera to cover the story. Buddy finished with the tire and put the pump away as Wilber took some photos and asked some questions about the fires. He answered as briefly as possible, since he didn't care to reveal how little he actually knew about what was going on.

There wasn't much to say, anyway. In fact, Buddy could

condense the entire past three weeks into a single sentence. Somebody in Cypress County was setting fires, and catching him was not going to be easy. Maybe that would be a good lead for his story, Buddy suggested to the reporter.

"On the record?" Wilber asked. "I mean, can I quote you?"

"What's wrong with that?" Buddy replied. "It's the truth. Isn't that what you're supposed to write? The truth?"

"Yes, but . . ." Wilber scribbled for a moment. "Thanks," he said.

As Wilber drove off, Buddy went into the plant to talk to Henry Biddle, who didn't have much to say, either, beyond what he'd already told the fire chief. He hadn't seen or heard anything unusual, and everything at the plant seemed to be operating pretty much as per normal, although, when prodded, Henry had to admit that it was a tad bit unusual to have that much valuable machinery stored in a shed.

"I'm filing a report," Henry said, with a gesture to a sheet of paper on his desk. "I'm just glad I don't have to tell the company that their new equipment got burned up in a fire."

"Yeah," Buddy said. "Good that you got out here this morning when you did. You come out every Saturday, do you?"

"When I have to," Henry said. "They don't pay me enough for Saturdays, too." He gave Buddy a lopsided grin. "Maybe I should ask for a raise. I mean, like a reward. Like, for discovering the fire because I was working overtime."

"Maybe," Buddy said. "I guess you could make a good case."

He thought about this on his way back to Darling, and before going to the office, he stopped at the bakery—The Flour Shop—where Mrs. Biddle worked. He asked her a couple of questions, took the half-dozen doughnuts she offered, and drove the short block to the sheriff's office. His deputy's old Chevy wasn't in its usual parking spot, which meant that Wayne must be out on a call somewhere. Buddy hoped he wasn't off to another fire.

The sheriff's office occupied a four-room frame house behind Snow's Farm Supply, catawampus from the courthouse and across the street from the bank. The jail was next door, on the second floor above Snow's Farm Supply, so it was easy to keep an eye on the occupants, if there were any—usually just a couple of fellows who had overindulged in the local moonshine. There was nobody in the lockup this morning, but there would be tomorrow, likely. Saturday nights were drinking nights and now that alcohol was legal again, there was a fair amount of celebrating, both in Darling and on the other side of the railroad tracks, in Maysville, where the coloreds lived.

In both places, the local moonshine was preferred to the more expensive stuff with the tax stamps on it. Almost nobody saw the wisdom of paying the government a tax just because the booze was distilled by a big company up in Kentucky or over in Missouri, when you could get it cheaper from a local shiner. Bodeen Pyle's was good. Mickey LeDoux's was better, and what was more, Mickey was out of prison and—according to local reports—back to shining at his old still over in Briar Swamp. Buddy hoped Mickey would do it privately enough that he didn't have to put him in jail again.

A scrawny black tomcat was sitting on the porch railing when Buddy came up the steps. He had belonged to the former occupant of the house, Miss Josephine Crumpler, who had gone to live with her niece in Nashville. At first, Buddy and Wayne had tried to evict the Beast, as they called the uncongenial creature. But they stopped trying when they realized that a gang of mice was poised to move in if the Beast should move out, which made him the lesser evil.

As Buddy unlocked the front door, the Beast leaped off the railing and followed him into what had once been the kitchen—and still was, since Miss Crumpler had left not just her cat but her stove and icebox. Wayne earned even less than Buddy, so to save money, he slept on a cot in the pantry (a handy arrangement, especially when there was a nighttime emergency) and cooked his meals in the kitchen.

Buddy put coffee and water into the percolator and got it started, then poured milk into a cracked china saucer, set it down for the cat, and went into Miss Crumpler's bedroom, now his office. He had finally got tired of looking at the flowered wallpaper and painted over it, which hadn't been such a bright idea. The weight of the paint had buckled some of the paper and it hung down in loose drapes, giving the room a rakish look. When he got a little time, he'd strip it to the plaster and try again.

But not today. Today, he had to write up the report on the fire at the Coca-Cola plant, find out how to get in touch with the state fire marshal's office (probably closed on Saturday, like civilized people), and finish his budget proposal for the county commissioners. He was asking for raises both for himself and Wayne. The last time he'd done that, they'd said sorry, no, so this time, it had to be good. Not that he blamed the commissioners. These days, the county had a tough time collecting taxes, and it was taxes that paid his salary. But he sure wished for a bigger paycheck so he and Bettina could go ahead and get married.

He pulled out a yellow tablet and the green-covered office account ledger, sharpened a couple of pencils, and turned on the Zenith radio on the shelf behind his desk. He turned it off again, though. Somebody was reading the latest commodity markets and Buddy had no interest in the price of pork bellies. Be nice if they'd play some Gene Autry songs, though.

When the coffee had perked long enough (but not too long), he poured a mugful and got started on the Coca-Cola report.

He had just finished when he heard tires crunching on gravel and looked out the front window to see Wayne's battered Chevy pulling up. A few minutes later, his deputy was standing in the doorway, fingers hooked in his belt loops.

"Mornin', boss," he said. It was about as far as Wayne ever got with the social niceties.

In his midthirties, Wayne Springer was tall, lithe as a swamp willow but muscular and dark-haired, with high cheekbones and the bronzed skin and easy grace that hinted at a Cherokee or a Creek somewhere back in the family. Buddy had been happy to hire him because he came with five years of law-enforcement experience and a reputation for deadeye accuracy with both his .38 Special and his long gun. There was a mystery that Buddy had not yet solved, however: why Wayne seemed satisfied to hire on for the pittance that Cypress County paid its one and only deputy. He could have earned more in a big city.

Wayne's other good point (as far as Buddy was concerned) was that he claimed no local friends or kinfolk. Most Darling folks couldn't spit without hitting an uncle or a cousin. Buddy hadn't been sheriff very long before he decided that if he and his deputy were on the hunt for a bank robber, he didn't want the deputy wondering whether the guy they were after might be his mother's great-uncle's second boy. He might hold his fire—or conversely (and just as likely), might shoot to kill when that wasn't strictly necessary. Buddy had the feeling that an outsider like Wayne was more likely to take the objective view, which could in the end save a couple of bushels of trouble.

He put down his pencil. "Coffee's on the stove," he said, and held out his mug. "Mine's empty." Wayne took it and reappeared a moment later.

"You been out on a call?" Buddy asked, leaning back in his chair with his coffee.

Wayne sipped his. "Mrs. Custer left a pair of Mr. Custer's

overalls on the clothesline overnight. When she got up, they were missing." He propped himself against the door frame. "Her husband works out at the prison farm and is gone all week. I thought she'd feel better if somebody showed up to take a look."

Buddy liked that about Wayne. He wasn't just doing a job. He cared about people—although sometimes that seemed a little at odds with the other part of him. The Deadeye Dick part. Another one of Wayne's mysteries.

"The Custers are what?" Buddy asked. "A half-block from the depot? Likely somebody rode in on the last freight yesterday and helped himself to what was handy."

"That's what I figured." Wayne grinned slightly. "I went over to the church to see if I could spot a clean pair with a patch on the right knee. And there was this young fella with his chin in a bowl of grits one of the ladies had just served up. Mr. Custer's britches went back home and the kid was told to take a pair from the giveaway shelf at the church. He also got a lecture from me and a morning's worth of chores for Mrs. Custer. Reckon he'll be glad to get back on the road."

Hobos didn't always understand that Darling was on a dead-end spur, not a through track, which meant that those who came in late were stuck in town until the first train out the next morning. In fact, there had been so many overnighters recently that the First Baptist ladies, with help from their Methodist and Presbyterian sidekicks, had set up a refuge of sorts in the church basement. The hobos—mostly young men and boys, some with fevers and wracking coughs, others with scrapes and sprains and bruises—were invited to supper, a blanket, and breakfast. Riding the rails was a hard-luck life, and hot biscuits with butter, a bowl of grits or soup, and a safe place to bed down were welcome. There were often a dozen or more transients sleeping at the church. Reverend Couch stopped in before lights out, counted noses, said a prayer for safety on the road, and counseled the wanderers to be on their way after breakfast. Mostly, there was no trouble. But every bushel had at least one bad apple. Hence Mr. Custer's missing overalls.

Everybody knew that Darling wasn't alone in this situation, of course. The New Deal was providing work for many but by no means all, and thousands of the jobless and homeless were constantly on the move, hoping to pick up enough money for a meal and cigarettes—maybe even find a place where they could put down roots and start a new life. Towns on the railroad or a main east–west highway saw the most traffic, of course. Buddy had read that Deming, New Mexico, which was home to only about 3,000 souls, was counting 125 transient arrivals every day. Double that in Tucson. Double again in Kansas City. Many towns set limits on how long transients could stay or arrested them for vagrancy and sentenced them to a week in jail, where they at least had meals and a bunk. Darling didn't do that—yet.

"I was at the church when I heard the siren," Wayne said. Taking another sip of coffee, he made a face. He preferred it strong enough to get out of the cup and do bench presses. Buddy's coffee was always too weak. "Where was the fire? Did you go?"

"Yep. Just finished the report," Buddy said. "It was in some lumber piled up against a lean-to shed at the rear of the Coca-Cola plant. They work a five-day week out there, but Henry Biddle said he needed to do some paperwork so he drove out this morning and spotted it when he got out of the car. Said he smelled kerosene, and Archie Mann turned up another delay device." He tossed it onto his desk. "And in this case, there could have been a substantial claim. Henry says they're storing nearly four thousand dollars' worth of new equipment in that shed. Insured."

Wayne arched an eyebrow. "Biddle phoned in the alarm himself?"

"That's right. But if you're wondering whether he set the fire and called it in so Coca-Cola would think he was a hero, the answer is no." He paused, considering. "Or not likely, anyway. On my way back to the office, I stopped at the bakery and had a little talk with Mrs. Biddle. She says her husband left the house at five past nine, and it's just ten minutes to the plant. Violet got his call at nine-nineteen. So it was already going when he called it in."

Unless, he thought, Biddle had called it in and *then* lit it. Which, he supposed, was a possibility he should keep in mind. But if that's what happened, where was the evidence? As Mr. Moseley always said, you couldn't arrest a man on a possibility. You needed proof—or at least something that looked enough like proof to get an indictment out of the grand jury.

"You checked the shed, I reckon." Wayne was following along with his thinking. "You got a look-see at what was inside?"

Buddy nodded. "I had Biddle open the crates and both of us had a look. He says the equipment is all there, and he had the manifest to prove it. The fire wasn't set to cover a theft."

"And that's it? Nothing else?"

"That's it," Buddy said with a sigh. "I had a good look around, thinking there might be a gasoline can, a cigarette package, something, anything. Of course, the boys working the fire weren't especially watching their feet. They might have destroyed any evidence on the ground. Footprints, tire prints, and the like."

"That's what makes arson so tough," Wayne said. "Fire eats up whatever evidence there is, and the firefighters trample the rest underfoot. We had a string of cases over in Jefferson County that stretched out for the better part of two years before we finally caught up with the arsonist."

"How'd you do that?" Buddy asked.

"We had a little help." Wayne grinned. "The firebug was a teenager in it for the excitement. His mama found out what he was doing and told him to lay off. When he lit the next one, she turned him in. All we had to do was arrest him. That lady made the case for us."

Buddy laughed. "I don't reckon we can look for that kind of luck. I was thinking, though. I might could ask Mr. Duffy if the bank would put up some reward money—twenty, twenty-five dollars, maybe."

Wayne pursed his lips. "That could work. Charlie Dickens could print a story in the newspaper. And maybe the boys would broadcast something on WDAR. You know, something like 'Keep an eye peeled for our firestarter. Your house could be next.'"

"Now, that's an idea," Buddy said approvingly. "I'll stop in and see Charlie today about a story in the *Dispatch*. I've already got an appointment with Mr. Moseley." The newspaper and the lawyer's office were in the same building. "You want to talk to Tommy Lee or Benny about getting it on the radio?"

A few months earlier, Tommy Lee Musgrove and Benny Biddle had launched radio station WDAR out of Mr. Barton's garage. They stuck their antenna on top of the Darling water tower and were getting pretty good reception in a radius of seven to ten miles, depending on the weather. They broadcast news and markets, weather forecasts, local programs (like the Flour Hour, from the bakery on the square), and music that Tommy Lee played on his Victrola in the garage studio.

"I'll do it." Wayne straightened up. "I was also wondering about deputizing a few of the guys and telling them to keep an eye out around town for unusual vehicles, somebody hanging out where he's not supposed to be, especially at night. What do you think?"

"Also a good idea," Buddy said. "I'd start with Jed Snow and Hank Trivette, maybe Artis Hart, at the laundry. Roger Kilgore, too." He frowned. "No guns, though. Tell 'em no guns. People are spooked enough by these fires. They don't need to see a bunch of vigilantes walking around with guns on their hips." He cast a look at Wayne, whose .38 was prominently slung on his left hip. Wayne was faster with his left hand than his right.

Wayne nodded. "You and me still aimin' to go to the hot dog supper this evening?"

"Yeah, but there's a new wrinkle," Buddy said, and told him about Archie Mann's request for a couple of votes to counter Rufus Radley's offer of a five-dollar bonus. He didn't mention the Gene Autry cowboy hat, though. He wanted to think that Archie was joking about that. And anyway, Archie had offered only one hat, for Buddy. Wayne wouldn't get one. He wouldn't want one, either, Buddy thought. Wayne wasn't a fan of cowboy movies. When it came to outlaws, he was more interested in folks like John Dillinger and Bonnie and Clyde, who'd been mowed down last year in Louisiana by a Texas posse.

"What do you think?," he asked. "Is it legal for Rufus to offer that money—in return for votes?"

Wayne shrugged. "You got me. We're talking a private organization here, not state or municipal, right?"

"I guess so," Buddy said. "Although I think the town—or maybe the county—gives the chief a little something to keep the trucks running."

"Well, I suppose the VFD can make its own rules, but you'd better ask Mr. Moseley. I could be wrong. Either way, though, I don't think I'll vote."

Buddy had pretty much made up his mind that he wouldn't, either. "Oh, and there's something else, too," he said. "When I was talking to Mrs. Biddle at the bakery a little while ago, she told me that Huey P. Long will be in Darling next week.

Wednesday, she said. He's giving a talk at the Masonic Lodge over in Birmingham the night before. The local Share Our Wealth Club invited him to stop here on his way back to Baton Rouge and he said yes."

"You bet he said yes," Wayne replied dryly. "That man would stop and talk politics to a gaggle of geese, if they'd give him a soapbox to stand on. Where is the club planning to put him?"

"On the courthouse steps. Mrs. Biddle said they'll probably start around two or three, or whenever his motorcade gets over here from Birmingham. They'll have a microphone and a loudspeaker. And maybe get the Academy band to play some marching music."

"If they ask him what he wants the band to play, he'll tell them 'Hail to the Chief,'" Wayne said.

"You think?" Buddy asked, surprised. "But Long is a Democrat, isn't he? FDR beat Hoover in a landslide. Won't the Democrats run *him* again?"

Wayne looked grim. "One way or another, Huey will run. And we'd better expect a crowd. I heard the man talk in Shreveport a couple of years ago, when he was still the Louisiana governor, running for senator. He draws crowds. *Big* crowds."

"Well, if that's the case," Buddy said, "we'd better block off traffic on the courthouse square on Wednesday. Probably need to round up some guys to help."

"We can do that." Wayne looked thoughtful. "I hear that the senator is paranoid about getting shot, so he never goes anywhere without three or four bodyguards. Over in Louisiana, they call them the Cossacks. You don't want to get crosswise of them."

Buddy thought about that for a moment. At last he said, "Well, I guess I'm not surprised he needs bodyguards. He likes to call people names and say things that are bound to piss folks off. Anyway, if he brings his own protection, we won't have to look after him. All we'll have to do is manage the traffic."

Wayne raised an eyebrow. "So if somebody does take a shot at him, it's the bodyguards' lookout? It's not on us?"

"You got it," Buddy said promptly, and opened the ledger. "But let's hope that doesn't happen. Not here in Darling anyway."

It was a remark he would remember for years afterward.

# CHAPTER FOUR

# ALL'S FAIR IN WAR AND POLITICS

*Monday, September 2, 1935*
*Labor Day*

CHARLIE DICKENS, THE EDITOR OF THE *DARLING DISPATCH*, turned down the volume on the radio beside his desk and dropped Elizabeth's Lacy's story about the garden contest into his wooden outbox. Liz (who also wrote a regular column called "The Garden Gate") was an excellent writer and he rarely had to take a pencil to her work. This piece—"Red Hot and Gorgeous"—was ready to go on the Linotype whenever Wilber got around to it. The topic was the red hot poker lily that had helped Bessie Bloodworth and her Magnolia ladies win the August garden prize.

Charlie picked up the last bite of Twinkies from the package on his desk and popped it into his mouth. As he did, he frowned, thinking of his conversation with Mrs. Hancock, the proprietor of the grocery store next door. He had been paying for the Twinkies when she told him that the Voodoo Lily had stopped in that morning for a sack of grits. She had told Mrs. Hancock that a hurricane was going to slam into the Florida Keys on Labor Day.

"Lil says it'll be the worst one ever," Mrs. Hancock reported with evident satisfaction. She always looked forward to disasters—the more catastrophic, the better. "And there's more to come after that, she says. And you know Lil. She always gets it right." She rang up the nickel he had given her for the Twinkies. "Could be a story for the paper, you know."

Charlie might have told her that newspaper stories came in on the wire services, not through the local soothsayers, even the good ones. But he didn't. He just thanked her, took his Twinkies, and left. He was seriously concerned, though. Big Lil—the Voodoo Lily—had favored him with a number of tips in the past and he had found her predictions eerily, even astonishingly accurate. And Charlie had lived in Key West for a time. He had friends there. He knew just how vulnerable the islands were.

If he was hoping that Big Lil was wrong, he was about to be disappointed. The radio on the shelf behind his desk was tuned to the new local station, WDAR. Tommy Lee Musgrove, one of the two teenagers who launched the station a few months before, had just read an AP news bulletin. Just as the Voodoo Lily had predicted, a powerful hurricane was barreling up the Florida Straits, the channel between Florida and Cuba. It was headed directly for the Keys and somebody—Charlie didn't catch who—was getting ready to send a special railroad train to pick up a big group of veterans of the Great War. They were working on the new Overseas Highway from the mainland to Key West.

A veteran himself, Charlie knew those men. They were the sad remnants of the Bonus Army that had marched on the capitol three years ago, petitioning then-president Hoover and the Congress for an early payment of their army bonuses, not due for another ten years. Hoover had refused to listen and had even ordered General MacArthur to drive them out of their Hooverville on the bank of the Potomac. It was a debacle involving tanks, the cavalry, and armed soldiers, and Hoover paid dearly for it. It was one of the principal reasons why FDR defeated him so handily in '32.

A smaller group of vets was back the next year, though, and the year after that. While Congress debated the bonus payment, FDR offered them jobs in the just-established Civilian Conservation Corp, and nearly seven hundred took him up on it. They were sent to Florida to work on the new Overseas Highway.

Yes, it was work, which they wanted. And of course it was money, which they desperately needed. But it was a bad situation for many of the men. They were away from their families, in malaria country. They had nothing to do but fish, get drunk, and brawl. And sure enough, in early August, Harry Hopkins, the head of the CCC, had announced that the three Florida work camps would be closed in November. The vets would be going home.

Charlie was thinking about this and hoping fervently that the train would get to those men before the hurricane did, when the bell over the door jingled and Wilber Casey came in. He slung his cap on the peg beside the door and came around the front counter to Charlie's desk. They hadn't had a chance to talk since Saturday morning, when Wilber went out to cover the fire at the bottling plant.

"No rest for the wicked," Wilber said. "Even on a holiday weekend."

"How was it out there?" Charlie asked, around the cigarette at the corner of his mouth. "Much of a blaze?"

"Could have been but wasn't," Wilber said. Slight and thin-shouldered, the young man had ginger-colored hair and blue eyes behind round, wire-rimmed glasses. "It was in a pile of boards behind a shed built smack-up against the back wall of the Coca-Cola plant. The building is frame construction, so it was a good thing Mr. Biddle happened to see it when he did. The firemen got to the fire before the fire got to the shed. There wasn't any serious damage."

Charlie dropped the butt of his Camel into the root beer

bottle on a corner of his desk and leaned back in his chair, clasping his hands behind his head. "That makes what—six?"

"Yeah," Wilber said, "if you count the fire at the parsonage, which Chief Mann doesn't, since the preacher started it by being careless. I missed the chief at the fire, but I stopped at the VFD barn and got a couple of quotes from him. By his count, it's number five, and he's calling it arson, without a doubt." He leaned forward eagerly. "They're *all* arson, Mr. Dickens, so we've got ourselves a firebug. I got a couple of quotes from Sheriff Norris too," he added. "And some photos." He grinned. "I'll get them developed tonight. And I'm going to get out there on the street and interview a few people—hear what they're thinking about these fires. You know, whether they're scared and lying awake or sleeping okay at night. Right now, though, I'm rarin' to hit the typewriter."

Charlie gave the boy an approving look. For a cub reporter in his first newspaper job, Wilber was shaping up to be first rate. He had an eye for detail, a passion for the story. And a pretty good sense of how to make it sing. What's more, he had learned to operate the balky old Linotype as easily as if it were a typewriter, which it definitely wasn't. He was no slouch when it came to selling advertising, either.

In fact, although Wilber had only worked at the *Dispatch* for a few months, he was already so all-fired good at what he did and so eager to learn how to do it better and faster that Charlie had begun thinking of how he could put that can-do spirit to work to build up the newspaper. And for another plus, he not only had Wilber Casey to do the reporting and write the stories but Osgood Fairchild to arm-wrestle the old Babcock press into submission and Baby Mann to run errands and keep the place looking halfway clean. His little team was so competent that he had recently taken a week off for a trip with his wife Fannie— the first since they were married.

The trip had given him some thinking time, and the idea he had come up with was pretty . . . well, challenging might be a good word. Expensive would be another. So today, he was having lunch with Alvin Duffy, the president of the Darling Savings and Trust, to discuss a loan. He had talked it over with Fannie, who liked what she'd heard and said she could help a little with the funding. Against all odds, Fannie's millinery partnership with famous designer and fashion merchandiser Lilly Daché was going very well. It appeared that there were still quite a few women who had enough money to afford a pricey new hat for the season. Lilly Daché knew where to find them and Fannie knew exactly what they wanted.

Charlie unclasped his hands and sat up straight. "Okay, Wilber. You write me a dynamite story and we'll run it top of page two." Page one was the pre-print national news Charlie bought from Western Newspaper Union, a syndicate that provided the latest wire-service news to small-town newspapers all across the country. Page two was where they ran the local headline news story. "That is," he added, "unless something else comes along and knocks it off."

That didn't seem likely. Darling had been quiet for the past few weeks. Besides the arsonist, the only other news was the unexpected election of Rufus Radley as the new fire chief (Archie Mann had been thought to be a shoo-in) and Liz Lacy's story about the little old ladies who had won the August garden prize.

In contrast, the arson story had everything going for it: thrills, chills, mystery, and above all suspense. Nobody knew who the firebug was. Nobody could predict his next target. Would it be somebody's house? Somebody's business? The school, a church, the post office? The town could talk of nothing but those fires. They probably ought to increase the print run for this week's issue, Charlie thought. The arson story could be a winner.

But Wilber had a surprise for Charlie. "Well, here's something that could knock that story off," he said. Wilber's glasses always slid down his nose when he was excited. They slid down now, and he pushed them up again. "You ready for this, Mr. Dickens? Hold onto your hat." He paused for dramatic effect. "Huey P. Long is coming to town!"

Charlie felt his jaw drop. "Huey P.?" he exclaimed. "Hell's bells, Wilber. What does he want to come to Darling for?"

But Charlie knew very well why Huey P. Long wanted to come to Darling—or anywhere else that promised even a handful of voters. The 1936 presidential election might still be fifteen months away, but Senator Long of Louisiana (recently Governor Long) was already making it clear that he intended to be President Long. He had just finished a swing through Iowa, Missouri, and the Dakotas, grabbing headlines, holding rallies, firing up the crowds. Now, he was campaigning across the South.

And FDR? The man who had saved the banks and kept America's credit from crumbling? Who had found work for thousands of people who had lost their jobs? Who had dragged the country out of the Slough of Despond by the sheer force of his will, the magic of his smile, and the persuasive power of his fireside chats? What did FDR think about Senator Long?

Well, it just so happened that the answer to that question was no mystery to Charlie. He and Fannie had recently driven to Warm Springs, Georgia, to visit Fannie's son Jason. A polio survivor, Jason was undergoing long-term therapy at the Roosevelt Warm Springs Institute, where he could get daily attention from physical therapists and spend time in the therapeutic springs. The president had been there, too, staying in the recently built Little White House. FDR had had plenty to say about Huey P. Long, none of it good. And Charlie happened to be there when he said it.

When he was at Warm Springs, the president liked to eat supper with the residents in the Institute dining hall. The first night Charlie and Fannie were there, FDR happened to sit across the table from them. Fannie was charmed by her first meeting with him. But Charlie had met him before. In fact, as a reporter for the *Cleveland Plain Dealer*, he had covered Roosevelt's first national political campaign, in October 1920, the year before FDR contracted polio. Roosevelt was running for vice president on the Democratic ticket with James Cox of California. Charlie, lately back from a couple of years with the *Stars and Stripes* military newspaper, was assigned to Roosevelt's whistle-stop campaign train. The candidate gave twenty-minute stump speeches, glad-handed with the local bigwigs in every one-horse town the train passed through, and engaged in friendly personal banter with reporters wherever he stopped. FDR liked to be on good terms with the newspapers.

It happened that Charlie had a reputation as an excellent poker player, so FDR invited him to join the nightly poker game, which also included Steve Early, the campaign's advance man and (as another former *Stars and Stripes* reporter) one of Charlie's newspaper buddies. When FDR was dealing, he usually preferred seven-card stud with one-eyed jacks wild or Woolworths with fives and tens wild. He insisted on playing nickel-ante, though. Nobody lost very much, and Charlie and FDR (whose Democratic ticket was soundly defeated by Republicans Warren G. Harding and Calvin Coolidge) often split the pot.

Which was why, when the president wheeled himself to the opposite side of the dining table that night in Warm Springs, he remembered Charlie with pleasure. "We may have lost that first one, Dickens," he said cheerfully, referring to that 1920 campaign, "but we've won every election since."

True, of course. In 1928, on a long shot, FDR had beaten Al

Smith (and the Tammany Hall machine) for the governorship of New York. In 1932, he had whipped Herbert Hoover.

Somebody went to the old upright piano in the corner and began to play FDR's campaign song, "Happy Days Are Here Again." Beaming, the president leaned across the table. "Say, how about joining us for a little game tonight?" he asked. "At the house, about eight. Steve Early will be there, too—as I remember, both of you were *Stars and Stripes* reporters, back in the Great War." FDR's memory was phenomenal, especially when it came to people he'd played poker with.

Charlie had, of course, agreed. (Who wouldn't? It was the president asking.) He left Fannie playing checkers with Jason, a handsome little boy who bore his disability with exceptional patience. As he walked through the quiet Georgia woods, he thought with mild surprise about the rare sight of the president in a wheelchair. He had heard from wire-service friends who covered the White House that FDR never appeared in a wheelchair in public and that all his events were carefully choreographed so that his audience wouldn't be aware of his paralysis. He apparently felt at home in Warm Springs, where—in one way or another—everybody lived with the devastating effects of polio.

At the white-porticoed Little White House, Charlie joined the president; Steve Early, now FDR's press secretary; Louis Howe, his right-hand-man and political advisor; and Missy LeHand, the president's pretty, vivacious secretary and a poker whiz. They played until nearly midnight, when Charlie called it quits and Roosevelt and Early split the pot.

The subject of Huey Long had come up during the course of that poker game. In a jocular tone, Early asked Howe if he'd heard about Huey's latest book, scheduled for publication in October. "It's called *My First Days in the White House*." He made a disgusted noise. "Can you believe the nerve of that guy?

The book is supposed to be set in 1937, after he's moved into the Oval Office."

"I understand that I'm to be offered a position in his cabinet," FDR said, his ivory cigarette holder at a rakish angle. "Secretary of the Navy. Huey says it's a promotion."

Laughter rippled around the table. But Long had a gift for targeting his insults, Charlie thought. Roosevelt had been Assistant Secretary of the Navy in Wilson's administration, twenty years before. The Navy ran in the Roosevelt family. FDR's cousin Theodore had had the same job in the McKinley administration, before McKinley was assassinated and TR moved to the White House.

Early sucked on his cigar. "Long is a fool. You've heard about the gold toilet seat medal, Dickens?"

Roosevelt rolled his eyes. "Doesn't bear retelling in the presence of a lady."

"Long is a rude, crude, boorish clown," Missy LeHand said fiercely, stubbing out her cigarette. "I heard that once he got himself elected governor of Louisiana, he tore down the old governor's mansion and built an exact replica of the White House, only smaller." She pressed her lips together. "Nobody can take a fool like that seriously."

"*I* take him seriously." Louis Howe's cadaverous face, ravaged by chronic illness and wreathed in cigarette smoke, was somber. "So does Farley. He fielded a secret poll a couple of months ago to find out just how much of a threat Huey poses."

"Farley is the chair of the Democratic National Committee," Missy explained sotto voce (and unnecessarily) to Charlie, who knew that Jim Farley was the most powerful man in the party. Farley and Howe, together, would manage FDR's reelection campaign.

Howe went on. "Turns out that nearly twelve percent of the voters prefer the Kingfish on a third-party Share Our Wealth ticket over either President Roosevelt or a Republican candidate. Which is substantial."

"But he promised there won't be a third party," Missy protested.

"If you believe that, I can sell you the Brooklyn Bridge," Early muttered.

Howe ignored them both. "Huey will grab some six million votes in a third-party bid, according to Farley. In crucial states, he'll siphon off enough Democrats to hand the Electoral College to the GOP."

Charlie had heard this calculation before. Roosevelt would need at least 266 electoral votes to win a second term. His supporters were already jotting down numbers on the backs of envelopes. If Long was in the picture, FDR could come up thirty or forty votes shy.

Missy squared her shoulders stubbornly. "I don't believe that."

"I do," Roosevelt said—rather nonchalant, Charlie thought, given the subject.

"Believe it." Howe took a last pull on his noxious Sweet Caporal cigarette. "After he's split the party in '36, he'll run in 1940. And after four more years of a stagnant economy, he'll win."

"A third-party ticket." Early shook his head gloomily. "Slick. Very slick." He narrowed his eyes at Charlie. "This conversation is off the record, Dickens. I don't want to read anything about it in your little rag. Or elsewhere."

Charlie nodded, half amused by the thought of FDR's press secretary actually reading a page in the *Darling Dispatch*. Of course, if he'd still been reporting for the *Plain Dealer*, this might have been a hard pill to swallow. But he understood why FDR's political strategists wanted to keep those poll numbers under their hats. They were scary as hell. Long clearly had the potential to divide the party next year, to the benefit of nobody but himself.

And then, no longer nonchalant, the president said something so frank and forthright that Charlie knew he would never forget it. "Huey Pierce Long is one of the two most dangerous men in America."

"You really think so?" Charlie asked, surprised.

"I do." FDR's voice was suddenly and uncharacteristically sharp. "Long is undisciplined, perpetually angry, and narcissistic. He's like a kid with a red hot poker, jabbing at everybody, trying to get them all fired up and mad about something, anything." He smacked the flat of his hand on the table. "Worse, he's a pathological liar who knows full well that he can never implement that phony 'make America wealthy again' scheme he's ginned up to win votes. A corrupt politician who uses his elected position for his personal gain. And a rabble-rouser who manipulates people's emotions, particularly those who are less well-educated and uninformed. They'll follow him like rats after the Pied Piper."

Charlie was surprised by the vehemence of FDR's assessment but had to agree with it. For the past decade, he had been reading newspaper accounts of Long's rise to power in the *New Orleans Item* and the *Times-Picayune*. A number of the stories had been written by Virgil McCone, another friend from his *Stars and Stripes* days, now a reporter for the AP news service. Long's four years as Louisiana governor had been scarred by the blatant corruption that had finally resulted in his impeachment, although he had managed to escape conviction on a technicality. Charlie had also read about Long's opposition to the New Deal in his home state—for instance, his refusal to allow the work relief program to be implemented—since he couldn't control the distribution of those funds. A United States senator for going on three years, Long preferred to be the man who handed out the jobs, the money, and the political appointments. That was the way he bought loyalty.

But Charlie had another question for the president. "If Huey is one of the two most dangerous men in the country, who's the other?"

"You can't guess?" Missy asked coyly.

When Charlie hesitated, Steve Early spoke up. "Douglas MacArthur," he said, one crooked eyebrow raised.

"Ah," Charlie said. "Of course."

General MacArthur had fallen into disgrace when he ordered federal troops to break up the encampment of peaceful Bonus Army veterans a couple of summers before. What's more, his tenure as chief of staff of the Army had been punctuated by budget quarrels with the White House—rancorous quarrels so loud they made it into the newspapers. A relentless self-promoter, MacArthur was especially popular with Midwestern conservatives who distrusted Roosevelt's New Deal. Like Huey Long, the general was also said to nurse presidential ambitions.

"MacArthur is on his way to the Philippines," FDR remarked with acid amusement. "As Grand Poobah."

"The Philippines?" Charlie asked, although he thought he knew the answer. "Now, why under the sun would he want to go *there*? Who is he going to fight in the Pacific?"

"He's supposed to keep an eye on the Japanese," the president said innocently. "Who knows what the devil they're up to."

"The boss reassigned him," explained Howe with a grin. "Military advisor to the Philippines' new president." Out of the corner of his mouth, gangster-style, he added "Sidelining the general so he can't decide to run for president."

"All's fair in war and politics," the president said, still innocent.

"If Senator Long doesn't watch out, somebody's going to

sideline *him*," Missy said in a stern tone. "For a clown, that man has an astonishing number of enemies."

"How about sending *him* to the Philippines?" Early suggested.

"How about Timbuktu?" FDR sighed. "Unfortunately, I've got no say over damfool idiot senators. Your deal, Dickens."

So that was how the president felt about Senator Long—a feeling that Steve Early had elaborated on as he and Charlie left the game and strolled to their cabins through the quiet Georgia night.

"Is the president really concerned about Long or was he just spouting off?" Charlie asked.

"You bet he's concerned." Early's voice was dark. "He'd never say it in public, but he knows that Long is a dangerous man. The fellow is no populist. He doesn't give a damn about public policy or what's good for the country. He has no principles. All that 'every man a king' crap—it's just a con to get people all fired up, make them think they're part of a movement. No, sir. Power for himself, personal power. That's the only thing Long is after."

"And there's nothing anybody can do to stop him?"

"Nothing short of bloodshed," Early hunched his shoulders. "Forget I said that."

Now, Charlie swung his attention from that remembered conversation to Wilber, still sitting in front of him. "When is Huey's circus coming to town?"

"Wednesday afternoon. He's speaking in Birmingham and stopping here on his way to Mobile. The local Share Our Wealth Club is supposed to be organizing it."

"Well, you're right about one thing," Charlie said. "That knocks your arson story below the fold."

"I figured." Wilber got to his feet. "Guess I'll get started writing."

"You do that." Charlie pulled out his desk drawer and began

pawing through the disorganized litter of business cards. "Virgil McCone," he muttered. "Virgil, where are you, buddy? You covering the Kingfish these days?"

He was still looking for Virgil's card when the phone rang. "Long distance for you, Mr. Dickens," the girl on the Darling switchboard said. "Please hold."

There was a brief series of clicks, and then a strong male voice said, "Hey, Charlie-boy, how you doing? Virgil McCone here."

"Well, speak of the devil," Charlie said in amazement.

# CHAPTER FIVE

# OUT OF THE FRYING PAN

UPSTAIRS OVER THE NEWSPAPER OFFICE AND PRESS ROOM, ELIZabeth Lacy finished typing the last page of the brief, rolled it and its carbon out of the Underwood, and put it with the other pages. Then, instead of quitting, she picked up the draft of the letter Mr. Moseley had left for her.

*This won't take more than a few minutes,* she told herself as she rolled a clean sheet of paper into the typewriter. There were plenty of things she liked about working for Bent Moseley, but typing legal briefs—with carbons—wasn't one of them. Especially on a Labor Day Monday, when the office was supposed to be closed. And especially after she'd stayed up late the night before, retyping the first three chapters of her novel.

Her *second* novel. Miss Fleming, her literary agent, wanted to see the chapters before Lizzy sent them to Maxwell Perkins, her editor at Scribner. Lizzy wasn't happy with the chapters or with the progress she was making on the book, a sequel to *Inherit the Flames.* To tell the truth, she was stuck, and it wasn't a pleasant feeling. Was it writer's block—or something else? She kept asking herself *Where am I going wrong? What can I do to fix it?* But she hadn't come up with any answers.

She sighed. Well, the brief was done, anyway. There was only the letter, and it was much shorter. She had already made coffee. She would have a cup before she started on it. She was just pouring it when the outside door opened and Verna Tidwell came into the office.

"I thought I saw your light on, Liz. You're working on a holiday?"

Verna was looking especially summery on this hot morning, in a light blue voile dress with a V-shaped white collar and a swingy bias-cut skirt. She wore her dark hair in a Louise Brooks bob, short and sleek with straight-across bangs—a 1920s look, she admitted, but easy care, and it suited her. She had little patience with bobby-pin curls and even less with makeup. A quick comb-through, a slick-down with a little Vaseline hair tonic, a dash of fire-engine-red lipstick, and that was it. The Cypress County clerk (the only elected female county clerk in the entire state), Verna worked on the second floor of the courthouse, just across the street. In fact, Liz could see her office window from the front window of the Moseley office.

"Had to type a brief," Lizzy said with a smile. "And a letter." She reached for the dial on the radio behind her desk and switched it off. She liked music while she typed, and WDAR usually played recordings of big-band instrumentals. "I hope *you're* not working today."

Verna gave a casual shrug. "I thought I'd spend a couple of hours on paperwork while the office is cool—well, cooler. And quiet. I'm digging into some out-of-the-ordinary property filings, and it's easier when there are no distractions. But I noticed your light and thought I'd drop in for a quick hello."

Whatever those unusual property filings were, Lizzy knew that Verna was perfectly capable of handling them. She was one of those people who seemed to have been born with a rather dim view of human nature, nurtured by her habit of peering "under the rocks," as she put it. Since she was responsible for collecting the county's taxes and paying the county's bills,

Verna's mistrustful nature ideally suited her to her job as Cypress County's most relentless detective.

Not long before, for instance, she had gone through a stack of invoices and discovered that the contractor who won the bid to build a new bridge over Jericho Creek had billed the county for twice the amount of cement he put into the bridge—and sold the rest of it to his cousin, who'd been hired to pave the parking lot at the Academy. She was always on the lookout for that kind of chicanery, especially now that times were hard and people were perpetually short of money. In the course of her job, Verna met a great many folks who did whatever they thought they could get away with. In the case of the bridge contractor, it was up to her to blow the whistle. So she did.

Now, she held up a brown paper bag. "It might be a holiday, but The Flour Shop was open. I stopped in just as Earlynne was putting out fresh doughnuts." She opened the bag. "Thought I might tempt you to tell me about your book tour."

"A doughnut sounds swell," Lizzy said. She and Verna hadn't had a chance to talk for weeks. She was eager to share some of the details of her trip and hear what was going on in her friend's life. She waved a hand at the electric percolator on the shelf behind her desk. "I was just ready for fresh coffee. A cup for you?"

"Wonderful," Verna said. A few moments later, she was taking the cup Lizzy handed her, with a small white paper napkin.

Verna frowned at the napkin. "This is something new?"

"They've been out for a couple of years, I think. I saw them in New York and bought a box to show my mother. She ordered them for the dime store." Lizzy's widowed mother had recently (and rather surprisingly) married Mr. Dunlap, owner of Dunlap's Five and Dime, on the south side of the courthouse square. She was now happily employed as the store's manager—happily for Lizzy, too, since the work kept her mother occupied.

"Looks like a good idea," Verna said. "Expensive?"

"Not very. Sixty for a nickel." Lizzy lowered her voice. "Mother has also ordered some tampons. Tampax, they're called. I got a box of them in New York, too."

Verna smiled. "Tampons! I've read about them. Now, that's an innovation I'll go for—if they don't cost too much."

Lizzy nodded. "They're only six for a quarter. Mother said she'd keep them under the counter, so pass the word. If we want them, we have to ask. Not Mr. Dunlap, of course," she added hastily. "She hasn't told him about the tampons yet. Remember how embarrassed he was when he first started selling Kotex a few years ago? It was self-service and all very hush-hush. You'd pick up the box from a bottom shelf at the very back of the store and drop the money in a coffee can on the counter."

"He did the very same thing when he first started selling sanitary belts," Verna reminded her with a wry smile. "But tampons! Jeepers! Times *are* changing."

Supplied with doughnuts, coffee, and paper napkins, they went to sit at the open second-floor window that looked out across Franklin Street to the old red brick courthouse where Verna worked—in many ways the heart of Darling. For her, a practical, get-it-done woman, it was the place where people came to meet their obligations as citizens: to get a marriage license, register the births of their children or the purchase of a piece of property, settle a disagreement, file a death certificate, probate a will.

Lizzy, on the other hand, was rather more idealistic. She saw the courthouse as Verna did, but more. To her, the old place had always seemed to represent the civilizing and stabilizing power of justice in their small community. It was the place where Darling people went to see things made right under the law—a law they knew they could trust.

Now, some people might say that Liz was being a little too

idealistic, perhaps, especially given the fact that the Klan still operated in Cypress County and that Governor Bibb Graves once served as the Grand Cyclops of the Montgomery Klavern. It was certainly true that her optimistic views about the law had been tempered in the years she had worked for Mr. Moseley, as she learned that the courts didn't always administer justice evenhandedly and that "fairness" and even "equality" could be debatable terms.

But Lizzy clung to her optimism and her faith in the law and justice even when it was sorely tested by people who managed to get away with doing things that she knew were just plain *wrong*. Like the arsonist who was setting all those fires around town—for what? For fun? Excitement? The thrill of seeing that new fire engine racing down the street? And Rufus Radley had been elected as Darling's new fire chief, even though the man had no experience whatsoever when it came to fighting fires. It was a narrow victory—he'd won by only three votes—and the mystery of how that happened had been cleared up when Buddy Norris told Mr. Moseley about Rufus Radley's promise of a five-dollar "bonus" to any volunteer who voted for him.

"Would that make the election illegal?" he had asked.

Mr. Moseley said it wouldn't. For one thing, that bonus business was just an allegation—at least, until somebody came in with hard-and-fast proof that Radley was buying votes. And even if that happened, he didn't think any laws had been broken. The VFD was a private organization of volunteers. They made their own rules. If it pleased them to elect Mr. Parrish's red pig Ruby as their fire chief, they could do it.

"And then," he had added, "they'd have to live with the result. Elections have consequences—especially if you elect a pig. Or somebody who doesn't know what he's doing. Once Rufus Radley tries to take charge, I reckon they'll figure that out pretty quick."

"Well," Verna said, sipping her coffee, "you'll have to tell me all about your book tour. Was it fun? Did you like New York?"

Without a doubt, Lizzy's book tour was one of the most exciting things that had ever happened to her. After months of hard work and more revisions than she could count, her Civil War novel, *Inherit the Flames*, had at long last been published by Charles Scribner's Sons. The reviews had been excellent and the prepublication sales figures seemed quite decent, although Miss Fleming (Lizzy's agent) confided that the book would certainly have done better if it weren't for the Depression. When people had to choose between buying bread and buying a book, she said, they usually reached for the bread. Still, Lizzy had visited bookstores in New York, Boston, Baltimore, and Atlanta, where people *had* bought her book and asked her to autograph it for them—an enormous thrill.

But as Lizzy now told Verna, it was her three-day visit to New York and the people she met there that stayed in her mind. Maxwell Perkins, her editor (whom she was meeting for the first time) turned out to be a slender man with graying hair, a narrow face with a beakish nose, and a modest, self-effacing manner. But he had a passionate interest in young authors who showed promise. He had been the first to publish Scott Fitzgerald, Ernest Hemingway, Thomas Wolfe, and Marjorie Kinnan Rawlings. He had even sent Lizzy a copy of Rawlings' Pulitzer-nominated first novel, *South Moon Under*.

At Scribner's offices on Fifth Avenue, Mr. Perkins introduced her to the editorial staff and showed her around the building. He asked about her progress on her second novel and, to her surprise, Lizzy found herself telling him that she was stuck.

"And terrified," she confessed. "The first book just spilled out of my head and into the typewriter. This one . . ." She shook her head. "It's like pulling teeth. I'm not sure where I'm going with it."

His smile was sympathetic. "We call it sophomore slump. Many of my writers have suffered from it."

Although it was good to know she wasn't alone in this daunting dilemma, Lizzy had to ask, "But what can I *do*?"

For a moment, Mr. Perkins didn't answer. Then he said, "One of my writers once told me that writing a book is like driving down a road in a pouring rain—at night. You can see only as far as your headlights, and sometimes your wipers don't even clear the windshield. But if you keep your foot on the gas and manage to stay out of the ditch, you'll eventually get where you're going." He smiled. "Just write, Elizabeth. Every day. You'll get through it. Your next book will be easier. And the one after that."

*Next* book? She shuddered. She had the terrible feeling that there wasn't going to be a second book, let alone another after that.

For lunch, they walked to the nearby Brevoort Hotel, where Lizzy was surprised and delighted when they were joined by Miss Rawlings, in town to discuss last-minute editorial details on her second novel, *Golden Apples*, due out in October. Marjorie (they were quickly on first-name terms) owned a small orange grove in a Florida scrub-country hamlet called Cross Creek.

Miss Rawlings, a petite, plumpish woman with dark hair and an attractive face, was lively and full of stories about her life in Florida and the fascinating people she had met there. Before lunch was over, she had invited Lizzy to come to Cross Creek for a visit, and Lizzy had eagerly agreed. She had loved *South Moon Under*, which was about a moonshiner and his family—a subject that was well known in Darling, where a couple of moonshining families played a prominent role in the town. Marjorie said she was currently working on a new novel about a boy and his pet deer. *The Yearling*, she was calling it. Lizzy was amazed by (and deeply envious of) a writer who could produce a book and several outstanding short stories every few years. And here she was, stuck on her second book!

During lunch, Mr. Perkins entertained them with stories about his work as an editor. About wrestling with Thomas Wolfe over the ninety thousand words Wolfe had finally agreed to cut from the manuscript of *Look Homeward, Angel*. About going driving with Scott Fitzgerald's wife Zelda and ending up waist-deep in Long Island Sound. About nearly losing his job when Ernest Hemingway's manuscript of *The Sun Also Rises* (which Mr. Perkins had bought sight unseen) turned out to be blistered by four-letter words.

The three of them were enjoying cherry tarts with their coffees when they were abruptly joined by Ernest Hemingway himself. Lizzy had admired *A Farewell to Arms*, but she quickly discovered that she wasn't impressed by its author. Hemingway might be a world-famous writer but was patronizing, profane, and more than a little drunk. He completely ignored Lizzy and Miss Rawlings and focused his attention on Mr. Perkins. And all he wanted to talk about was his new thirty-eight-foot sport-fishing yacht, which he called *Pilar*, the nickname he had given to his second wife, Pauline. He was paying for it, he told Mr. Perkins with a note of triumph, with an advance from *Esquire* "on future articles." (Mr. Perkins had apparently been unable to advance him anything because he wasn't making much progress on the next book.)

But that was the only unpleasantness. Both Lizzy and Marjorie were staying at the Grosvenor Hotel, where Willa Cather had lived while she was writing *Shadows on the Rock*. Marjorie had once lived in the city and volunteered to show her around, so the two of them took a taxi up Fifth Avenue to Times Square, where they wandered around for a while looking at shop windows. Then they went to dinner at the Algonquin

Hotel, the famous gathering place for writers Dorothy Parker, Robert Benchley, Edna Ferber, and Noël Coward. After dinner, they taxied to the Alvin Theater on West Fifty-Second to see *Anything Goes*, the exciting Cole Porter musical everyone was raving about, starring the unforgettable Ethel Merman. Back at the Grosvenor, Lizzy fell asleep with "Anything Goes" echoing in her dreams.

And yes, it seemed that "anything went" in New York City. The streets could be dirty with discarded refuse but electric with the energy of people hurrying off to exciting places to do exciting things. They could be raucous with the honking of cars and taxicabs but intriguing with the babel of different languages and different costumes. They could be smelly with last week's garbage but fragrant with exotic foreign cuisines.

And there was always some new vantage point to look from and something new and exciting to see. During her visit, Lizzy had ridden three elevators, one after the other, to the top observation deck of the new Empire State Building, where she could see all of New York at her feet, as well as two rivers, six states, and an ocean that stretched beyond the horizon. She had climbed 393 steps from the base of the Statue of Liberty into the crown, where she looked across New York Harbor toward Brooklyn and lower Manhattan, Staten Island, and the tidal straits of the Hudson River. Back in mid-town, she went to the Museum of Modern Art, where she stared, puzzled, at paintings by Pablo Picasso and Paul Klee. After that, she went shopping at the glittering Bergdorf Goodman, where she paid too much for a new leather handbag. Then to the elegant Saks Fifth Avenue, where she bought a pair of smart blue kid-leather gloves.

But what stayed with her longest were the lines of hopeless-looking men, women, and children queued up for the soup kitchens—lines that wrapped around the block. And the notorious Central Park Hooverville, a filthy shanty town of tents and packing-crate-and-canvas shacks sheltering the homeless people who had lost their jobs and their livelihoods to the Depression.

Perhaps it was those tragic contrasts—the glaring luxuries of the very rich and the terrible poverty of the down-and-out—that had made Lizzy so glad to find herself at home once again. Most Darling people didn't have very much, the movies were second- or third-run, and it might take a couple of years for an innovative product—like paper napkins or tampons—to show up on a store shelf (or under the counter).

But people cared enough to plant extra vegetables for their out-of-work neighbors and to provide a hot meal, bedding, and clean used clothing for the hobos who bunked in the First Baptist basement. Liz had enjoyed her few days in New York, but she knew she was a small-town girl at heart.

"Sounds like a marvelous trip," Verna said when Lizzy had finished telling her all about it. "Are you ready to go again?"

"I'm ready to settle down and get back to work on the next book," Lizzy said ruefully. "Mr. Perkins says that if I can finish in a couple of months, he can put it on next year's fall list. But we've been really busy here at the office." She sighed. "And by the time I get home, I don't have the energy to work on it."

That wasn't the whole story, of course. She was stuck and she didn't know what to do about it—except follow Mr. Perkins' advice. Keep her foot on the gas and stay out of the ditch.

"Of course," Verna said in a comforting voice. "And you can't just work. You need a little social life." She cocked a teasing eyebrow. "Wasn't that you I saw with Benton Moseley, driving down Rosemont the other evening?"

Lizzy nodded. "We were on our way to Monroeville for a movie. *Forty-Second Street.*"

She wondered whether Verna had also seen Bent's arm across the back of the seat, his fingers on her bare shoulder, and colored a little as she remembered the quick, almost shy kiss he had given her when they said goodnight on her front porch. It was still "Mr. Moseley" when they were in the office, but "Bent" when they went out together—as they did occasionally now, but always casually. When Lizzy had first come to work in the office, she had yearned for him with an achingly adolescent puppy love. But she had outgrown that years ago. And if she wanted their relationship to grow into something else (did she? She wasn't sure) it appeared that it wasn't.

And wouldn't, she told herself, as long as Moira Skelton was in the picture. One of Lizzy's jobs was keeping Mr. Moseley's calendar. She knew that whenever he went to Montgomery on legal business, he saw Miss Skelton, the politically connected daughter of an Alabama state senator. The lady was undeniably gorgeous, with a striking figure, exquisite taste in clothes and jewelry, and a reputation for putting on the most fabulous parties in town. Since Mr. Moseley had an office in Montgomery, he was there quite often. In August alone, he had made three separate trips to the capital city.

Lizzy had also heard (confidentially, from Doc Roberts' wife, Edna Fay) that Miss Skelton was a "duplicitous" woman whose "dangerous" political liaisons were personally hazardous to Mr. Moseley. Edna Fay clearly hoped that Liz could do something about that, but of course she couldn't, even if she had wanted to. Mr. Moseley was going to do what he was going to do, and whatever it was, it was none of her business.

Verna gave her a quick smile, as if she had understood the thoughts that had just gone through Lizzy's mind. Then she added, in a different tone, "And coming out of the Old Alabama dining room with Mr. Nichols?"

"Well, yes." Lizzy picked up her half-eaten doughnut. It wasn't exactly easy to talk about Bent, even to Verna, who was her closest friend. And she felt just as diffident when it came to talking about Ryan. "Mr. Nichols comes to Darling to look in on Ophelia's work on the Federal Writers' Project," she added a little primly. "In fact, I understand that he'll be in town tomorrow."

She knew this because he had called to tell her—and had asked her to meet him for dinner. The thing was, he had said, that he didn't know exactly what time he would be finished.

"Then how about dinner here, instead?" she had suggested. "I'll plan something that we can eat whenever you arrive." So that was what they had agreed. She was looking forward to it.

"I've heard about the project," Verna said. She was folding her square paper napkin along the diagonal. "Ophelia certainly seems to enjoy working with Mr. Nichols." She glanced up at Liz. "A very great deal, actually."

"I hope she does," Lizzy said, her mouth half full of doughnut. "I wouldn't like to think I talked her into taking a job she hated."

Ryan had first asked *her* to work with the Federal Writers' Project, but after giving the offer serious thought, she had decided to say no. Her second novel needed as much time and attention as she could give it, and she hadn't felt right about leaving Mr. Moseley in the lurch. She had recommended Ophelia instead.

Verna looked back at Lizzy. "Oh, I don't think there's any danger of her hating the job, do you?" She folded the napkin again and creased it, hard. "In fact, when I was with Ophelia the other evening, she couldn't stop talking about it." She slid Lizzy a look. "About Mr. Nichols, too. I'm sure you've noticed this."

"She's certainly excited about the job." Lizzy agreed. She frowned at the odd emphasis in Verna's words. "But then, that's just Ophelia. To me, she seems pretty much the same as always."

But was that true? Her frown deepened. Now that Verna mentioned it . . .

Lizzy had always valued Verna's habit of careful observation, which stood her in good stead in the bare-knuckle world of county politics. She might not have a lot of empathy, but she had a sharp, penetrating intelligence that prompted her to measure people and events with a critical, attentive gaze. In fact, Verna seemed to have an almost uncanny ability to see right through people. This was sometimes a little unnerving to her friends, for she often seemed to understand their motives when even *they* weren't entirely sure why they were doing whatever it was they were up to. A devotee of detective novels and true crime magazines, she liked nothing better than a good mystery. Erle Stanley Gardner's Perry Mason legal thrillers, for instance, or Dashiell Hammett's hard-boiled detective fiction—neither of which, Lizzy thought, did anything to brighten her friend's sometimes dark and mistrustful view of the world.

Verna folded the napkin again, obviously unwilling to leave the subject. Hesitantly, she said, "You haven't noticed the way she talks about him?"

Lizzy finished her doughnut and licked her fingers. "Why don't you tell me what you're thinking about."

Verna sighed. For a moment, she said nothing. Then she launched her napkin into the air. It flew a few feet and took a nosedive onto the floor. "Makes a better napkin than an airplane," she remarked. She turned back to Lizzy.

"I know I have a habit of sticking my nose into things that don't concern me. But I can't help being just a little concerned about Ophelia." A pause. "To be perfectly blunt about it, Liz, I think our sweet Opie has a crush on Mr. Nichols. You must have noticed—haven't you?"

Lizzy's first response was to rush to Ophelia's defense with a denial. "A *crush*? On Ryan Nichols?" She chuckled. "Really, Verna. Don't you think that's a little ridiculous? Opie has been happily married to Jed for nineteen or twenty years. She has two teenage children. What's more, she comes from a religious family. Her father was a preacher, you know. And she has always been far too adult and sensible to let herself be . . ."

But Lizzy had let her voice trail off. She was suddenly remembering a few little oddities that had puzzled her when she and Ryan and Ophelia had been together. Tiny things, really—Opie's slantwise glance at him, a catch in her voice, a quickened breath, a rising flush in her cheek. Little things Lizzy had seen and then forgotten in the surging excitement she always felt when she was with Ryan.

Yes, *excitement*. There was no other word for it. An electrifying excitement, an intense exhilaration that energized her when they were together and kept her thinking of him when he had gone away again—scribbling little notes to him in her journal, notes that she knew she would never send. She suspected that he could even be one of the reasons, perhaps even the main reason, for her troubles with her second book. Concentrating on a Civil War–era story was hard when her mind kept darting into warm memories of their private time together, times when—

Lizzy drew in a breath. She knew Ryan. He wasn't the kind of man who would make improper advances to a married woman.

But that didn't mean that Ophelia wasn't *imagining* that he would.

Was it possible that her friend might be hoping . . .?

That Opie might be feeling the same way *she* felt about Ryan? She gulped. But that would be—

"I see." Verna's voice was quiet, deliberate. "You *have* noticed." Quickly, she added, "I'm not blaming her, Liz, and I'm sure you aren't either. And you're right in everything you say. Ophelia is a model wife and mother. She is always completely conscientious about simply everything." She paused. "We're both of us just recognizing something that Opie herself may not see. And I doubt very much that Mr. Nichols is encouraging her—or has any idea what's going on." She opened her handbag and took out a pack of Old Golds. "But he is just about the best-looking man any of us have ever laid eyes on. And he's always such a gentleman." She flicked a lighter to her cigarette. "I wondered what you know about him," she added casually.

Well, he was certainly *that*, Lizzy had to agree—good-looking *and* a gentleman. "Know about him?" she repeated slowly. "Well, I know that he's head of the Federal Writers' Project for the southern region. He reports to the director, Henry Alsberg. He works in Washington and travels a great deal. He oversees projects in eight states."

There were plenty of other things to know about him, of course. That he was a fabulous dancer who made you feel like Ginger Rogers even when you had two left feet. That he could tell the most interesting stories in the *most* interesting way. That he was a very good listener who paid close attention to everything she said. That when he was kissing her, it was impossible not to want—

"He lives in Washington, too, I suppose." Verna had raised her voice and Lizzy had the feeling that she had repeated this remark at least once.

"I believe so, yes," she said quickly.

"And he's a bachelor?"

"Actually, he's divorced," Lizzy replied. "He and his wife were married very young. They didn't have any children and they realized early on—years ago, actually—that it wasn't going to work." She frowned. "Verna, what are you thinking?"

Verna looked as if she were about to say something. Then she paused and after a moment, said, "Oh, nothing, really." She blew out a stream of smoke. "You know me, Liz. I'm always poking around where I have no business to be. Of course, it's fine for you to go out with Mr. Nichols—you're single and you have no obligations. You can take care of yourself. It's Ophelia I'm worried about. And you know the old saying—out of the frying pan, into the fire. Ophelia and Jed have been married forever. Maybe her husband doesn't exactly light her fuse these days—marriage has a way of cooling you off after a while. But getting involved with her boss isn't the answer." She gave a little shrug. "I don't want her to get hurt, that's all."

*Out of the frying pan?* Well, yes, Lizzy supposed that Ophelia *might* get herself into trouble, but she didn't think so. Opie was too level-headed. And she was half amused at her friend's confidence. Verna thought she could take care of herself? Could she, really? She was half in love with Ryan, whatever that meant. More than that maybe. The last time they were together, she had been ready to give . . .

She pushed the memory away. "Verna, about Ophelia. I really don't think she—"

But Verna was changing the subject, as if they had taken this discussion farther than she intended. "I haven't told you about the trip that Alvin and I made to Pensacola," she said brightly.

For the past year or so, Verna (a widow) had been going out with Alvin Duffy, the level-headed president of the Darling Savings and Trust and a definite match for Verna's sharp intelligence. Everybody wondered when they were going to get married, but Verna (who could be very obstinate when she wanted to) was in no hurry.

"We had fine weather," she said. "Hot, naturally, but the beach was splendid. We took Clyde, who had a glorious time playing in the sand. He even went for a dip in the Gulf and played catch with Alvin like a civilized dog."

Relieved that they were no longer talking about Ophelia and her presumed and possible crush on Ryan Nichols, Lizzy found herself laughing. Clyde, Verna's fierce little black Scotty, was notoriously possessive when it came to his mistress. Verna had told her that Mr. Duffy had once left his necktie draped over a chair in her bedroom. While the two of them were occupied with other matters, Clyde had snatched the tie and dragged it out to the backyard with the clear intention of burying it with his bones and other spoils of war.

"If Clyde is able to declare a truce with your Mr. Duffy, who knows what's next?" Lizzy said, teasing. "Wedding bells?"

Taking her seriously, Verna shook her head. "No, no, Liz. Alvin is a lovely man and I'm glad for his companionship. But I meant what I said about marriage cooling you off. I'm personally enjoying the fire." She smiled crookedly. "I even enjoy cooking for him—as long as I don't have to do it every night."

"Really?" Lizzy was quizzical. If Verna invited you to dinner, she was likely to present you with a grilled cheese sandwich.

"Really. The other night, we had a cheese custard pie—something the French call a *quiche*—and a summer salad and an orange whip, all out of that new *Joy of Cooking* cookbook. But marriage . . ." She squared her shoulders. "I did that once. It's not a mistake I'll make again—no matter how I'm tempted." She waved a hand, obviously ready to change the subject once more. "I suppose you've heard the latest news."

"Which news? About the fire at the Coca-Cola plant this weekend—and the four or five *other* fires we've been seeing? Or maybe you're thinking of Rufus Radley, the new fire chief." Both of these had been the main subjects of conversation at the church picnic after service on Sunday. It seemed that everybody was worried about those fires. And *nobody* thought that the Hot Dogs had any business electing Rufus Radley as their new fire chief.

Verna shook her head. "About Huey P. Long's visit to Darling."

"You're kidding." Lizzy stared at her. "Senator Long? Why would *he* come *here*?"

"Not kidding," Verna insisted. "He'll be here on Wednesday. Day after tomorrow. I heard it from Earlynne just this morning. The Share Our Wealth Club is making all the arrangements.

Earlynne is beside herself with excitement—you know she's a Long supporter."

"Yes, I know." Lizzy wrinkled her nose. "Mildred, too. I'm afraid I can't share their enthusiasm."

"I can't either." Verna pulled on her cigarette. "And neither can Al. He says that if you add everything up—the annual income, the pension for people over sixty-five, free college education, veterans' benefits, federal assistance to farmers—Huey's tax on millionaires wouldn't begin to pay for it. He knows he can't make the numbers work. He's just pushing those ideas because he thinks they'll get him elected."

"But he's able to make people *believe* that his plan will work," Lizzy pointed out. "Even smart people. Like Earlynne." And like her mother and Mr. Dunlap, both of whom believed every word that spilled out of Huey P. Long's mouth.

Verna blew out a stream of cigarette smoke. "Well, like it or not, the man's coming to town. Earlynne says he'll be speaking on the courthouse steps. Right down there." She pointed out the window.

"I suppose we could watch from here," Lizzy suggested. She gave a small smile. "We already know what he's going to say, so it won't matter if we can't hear him."

"We can do that," Verna agreed. She bent over to pick up her handbag, then stood. "Well, those property filings are waiting for me. I guess I'd better get going." Impulsively, she reached out and put her arms around Liz. "I always feel better when I talk to you, Liz."

"I know," Lizzy said, returning the hug. "Me, too."

When Verna had gone, she went back to her desk to finish typing Mr. Moseley's letter. She turned the radio back on, hoping that WDAR would be playing some music. But Tommy Lee Musgrove, who announced the daytime programming, was doing the weather forecast. As she began typing the letter, she listened with only half an ear. It would be more of the same, she supposed. Hot and dry, with the smoke-colored haze of Great Plains dust hanging in the air.

And yes, it was more of the same—but something was different. At the end of his usual weather report, Tommy Lee read an Associated Press bulletin he had picked up from WIOD in Miami. A powerful hurricane was approaching the tip of Florida. It looked as if the storm might slide between Cuba and the Florida Keys and head into the Gulf. There was something about a special train that she didn't quite catch.

*Into the Gulf?* Lizzy turned to listen, paying full attention now. Some years before—in September, wasn't it?—a major hurricane had slammed into Miami, skipped across Florida and then northwest across the Gulf, targeting the Alabama coast. It made landfall just east of Mobile and stalled out, dumping over eighteen inches of rain on Darling. The town's streets were flooded, the Monroeville Highway was washed out, and the bridge over Jericho Creek was destroyed.

Darling could certainly use a good rainstorm, Lizzy thought. This hot, dry weather was awful. They needed a good hard rainstorm that would cool everybody off—including their firebug, maybe. But she didn't like to think about the threat of another hurricane. That could be worse than the heat.

She shook her head. What was it Verna had said? Out of the frying pan, into the fire? From a bad situation to something worse. Maybe much worse.

And there wasn't a darn thing anybody could do about it.

# CHAPTER SIX

# I DON'T *SPY*

AT THE DARLING DINER, NEXT DOOR TO THE DISPATCH OFFICE, Myra May Mosswell put the broom away and surveyed the dining area, checking to see that everything was in order. It had been business as usual for breakfast this morning, no matter that today was Labor Day and a holiday. Most of the folks who came in on workdays for bacon and eggs or ham and grits and fried green tomatoes also came in on weekends and holidays—except for maybe Thanksgiving and Christmas.

The Dr Pepper clock over the coffee urn said that it was just past eleven. The early crowd would be clamoring for lunch any minute now. In the kitchen, Euphoria Hoyt was tending to the items on the lunch menu that Myra May had chalked up on the blackboard behind the counter. Meatloaf, chicken livers, fried catfish, and pulled pork on a bun. Sides of mashed potatoes and gravy, mac and cheese, corn oysters, sweet corn, green beans, coleslaw, and bacon-fried grits (leftover grits from breakfast mixed with crumbled bacon, chopped green onions, and red pepper flakes and fried in hot bacon grease). Raylene, Myra May's mother, was taking three peach pies out of the oven and putting two blackberry pies and a strawberry pie in. Priceless Perkins, home for the holiday weekend from her second year of nursing school at Tuskegee University, was still at the sink, having just finished washing the breakfast dishes. Priceless had been a regular helper at the diner until she went off to college.

Out front, Myra May had swept the floor, straightened the chairs, wiped off the tables and the long counter, refilled the condiment caddies, and brewed another urn of coffee. The air was filled with the enticing fragrance of the pork shoulder Raylene had slow-baked overnight with barbecue sauce, cider vinegar, and her special spices. And since the diner's front door was open, Myra May knew that the richly tantalizing odor of pork and barbecue sauce would bring in an even larger lunch crowd than usual.

Meanwhile, back in the Darling Telephone Exchange at the rear of the diner, Violet Sims, Myra May's partner, was training their new operator, Paulette, in the complexities of the recently upgraded telephone switchboard. Their adopted daughter Cupcake—now four-and-a-half—was there, too, and every now and then, Myra May could hear the little girl singing to her Cupcake doll: formerly a Shirley Temple doll, now dressed in red overalls and a yellow shirt, with her strawberry blond hair braided like Cupcake's.

Cupcake, who loved to sing and dance to tunes like "On the Good Ship Lollipop" and "Animal Crackers in My Soup," was an even bigger hit with her moms' customers than her Grammy Raylene's pulled pork. In fact, she was such a popular little girl that Earlynne Biddle had telephoned earlier that morning to say that she was in charge of the details of Huey P. Long's big event on Wednesday. The Academy band was going to play some Sousa marches and the "Star Spangled Banner." She was calling to ask if Violet and Myra May would allow Cupcake to sing the senator's campaign song, "Every Man a Millionaire."

Earlynne read a verse of the song for Violet, so she could get the idea. It promised "castles and clothing and food for all" if everybody shared whatever wealth they had. That would make them all millionaires. "Uncle Hiram Bond has agreed to play it on his accordion," Earlynne added. "I'm sure the senator will love it even more if sweet little Cupcake sings it for him."

Violet, of course, agreed immediately to this idea and ran to ask Raylene if she could whip up a red, white, and blue costume for Cupcake. "And we'll work out a tap dance, too," she had said excitedly. "It'll be a great opportunity for our little girl!"

Myra May hadn't been quite so enthusiastic. A few months before, Violet had been scheming to take their daughter to Hollywood so she could be discovered by David O. Selznick or Darryl Zanuck and turned into a movie star as famous as Shirley Temple or Jackie Cooper or Mickey Rooney. This chilling thought had nearly paralyzed poor Myra May, who was frightened almost to death by the thought of losing both Violet and Cupcake to the pursuit of fortune and fame.

But there had been no trip to Hollywood. Myra May had never understood exactly what changed Violet's mind—Raylene hinted that it had something to do with a nighttime visit to Big Lil's shanty deep in the middle of Briar Swamp and a mysterious conjure trick or two, and maybe it did.*

Whatever had transpired, a trip to Hollywood no longer seemed to be in the cards, and Myra May was enormously relieved. Still, she wasn't sure it was smart to allow Cupcake to sing—and dance—for Senator Long, who people said was already running for president. Everybody who saw the little girl fell in love with her. What if the senator offered to put Cupcake to work in his political campaign?

Myra May gave an involuntary shudder. Maybe she was being paranoid, imagining something so wildly unbelievable. But what if she wasn't? What if the senator liked Cupcake so

---

* You can read this story in *The Darling Dahlias and the Voodoo Lily.*

much that he offered her a job—or even arranged a movie contract for her? Would Violet agree to *that*?

And there was something else, too. Myra May thought of the words of the senator's campaign song, which promised that if everybody shared what they had, they would all be millionaires. That sounded awfully . . . well, communistic, didn't it? If Huey Long got to be president, would she and Violet be expected to share the product of their hard work—their diner and the telephone exchange—with every lazy Tom, Dick, and Harry in town? That didn't sound right to her.

The screen door opened and a man in a rumpled seersucker suit and straw boater came in, heading for his usual table. Mr. Dickens, the *Dispatch* editor and a regular, especially when his wife Fannie was out of town. She'd driven over to Georgia, to Warm Springs, to see her son, so Mr. Dickens would likely be eating all his meals in the diner. Myra May filled a glass with sweet iced tea and added a wedge of lemon—that's how he liked it—and took it to his table.

"Ready to order?" She took out her order pad.

He took off his hat. "It might be a bit," he said, reaching for the tea. "There'll be two of us. But while I'm waiting, you can bring me a plate of Euphoria's corn oysters and some butter. That'll get me off to a good start."

❀

On the other side of the courthouse square, Alvin Duffy came out of the bank, heading for the diner. The bank was closed for the holiday, but that didn't mean he had the day off. He was having lunch with Charlie Dickens, who wanted to talk over some plans he had in mind for the *Dispatch*—and likely hit up the bank for a loan.

But Alvin wasn't thinking about the newspaper. Earlier that

morning, he had gone across the street to the sheriff's office for a meeting with Sheriff Norris and Deputy Springer; the former fire chief, Archie Mann; and Emmet Piper, Darling's local insurance agent.

The sheriff had told them that five of the recent fires were now being investigated as arson. So far, there were no suspects and (this was the lucky thing) no losses to speak of—not even any insurance claims, Emmet Piper had reported. Until the incident at the bottling plant, the fires had all been minor grass fires. No structures were threatened and the VFD had arrived on the scene in time to contain every blaze. The weekend had been tense, but the siren hadn't gone off once since the Coca-Cola fire, giving the Hot Dogs a chance to go to church on Sunday morning and get a good nap after Sunday dinner.

But Agent Piper had nervously pointed out that the Saturday fire was not a minor matter. If the VFD hadn't arrived when it did, that shed would have burned—a shed where Henry Biddle had stored several thousand dollars' worth of new equipment. The plant could have burned, too, in which case there would have been a massive insurance claim and a dozen men out of work. It looked like whoever was doing this might be getting serious.

Or—Archie Mann had reluctantly suggested—they could be dealing with a copycat situation. That is, somebody had latched onto the arson idea, but with bigger ambitions.

To which Alvin Duffy had added that if his employees at the bank (the tellers and the ladies who worked in the office) were any indication, the town was getting extremely nervous. People were spooked, and rightly so. Every time that new siren went off, they jumped like somebody had lit a bottle rocket in the office. Nobody knew where or when the next fire was going to blaze up, or how big it was going to be.

"I think we should turn that damfool siren off," Emmet Piper said. "It's causing more trouble than it's worth."

"But it gets the Hot Dogs to the fire faster," the deputy replied. "Isn't that what it's for?"

"We need to catch this fellow as fast as we can," the sheriff said. "We have a clue or two, but neither Wayne nor I are trained in arson investigations. I put in a call to the state fire marshal this morning to see if they can send somebody down here. And Wayne is going to recruit a half-dozen or so men and deputize them as lookouts, so we can maybe catch this firebug in the act." He looked at Alvin. "Here's what you could do to help, Mr. Duffy."

Alvin had been quick to agree to the sheriff's proposal that the bank offer a reward. Twenty-five dollars, the sheriff had suggested. Alvin had upped it to fifty and pledged to go higher if they didn't catch the arsonist in the next few days. He had the ominous feeling that their lucky streak was going to snap sooner or later, probably sooner. Somebody was going to lose a house or a business—or a life.

And to make matters worse, on Saturday night, the volunteer firemen had been *stupid* enough to elect a man who had absolutely no experience of fighting fires. Rufus Radley, the new fire chief, had of course been asked to attend the sheriff's meeting. But he'd called at the last minute with an excuse. A new job had just driven into his auto repair shop and he couldn't make it. Was this going to be a habit? Would he be calling in absent to the next fire?

Alvin was about to cross the street when he was distracted from his troubling thoughts by the sight of Verna Tidwell coming down the courthouse steps. She was looking unusually pretty in a light blue summer dress with a wide white collar and a skirt that emphasized her slim waist and hips. She saw him and paused.

He quickened his pace. "You're not working on a holiday, I hope," he said, going up to her.

But he had the feeling that she was. Verna loved her work, especially when she was digging into something that promised a little intrigue—somebody trying to get by with something, for instance. That attitude appealed to Alvin, who as a banker had some of the same analytical instincts. It was one of the things that had attracted him to her. That, and her deeply logical mind.

The two of them had started going out together not long after Alvin had arrived in Darling to take over the Savings and Trust and try to keep it from closing. There had been too much benign neglect in the bank's office and too many non-performing assets on the bank's books: bad notes, defaulted bonds, uncollateralized loans. The bank had been on the brink of collapse and he'd had to practice some sleight-of-hand to set things right again. Most Darling residents had never realized just how close their little town came to losing its bank—and with it, the ability to function as an economic entity (not that many Darling folk understood what *that* really meant).

But Verna had understood, completely. What's more, she had helped Alvin make the special effort that had restored people's confidence in their local bank as well as their ability to spend money with the local merchants. *Real* money, not just Darling Dollars—the paper scrip they'd had to use for a while. Verna was responsible for the budget of Cypress County, the biggest employer in town. If she hadn't agreed to pay the county employees with scrip, the town could have said goodbye to its bank. Their friendship (Alvin liked to think it might be more) had grown from there.*

"Of course I was working," Verna said with a little toss of her head. "The job needs to be done. Today is a good day to do it."

---

* For the story of the Darling Dollars and Alvin Duffy's former life, read *The Darling Dahlias and the Silver Dollar Bush*.

That was another of the things Alvin liked about Verna. She didn't beat around the bush. If she said a thing, you could hang your hat on it. If she didn't—

And that was the trouble, wasn't it? The first time he had asked her to marry him, she'd said no. It was no the second time, too—and then she had told him to stop asking. She said she cared for him and wanted to be with him, wanted them to be close, intimate, even. And so they were. Intimate, that is, for Alvin found her body as attractive as her mind, and she was a generous woman.

But no to marriage. Which he found a little . . . well, puzzling. And vexing. They were clearly in synch where *that* was concerned. So why would she say yes to one thing and no to the other? Was there something lacking in him? Did she think he couldn't provide for her? Women were supposed to prefer the security of a marriage to the relationship they had, which was—as far as he was concerned, anyway—both eminently satisfying and infinitely frustrating, at the same time.

But Alvin was a man who had been schooled by hard fate to live by the bottom line. He had lost his first wife to cancer, his second (and a good bit of money) to his best friend, and his only child, a son, to a tragic trolley accident in New Orleans. Things were the way they were, he had learned, and all the wishing in the world wouldn't change them. Whether he liked it or not, the bottom line here was that marriage to Verna was not in the hand he'd been dealt. That wasn't going to change until she changed her mind, so he might as well get used to it.

Still, he wished he knew why. Another man, maybe? Verna had never seemed interested in anybody else in Darling, but he supposed it was possible that she was involved with somebody on the frequent trips she made to Montgomery—driving herself in that sporty little red LaSalle two-seater of hers. She was a private person who didn't share her innermost thoughts easily, at least, not with him, so he didn't know what was going on in her mind. In her *heart*—if she had one. Maybe she didn't. Feeling as if he'd been somehow wronged, he thought ironically that it was bankers who were usually accused of being heartless.

"You were working, too," she pointed out in a teasing tone. "I thought the bank was closed for Labor Day."

"It is." Alvin pushed his hat back with his thumb. "But I had a meeting at the sheriff's office about those fires and there was some paperwork on my desk, so I—"

"You see?" And now she was openly laughing at him. But she sobered quickly. "Actually, I was just thinking of you, Al. I was wondering—"

She broke off, biting the corner of her lower lip. She looked, Alvin thought, unusually serious. She nodded toward the stone bench under the magnolia at the corner of the courthouse lawn. "Could we sit down for a minute or two? That is," she added hurriedly, "if I'm not keeping you from something important."

"I'm on my way to lunch with Charlie Dickens," Alvin said, now curious. "But I'm a little early." They took their seats. "Something on your mind, Verna?"

She opened her handbag and took out a cigarette. "You've met Ryan Nichols, haven't you?"

"Nichols? Sure. Even talked to him a time or two." Alvin pulled his lighter out of his jacket pocket and held it to the tip of her cigarette, then took out one of his own. "He's that government fellow who comes to Darling every few weeks to check up on some sort of guidebook Mrs. Snow is doing." He lit his cigarette. "Works for the Federal Writers' Project."

"That's him," Verna said. "I wonder—when you talked, did he happen to mention anything about himself? Personally, I mean." She sounded uncharacteristically tentative. "Where he lives, for instance?"

It was another blazing hot day. The old magnolia cast a convenient shade, but the air was sultry. Alvin took off his hat and put it on the grass between his feet. He leaned forward, elbows on knees. "I got the impression that he lives in Atlanta." He paused. "Why?"

Verna answered his question with her own. "Not in Washington?"

"I don't think so." Alvin thought for a moment. "As I remember, he mentioned having to go to DC for a meeting with Henry Alsberg, the guy who runs the project. He complained about DC hotels."

"Well, I'm pretty sure it's Washington," Verna said.

He turned to squint at her through the curling cigarette smoke. "Why are you asking, Verna?"

She gave him one of her straight looks. "Don't laugh at me."

He was startled. "Why in the world would I laugh at you?"

"Because," she said slowly, "the last time he was here, I looked to see if he was wearing a wedding ring. What I saw was a band of pale skin that suggested that he *had* been wearing one—and recently, too." She took a breath. "But this morning, Liz Lacy told me he'd been divorced for a number of years. So I was curious about . . ." Her voice trailed off and she gave a little shrug.

Alvin frowned. He liked Liz Lacy. She had class. And ambition. He wouldn't want to see her hurt. "I've noticed Liz with Nichols a time or two," he said. "Is that why you're asking? You're wondering whether the guy is trying to pull a fast one on her? You want to keep her from making another mistake?" A mistake like Grady Alexander, he thought sympathetically. Somebody who makes a mistake like that twice has a right to feel snake-bit.

For a moment, he didn't think Verna was going to answer. Then her lips tightened. "No," she said reluctantly, as if she were forcing herself to be honest. "Not for Liz."

*Not for Liz.* Something cold knotted in his middle. "Then who?"

"That's not . . . not really important." She lowered her voice. "I mean, it's just too easy for a stranger to pretend to be something he's not, isn't it? And Mr. Nichols is a very charming man. I can see why Liz and . . . others are attracted to him."

"Charming." Alvin pulled on his cigarette. "Not bad looking, either." The knot grew harder, colder. She wanted him to believe that she was looking into this guy for a friend. But he had the feeling—a gut-wrenching feeling—that she was asking for herself. That was why she hadn't answered his question.

"Charming." She laughed a little. "Do men notice things like that about other men?"

"This one does," he growled. "I'm a banker. In my business, I'm paid to notice." It was true. Back in New Orleans, just before he came to Darling, he'd noticed some serious discrepancies in the details of a guy's loan application. He'd dug a little deeper and turned up three aliases, two felonies, and a stint of prison time. In another case—

Her voice was brittle. "Then you'll understand when I ask if you have a way of spying into Mr. Nichols' background." She said the word—*spying*—with an odd mixture of relish and distaste.

He almost said no. He didn't have to let her use him like this. He could just let *her* do the dirty work, for that's what it was, in his considered opinion. But he couldn't duck out that easily. And anyway, just suppose that Nichols was up to some sort of funny business. Suppose he'd fed some of them—all of them, maybe—a potful of lies. You didn't want a man like that hanging around Darling, where most people seemed to assume that most other people were as innocent and good-hearted as they were. A man like that could leave a trail of smoking wreckage behind him.

"I do, yes," he said slowly. "But I don't 'spy.' I do *research*. It's called a credit check. It's just part of the process. Bank rules require it."

"I see." Verna's eyebrow went up. "Does your research enable you to learn personal details, such as where somebody lives and . . . other personal matters?"

"Yes." There was a sour taste in Alvin's mouth. "Credit reports usually have personal details." He looked at her. "You *sure* you want me to do this, Verna? If I get you the answers to your questions, what will you do with them?"

She had the grace to look troubled. "I don't know, Al. It . . . depends."

He blew out a stream of cigarette smoke. Deliberately, he said, "Well, if you ask me, Liz Lazy can handle whatever life tosses into her lap. Look at the way she managed that business with Grady Alexander. If you're worried that she's going to get hurt—"

"It's not Liz I'm worried about," Verna said, her voice low.

There it was. He'd thought so. "Then who—"

"I can't tell you," Verna said, looking straight at him.

"You can't? Or you won't."

She pressed her lips together. "How long will it take? He'll be here tomorrow afternoon."

The knot tightened painfully. Well, he'd guessed as much. But he had agreed. He might as well play it like a gentleman.

He picked up his hat and got to his feet. "Okay, then," he said flatly. "I can't make any promises. Today's a holiday and the places I need to call are closed. But give me a day or so and I'll see what I can find out." He made a show of looking at his watch. "Dickens is waiting. I need to go."

"Fine," she said. She put out her hand. "And . . . thank you, Al."

He jammed his hat on his head. Nodding curtly, he walked away.

❀

AT THE DINER, CHARLIE LEANED BACK IN HIS CHAIR, TURNING his iced tea glass in his fingers. He'd finished his corn oysters—crisp and tasty, like hushpuppies. Al must have gotten hung up somewhere. He'd give him another few minutes and then he'd go ahead and order.

The Philco radio behind the counter, tuned to WDOX in Mobile, was playing a recording of "Brother, Can You Spare a Dime," the anthem of the Depression, sung by Rudy Vallée in that weird minor key. Charlie grimaced. He had once been full of "that Yankee Doodly Dum," thinking how swell he looked and how many Krauts he was going to kill. That was before the gods who looked after itinerant journalists had yanked him out of that hell and assigned him to the *Stars and Stripes*, so he could write about the boys in khaki suits and the kids with drums and get out of the Great War with body and soul relatively intact.

But many hadn't. The song made him profoundly sad, and then profoundly apprehensive, as he thought of the seven hundred veterans down there on the Keys with a hurricane coming. They were working on that highway because they had no other jobs, nothing else to do, nowhere else to go, nobody to turn to for help but Uncle Sam. And Uncle Sam had turned his back when they'd had the nerve to ask for early payment of their service bonus.

The last weather bulletin he'd heard made the Florida hurricane situation sound a little better, though. It now seemed that the thing was more likely to hit Havana. Still, the Weather Service had to rely on ship reports, and hurricane forecasts were notoriously unreliable. Charlie knew from his time on Key West that once a storm got into the Straits—

He looked up as Alvin Duffy came into the diner, hung his hat on one of the pegs by the door, and came over to the table.

"I was about to give up on you," Charlie said.

"Sorry," Al said shortly. He pulled out a chair and sat down. "Got waylaid on my way over. You order yet?"

"Waiting for you," Charlie said.

He gave his friend an assessing glance. How the heck did Al do it? It was hot as blazes outside and not much cooler in here, but Duffy looked like he'd just stepped out of a bandbox. His ivory linen suit was as crisp as a new dollar bill, his collar was immaculate, and his black Clark Gable–style hair and mustache were smartly trimmed. Every inch the banker, Charlie thought. Nothing at all like his rumpled seersucker self.

He signaled to Myra May and she came over, taking her order pad out of the cotton apron she wore over her tan slacks and brown plaid shirt. She wasn't the only Darling woman who wore trousers, but she was the only one who wore them all the time. Charlie preferred his wife's feminine way of dressing, but in spite of her mannish clothes, Myra May was definitely an attractive woman. You'd better not try to get between her and Violet, though. She could be fierce when she thought you were paying a little too much attention to her girlfriend.

"Yessir?" she asked pleasantly, setting a glass of iced tea in front of Al. Nothing fierce about her now. "What's your pleasure today, gentlemen?"

Charlie squinted at the chalkboard. "I'll have that pulled pork I've been smelling over at the newspaper office all morning. Coleslaw, too. Best in town, Raylene's coleslaw," he added appreciatively, which got a quick smile out of Myra May.

"The usual for me," Al said without even glancing at the board. Myra May scribbled on her pad. "And find another radio station, would you? I'm not in the mood to listen to somebody wanting to borrow a dime."

Myra May chuckled. "Not exactly a banker's lullaby, is it?"

"You said it," Al muttered.

When she had gone, Charlie gave his friend a critical glance. Usually, Al wore a cheerfully bland expression. Not today. "You don't look like you're on top of the world," he said. Not good news for what he had in mind—his grand plan for the newspaper and the possibility of a loan, to supplement Fannie's contribution. Maybe he'd better go slow.

Al gulped his tea. "I was at a meeting this morning. The sheriff and his deputy, Archie Mann, and Emmet Piper, the insurance guy. Those fires—they're calling them arson. All of them."

"All but the reverend's little trash fire," Charlie said, to show that he was already on top of the story. "Wilber covered the bottling plant fire Saturday morning. He talked to Chief Mann, who—"

"*Former* Chief Mann," Al amended dryly.

"Yeah. Former and ain't that a big can of worms," Charlie said, rolling his eyes. "How Radley ever got voted into that job is beyond me. He doesn't know diddly about fighting fires."

"I heard he bought votes," Al said. "Five dollars a pop. But he still only won by three." He added another spoonful of sugar to the already sweet tea and stirred. "Archie said he didn't believe it. He made them recount twice."

"Oughta be a law against buying votes," Charlie said glumly.

"Well, there isn't, apparently," Al said. "At least, that's what the sheriff said. He checked with Moseley. The VFD is a private organization. It can set its own rules. But I'm wondering what the state fire marshal might have to say about the situation. Emmet Piper's thinking about that, too. Said he's going to give the fire marshal's office a call and see whether there are any state regs that might apply in a case like this. And I hear that Archie Mann is refusing to step down. Says the job is too important to be turned over to somebody who doesn't have any experience."

"Huh," Charlie said. "I hadn't heard that. Suppose Archie can make it stick?"

Al grinned. "He says he's got the keys to the fire truck in his pocket." The grin vanished. "Listen, Charlie, there's something you can do. The bank's going to offer a reward. Fifty dollars for starters. Can you run an announcement in the next *Dispatch*? I'll get you the copy whenever you need it."

"Wednesday would be good," Charlie said, as Myra May came up with their plates. "It's a bright idea," he added. "Somebody out there is bound to know something. Maybe a cash reward will lure them out of the bushes."

"I hope so." Al picked up his fork. "So far, there's been no serious damage, but there's no telling where the arsonist will strike next."

"Bizarre, isn't it?" Charlie remarked. "Our torch isn't burning things down for the insurance money. So why is he doing it?"

"For fun?" Al hazarded. "Thrills and excitement? Somebody with something to prove? A bored kid with nothing else to do?" He shook his head. "Could be anybody."

There was a brief silence while they attacked their food. Then Charlie said, tentatively. "Are you inclined to listen to my idea for the *Dispatch*, or should I sit on it for a while?" He didn't want to do that, though. With WDAR eating into his market, the newspaper might be in danger of becoming irrelevant. If he put it off—

"Sure," Al said, to Charlie's relief. "Let's hear it. What are you thinking of?" He didn't sound enthusiastic, though, and Charlie wondered if there was something else on his mind beside the fires. He put down the bun he'd been working on.

"Okay, here's my sixty-second pitch," he said, wiping his

mouth with his napkin. "In a nutshell, Darling is doing okay, all things considered. The economy is looking up, and the *Dispatch* has the potential to grow in both circulation and advertising. I've got a terrific editorial and production team and I'm ready to do some building. Currently, we publish the paper on Fridays. I'd like to add a Tuesday edition. If that goes well— and I think it will—a Sunday edition. The content won't be a problem. The boys and I will just work a little harder and I'll look around for another reporter. I'm even thinking of giving up the ready-print pages and producing the whole thing right here. Ready-print is canned news. Darling deserves better." He paused for breath.

"But the Babcock was an antique when my dad bought it. I'd like to look for a replacement—a Campbell Country press, maybe. It would print two pages at a time, about seven hundred pages an hour. It's more versatile than the Babcock, and a damn sight more reliable. But this project won't be cheap. Three, four thousand, maybe more, depending on the price of the press and whether I can find another reporter who will work for peanuts, like the rest of us." He paused. "What I'm asking is, can you see your way clear to a bank loan? Or am I wasting my breath?"

Al chewed reflectively, swallowed, and took a drink of iced tea. "Collateral? When I came here, the bank was on a watch list for unsecured loans and low-end collateral. I've cleaned it up quite a bit. I have to keep it clean."

"Fannie said she can help out a little," Charlie said, "and there's the building. The newspaper has been located on the first floor since Ulysses S. Grant's second term. Moseley has a fifteen-year lease on the upstairs, with another ten years to run. The roof needs a little work but the place is still pretty sound." He didn't say that when they ran the Babcock on Thursday nights, the whole place shook as if it was being battered by a hurricane. He added, hopefully, "It might appraise at, oh, three, four thousand. Maybe higher."

"Okay." Al went back to his meatloaf.

"Okay what?" Charlie asked. "What are you saying, Al?" He leaned forward, feeling apprehensive. "It'll be good for Darling, you know. Two editions every week, home print if I can make it happen, which means a lot more local news coverage, more local advertising. With the presidential election coming up next year—"

"Charlie." Al held up his hand, palm out. "Ordinarily, I'd say yes right off the bat. But right now, I have to say I'll take it to the loan committee. You'll hear from us."

Surprised, Charlie asked, "Who's on the committee?"

"Me, myself, and I," Al said with a rueful chuckle. He paused. "Look, Charlie. I think you've latched onto a good idea. Tobias Bowser just bought fifty acres of timber from Miss Tallulah and is opening a lumber mill out on the Hanford Road. Kilgore Motors is expanding its repair business, and Pauline DuBerry expects to add a couple more cottages at the Marigold Motor Court." He pushed his plate away. "But—"

"But *what*, Al?" Charlie leaned forward, now feeling urgent. "I figured this would be a sure-fire proposal, with the building for collateral."

"Normally you'd be figuring right." Al's voice was quiet. "It would be a sure-fire thing. But we've had more foreclosures than I expected this quarter. I've already had to turn down a big renewal that I would have approved, under better circumstances." He gave Charlie a considering look. "The loan committee may have to tell you that the bank can't do a deal now. But we can revisit the question in six months or so. We'll get through another winter and maybe the picture will look a little brighter next spring."

*Next spring?* Charlie tried to swallow his disappointment.

Fannie's contribution would help, but it wouldn't be enough by itself. He needed the loan to make things happen. But what could he say? Alvin Duffy was a Darling booster. He'd make the loan when he could. *If* he could.

But that little *if* was threatening to sound like a mighty big one. What if six months went by and Duffy turned him down again? Charlie sighed. He should probably take it as a sign from the newspaper gods that it was the wrong thing to do. Or the right thing at the wrong time.

A number of people had come into the diner while Charlie and Alvin Duffy were talking. They had found seats at the counter and at nearby tables, and a buzz of conversation filled the room. On the radio, Tommy Lee Musgrove was clearing his throat to read the news, which he had no doubt pulled from other broadcasts, since the little station had no wire service.

As a newspaper publisher, Charlie had a built-in antagonism toward WDAR, which everybody else in town raved about. It might be a two-bit operation run by a couple of amateurs, but it was plenty capable of siphoning advertising dollars from the *Dispatch*. And every week, WDAR picked up more advertising and local news, to the point where Charlie gritted his teeth every time he thought about it. Still, he had to admit—grudgingly—that radio was more up-to-the-minute than print. His story about the Labor Day hurricane would have to wait until the *Dispatch* came out on Friday. WDAR, on the other hand, was covering it right now.

"According to Miami radio WIOD," Tommy Lee began, "a fierce hurricane with winds over 150 miles an hour is churning through the Florida Straits north of Havana this afternoon. The Coast Guard reports that no word has been heard from the passenger ship *Dixie*, bound from New Orleans to New York with 260 passengers and a crew of 140. The ship is thought to be traveling through the Straits and there is widespread concern for its safety."

Around the diner, the conversation had quieted and people lifted their heads, listening intently. "There are also worries for persons living on the Florida Keys," Tommy Lee went on. "It's been reported that a special railroad train is being dispatched to pick up a large number of veterans working on the new Overseas Highway. According to the Weather Service, the future path of the storm is quite uncertain and it is not clear what direction it will take tomorrow, when it reaches the Gulf of Mexico. Interests along the Upper Gulf Coast—the Florida Panhandle, Alabama, Mississippi, and Louisiana—should be prepared to take action."

With a shudder, Charlie shook his head. "God help those poor veterans. I lived on Key West for a while. That whole string of little islands is right at sea level. There's no escaping a surge. Anybody not in a very strong shelter is a dead man."

"Very bad news." Al was frowning. "Could that storm hit here, do you suppose? If so, when?"

"It could," Charlie said. "I wasn't here in '26, but my dad said the town took quite a beating from a hurricane that came in from the Gulf that September." He hazarded a guess. "Wednesday for landfall, maybe?"

Al's frown deepened. "I hear that we're in for another storm on Wednesday. Huey P. Long is coming to town."

"That's not a storm, that's a Barnum and Bailey circus," Charlie said. Remembering the phone call he'd gotten that morning, he added, "But it's big news for Darling. The *Dispatch* will cover it, of course, but the Associated Press will be here, too. Virgil McCone, a friend from our *Stars and Stripes* days, called this morning to let me know he'll be here. He's been covering Huey's campaign swing through the Midwest. Says the senator's definitely going to throw his hat into the ring in '36."

"Big *bad* news," Al said grimly. "And you're on the mark with the circus idea. Huey is a carnival barker. He enthralls the crowds with all this 'every man a king' bull hockey. But they love it. And they love him. They'd follow him anywhere. Right over a cliff, if that's what he asked them to do."

"That's what Roosevelt said." Charlie nodded. "He doesn't have a very high opinion of the senator." He related the story of the poker game at the Little White House. He concluded, "If Roosevelt could come up with a way to sideline Long, he'd do it."

Al shook his head. "Poker with the president," he said with more than a hint of envy in his voice. "Just how far do you think FDR would go to stop this fellow? Would he—"

But Al didn't get to finish his sentence. The air was ripped to shreds by an earsplitting mechanical shriek that rattled the dishes on the tables and made people cover their ears with their hands. It was the fire siren on the courthouse bell tower, across the street. All conversation had to come to a halt for over a minute.

When it finally stopped, there were a few seconds of silence in the diner. Then Al finished the sentence he'd started.

"—try to get rid of Long?" he asked.

Charlie was about to answer, but Violet Sims stepped out of the Exchange in the rear of the diner and raised her voice. "Chief says if there's any Hot Dogs here, the fire is over on Camellia Street, third block, on the south side. It's the Dahlias clubhouse—the old Blackstone cottage. The chief will get the fire truck and meet you there."

A glass crashed to the floor behind the counter. "The clubhouse!" Myra May cried. "Oh, no! I just painted that kitchen!"

There was a sudden loud hubbub of voices. Chairs scraped. Men scrambled to their feet. Somebody yelled "Which chief?" Somebody else laughed roughly.

"How should I know which chief?" Violet retorted. "Just get over there, guys. Don't let it burn! Hurry! *Hurry!*"

# CHAPTER SEVEN

# HOW TO USE YOUR LAUNDRY RINSE WATER

Labor Day might be a holiday for some folks. But at Magnolia Manor, over on Camellia Street, it was just another work day, and Bessie Bloodworth and Roseanne Stewart planned to spend the morning on their usual Monday chores. Roseanne was the Manor's colored cook and housekeeper. Bessie always rolled up her sleeves and worked right alongside her on their big jobs.

Like the sheets and towels, which they usually washed on Mondays. Out on the back porch, Bessie plugged in the big round Kenmore wringer washer, over a year old now and finally paid for ($87.25, including carrying charges, on Sears catalog's Easy Payment Plan: five dollars down and seven dollars a month). The Kenmore had seemed like an extravagance, and Bessie knew they really couldn't afford it. But the motor on the old wooden-tub Dolly Wonder machine had finally burned out and they had to replace it. Neither Bessie nor Roseanne wanted to go back to the corrugated tin washboards their mothers had used.

Roseanne filled the washing machine tub with water she'd been heating on the back of the stove. Bessie put in the Oxydol, a cup of Clorox, and the first load of sheets and pillowcases, then she and Roseanne let the Kenmore do its work while they went upstairs to strip the rest of the beds. Outdoors, the sun was bright and hot, with a breeze that lifted the leaves on the pecan tree in the backyard. It was a good day to dry sheets on the clothesline between posts along the hedge between the Manor and the Dahlias clubhouse next door.

There would be a dozen sheets and a half-dozen towels to wash because there were six residents at the Manor right now: Miss Dorothy Rogers, Leticia Wiggens, Mrs. Sedalius, and Maxine Bechtel, plus Roseanne, of course, and Bessie herself. Emma Jane Randall had unfortunately died in late spring—the least said about that the better. There was a new boarder, but she wouldn't be moving in for another week.*

Bessie had turned her family home into a boarding house after her father died some six or seven years before. It had been a desperation move, because her father's Civil War pension had died with him and there wasn't a penny coming in. Hoping to make enough money to get by, she'd had a wooden sign painted for the front yard, with the words MAGNOLIA MANOR in fancy script, embellished by magnolia blossoms and leaves. She had put advertisements in both the *Darling Dispatch* and the *Monroe Journal* for "older unmarried and widowed ladies of refinement and good taste, to occupy spacious bedrooms at the Magnolia Manor." The bedrooms weren't exactly spacious, but the house had been mostly full ever since.

While the Magnolia Manor managed to pay its bills, the place wasn't what anybody would call a gold mine. Nothing was these days, though, and Bessie knew she was lucky to have a good roof over her head, a garden to eat out of, and companionable friends to share it with. But it would be nice to have just a little extra money coming in, she often thought. She had

---

* Emma Jane Randall's mysterious demise is the subject of *The Darling Dahlias and the Voodoo Lily*.

considered charging more for board and room, but if she did, some of her ladies might have to leave—and where would they go? Certainly not to Mrs. Brewster's Home-Away-From-Home for Young Ladies, where the residents were so unmannerly that Mrs. Brewster had to set strict rules for their behavior. Or to Mrs. Meeks', the men-only boarding house over by the rail-yard. Or to the Old Alabama Hotel, where at $5.50 a week, the rooms were completely out of reach.

"There's no getting blood out of a turnip," she would remind herself with a sigh. "But a turnip isn't half bad, if that's all you've got for supper." Anyway, if she just had a little patience, it wouldn't be long before things looked up. On the fourteenth of August, after what seemed like endless squabbling in Congress, President Roosevelt had signed the Social Security bill. Once the program got underway, everybody who was over sixty-five and met the requirements would get thirty dollars a month. To her ladies, this was a fortune, and they all hoped to live long enough to take advantage of it.

Bessie was glad that the president had finally gotten it done, but she had to admit that he might have been pushed into it by Senator Long. The senator was lobbying for a guaranteed income of two thousand dollars a year for every family, as well as a monthly old age benefit. FDR, people said, might not have signed the Social Security Act if he hadn't been worried that the Kingfish would steal the nomination in '36.

But Bessie knew that while Senator Long had some good ideas, he made a lot of folks nervous. Some called him a corrupt politician who used his office to line his pockets and those of his friends. Others called him a demagogue who wanted to "Hitlerize" America. They pointed out that he had bragged that he was "Hitler and Mussolini both, rolled into one." Maybe folks were right to be afraid of him, Bessie thought, although she felt she didn't know enough to make up her mind.

But what she *did* know was that if Senator Huey P. Long had been the one to push Mr. conservative-at-heart Roosevelt into finally taking action, he deserved a round of applause. She would be in the front row when he came to town on Wednesday, along with the rest of the Share Our Wealth Club. She might even agree to carry one of the WE LOVE YOU HUEY! signs that Earlynne and the others were planning.

Bessie left Roseanne upstairs, making up the beds with fresh linens. Coming through the downstairs hall with her arms full of Miss Rogers' and Mrs. Sedalius' sheets and towels, she saw Leticia Wiggens with a feather duster. (All the Magnolia ladies volunteered to help with the housework.) Leticia—her silver-gray hair pulled back in a bun, her cane against her knee—was sitting in a living room chair beside the radio. Shoulders shaking, she held her head in her hands.

"Why, Leticia!" Bessie exclaimed, dropping the sheets in a heap and kneeling beside the old lady. "What's the matter?"

Leticia lifted her head. Her eyes were filled with tears and her cheeks were wet. "Somebody on the radio just read a little something Will Rogers said about dying," she whispered.

"Oh, I see," Bessie said sympathetically. The Magnolia ladies had always tuned in to Will Rogers' *Gulf Headliners* show on Sunday nights. They loved to listen to his simple, unpretentious humor and the homespun wisdom that often came with it. "Want to tell me what he said?"

Leticia swallowed hard. "I can try. Best I remember, it went something like, 'When I die, my epitaph is going to be *I never met a man I didn't like.*'" She hiccupped. "And then he said, 'I am so proud of that, I can hardly wait to die so they can carve it on my tombstone.'" Her voice broke. "And now he's *dead*, Bessie. Why, I feel just like I felt when my dear brother died!"

It was true, unbelievably. Just two weeks before, Will Rogers had been killed in a plane crash near Point Barrow, Alaska. He was with his friend, aviator Wiley Post, who was famous for being the first person to fly a single-engine plane around the world. Bessie gave Leticia a hug and gently wiped the tears from her wrinkled cheeks. For all Sundays to come, there would be a huge empty hour on the radio. And all across America, people would tell their children and grandchildren what a wonderful man they had lost. Nobody would ever forget Will Rogers.

But the laundry had to be done. Bessie gave Leticia one last hug, then picked up the sheets and towels and carried them to the back porch. The load in the washer was ready to rinse, so she turned off the dasher and began feeding the sheets through the wringer and into the rinse tub, being careful to keep her fingers—and her hair—out of the way. (She had heard terrifying stories about women getting *scalped* by their wringers.) A quick rinse in the tub and another pass through the wringer, and the damp sheets, still smelling of Oxydol, were all in the wicker basket, ready to be hung out on the clothesline.

This was usually Roseanne's job, but she was still upstairs, so Bessie grabbed the clothespin bag (attached to a wire coat hanger so it would slide along the clothesline), picked up the laundry basket, and went outdoors.

But as she took out the first sheet, shook the wringer-wrinkles out of it, and began pinning it to the clothesline, she paused, sniffing. What was that smell? Certainly not Oxydol. Was somebody on the block burning trash? She peered around the sheet and through the gap in the tall hedge that separated the Manor from the Dahlias' clubhouse. That's when she saw it.

*Smoke.* Wisps of gray smoke coming from the back of the Dahlias' clubhouse!

Her heart nearly stopped. "Fire!" she screamed. "Fire!"

Roseanne's head popped out of an upstairs window. "Fire?" she cried. "Where at, Miz Bessie?"

"The clubhouse!" Bessie shouted, forgetting all about the

sheets. She ran up the stairs to the back porch. "Phone the Exchange and tell them to sound the fire alarm!"

And with that, she grabbed up two empty pails and swiftly filled them, one at a time, in the rinse-water tub. Carrying both, she squeezed through the hole in the hedge and into the Dahlias' backyard.

The fire was at the back, beside the kitchen door. The old house, like many Darling homes, was built on brick pillars with an open crawl space underneath. Bessie could see what was left of a substantial heap of dry sticks and rags under the house. It had evidently been burning for a while, and the flames could have ignited the kitchen floor. She caught a brief whiff of lamp oil. This fire was no accident. Somebody intended to burn down the Dahlias' wonderful clubhouse!

At that moment, the shrill wail of the fire siren on the courthouse bell tower shattered Darling's quiet morning, but Bessie scarcely heard it. Bending over so she could see what she was doing, she emptied one of the buckets of rinse water onto the blaze, and then the other. The burning pile sizzled, produced a puff or two of steam, and subsided into scattered coals. But had it been burning long enough to catch the kitchen floor?

The back door was unlocked because the Dahlias were often in and out of the house—and because Darling folk, trusting as they were, rarely bothered to lock their doors. Carrying both empty buckets, Bessie opened the back door and dashed inside. Close to the ceiling, the air was hazy with smoke, and a widening ring of char and blisters seemed to be spreading across the linoleum floor.

Bessie hurried to the kitchen sink to fill one of her empty buckets, then left the tap running to fill the other bucket while she doused the floor, producing more steam and choking smoke. By that time, Roseanne had come in with another bucket and the two of them formed a short bucket brigade, filling buckets at the sink and handing them off to one another. They were still pouring water onto the floor when Archie Mann and a pair of Hot Dogs pulled up in Big Red.

"Sorry it couldn't be sooner," Archie Mann apologized at the back door. "I waited longer than I should for Chief Radley, but he didn't show up." He looked around. "Where's the fire?"

"I think we've put it out," Bessie said, wiping the sweat off her face. She knew she looked like a wreck but she didn't care. The clubhouse was safe. "But it was no accident," she added sharply. "Somebody set it. When I got here, I could smell kerosene."

About that time, Sheriff Norris drove up and after a conversation with Chief Mann—*former* Chief Mann—the sheriff got a flashlight from his car and disappeared under the house. Some minutes later, he crawled out with a couple of finds. A charred piece of blue cotton rag, wrapped around a length of rope. And a book of matches.

He held up the matchbook, carefully, by the corners, in case there were fingerprints. On the cover, it had a picture of a baseball player. "Dizzy Dean," he said. "Our man likes baseball."

"St. Louis Cardinals," Archie Mann said approvingly. "Dizzy's having quite a year. The Cards could wind up with the pennant."

"Not if the Cubs have anything to do with it," put in one of the firefighters, a young man named Joe who sometimes mowed yards in the neighborhood. "They are *hot* this year. Gabby Hartnett is batting better'n three-fifty."

"The Cubs?" Chief Mann chuckled dryly. "Afraid you're whistlin' Dixie, son."

The sheriff brought them back to the situation, pointing out that this was obviously arson, like the earlier fires. And even more worrying.

"Because it involves a residence," he said, "even though nobody lives here. The arsonist might have thought it was just another vacant house." He cast an apologetic glance at Bessie. "I know you and your club members use it regularly. But *he* might not have known that."

Bessie nodded. "We mostly use it for meetings, so we don't have much furniture—just folding chairs. If you looked through a front window, you might think nobody lived here."

"Let's hope torching vacant houses doesn't get to be a habit," Chief Mann said grimly. "The way things are these days, there are too many here in Darling." He bent over and peered under the house. "Well, looks to me like you ladies took care of things. But just to be on the safe side, we'll wet it down good before we go. Let's get to work, boys."

The sheriff left and Roseanne went back to the Manor to check on the washing machine. As Bessie watched, the chief drove Big Red around to the back of the house and the two young Hot Dogs pulled a firehose off the truck and sprayed water against the underside of the kitchen floor while Archie Mann gave instructions. When they were finished and packed up, he and Bessie shook hands.

"Maybe we should name you an honorary Hot Dog," he said with a grin. "Not only did you spot the fire and call it in, you put the gol-darned thing out—before we got here."

"Not by myself," Bessie reminded him. "Roseanne called it in and helped with the buckets."

He nodded. "I know Miz Roseanne. Her oldest boy, Amos, and me, we used to go squirrel hunting together. You tell her I said a big hoorah to her, too."

The fire truck had just pulled away when Wilber, the new reporter from the *Dispatch*, came riding up on his bicycle. "Where's the fire?" he asked excitedly, looking around. "Have I come to the wrong address?"

"The fire was right here," Bessie said, pointing. "We put it out with the rinse water." She told him what had happened and showed him the damage to the kitchen floor, which had burned through in a couple of spots just over the fire. The pretty yellow walls, recently painted by Myra May and Violet, were smudged and smoke-stained. They would have to be repainted.

Wilber wanted to take a photograph of her, but Bessie made him wait until she could get Roseanne to join them. "It was teamwork all the way," she said, as they smiled for the camera.

Wilber had just ridden off when Liz Lacy, the current Dahlias president, rode up on *her* bicycle. "I stopped at Hancock's for some groceries on my way home," she said, breathless. "Mrs. Hancock told me there was a fire here. What happened, Bessie? Is our house all right? Are *you* all right, dear? Should we ask Mr. Piper to come over and look at the damage, for the fire insurance?"

Liz was still there when Mildred Kilgore and Earlynne Biddle arrived. Tommy Lee Musgrove had just announced the news about the fire on WDAR. And then Mr. Greer stopped, on his way to the Palace Theater to set up the movie for that night's special holiday showing of *Little Women*, which Bessie had been looking forward to for the longest time. (Katherine Hepburn was one of her favorites.)

And after that, it was Miss Rogers, just back from the Darling Library and eager to hear what had happened. She was the one who pointed out the obvious: that the clubhouse was only a few yards from the Manor. If Bessie hadn't spotted the fire and if she and Roseanne hadn't managed to put it out, the clubhouse would soon have been engulfed in flames. And the wind was just right to catch the Manor on fire, too!

Roseanne had the second load of sheets hung up to dry by the time Bessie finally got back to the washing machine.

Rufus Radley, the *new* fire chief, never showed up.

# CHAPTER EIGHT

# WHERE THERE'S SMOKE

*Tuesday, September 3, 1935*

BEULAH TRIVETTE HAD CLOSED HER BEAUTY BOWER ON LABOR Day so she and Hank could take their two youngsters for a picnic at Pine Mill Creek, where somebody, years ago, had hung a rope from a big oak tree. Little Hank and Spoonie had had a wonderful time playing Tarzan and Jane, swinging over the swimming hole and dropping into its dark, cool depths. After an hour in the water, there were plates heaped with Beulah's fried chicken, potato salad, and deviled eggs; ears of corn roasted in the ashes of a hot fire and slathered with butter; and—late in the afternoon—chunks of watermelon carved from the fat green melon that Hank had floated in the river.

So for Beulah, Tuesday was the first day of a new week *and* a new month. With a private smile, she closed the door of the cupboard over the twin shampoo sinks. She had just checked her beauty supplies, making sure she had plenty of her favorite homemade setting lotion and that there was enough shampoo and conditioner to last until the next supply order came in on the Greyhound. It made her happy when events unfolded in a regular, predictable order, without interruptions and especially without too many appointment cancellations and reschedulings, which could throw an entire week into chaos.

Beulah had been especially happy when she slipped into

her ruffled smock this morning—pink, of course, her favorite color. She was already looking forward to today's beauty appointments, beginning with Ophelia Snow, who wasn't just a client but a special friend and a fellow Dahlia. She saw from today's schedule that Opie was coming in for a shampoo and set, no doubt because (Beulah had heard) her new boss would be in town later today and she wanted to look her best. Ophelia's lovely brown hair took to pin curls like a duck takes to water, so making her even more beautiful was always a pleasure.

But Beulah couldn't help sighing when she saw the next name on the list. She had learned long ago that while some people (like Ophelia) were all sunshine and smiles, others were scowls and thunderstorms. Leona Ruth Adcock was among the scowlers. *Her* skies were usually filled with ominous clouds.

In fact, Leona Ruth (whose sparse, graying hair was a challenge for anybody in the beauty business) reminded Beulah of the Wicked Witch of the West in Mr. Baum's magical book, *The Wonderful Wizard of Oz*, which she had read—over and over again—to Spoonie and Little Hank. Mr. Baum had written that the ugly old witch "had but one eye, yet that was as powerful as a telescope, and could see everywhere."

Well, Leona Ruth had two eyes and *both* of them were like telescopes. Whenever she could, she used them to peer into the private lives of Darling folk, like somebody peering through a knothole in the back fence or a gap in the bedroom curtains. What's more, she took a mean pleasure in telling tales about what she saw, although it was usually pretty hard to tell what was true and what was the product of Leona Ruth's vivid imagination. In Beulah's view, the woman was a tragedy, for she could have been just as beautiful as anybody else if she hadn't been such a witch.

Quickly, Beulah picked up a pencil and wrote Bettina's name

next to Leona Ruth's. Which was only fair. *She* had done Leona Ruth last time.

But the rest of the day was filled with friendly appointments, and beyond that, Beulah had plenty of other reasons to be happy. There was Hank, who might not be the best-looking guy in town but was certainly the sweetest and most helpful. After all, he had built the Bower for her, enclosing the screened porch at the back of their house, wiring it for electricity and a new hot water heater, and installing the twin shampoo sinks and hair-cutting chairs and mirrors. Beulah herself had done the rest, painting the wainscoting her favorite shade of bright pink, wallpapering the walls with lovely pink roses, and spatter-painting the pink floor with blue, gray, and yellow. Beulah's life had begun on the wrong side of Darling's railroad tracks, so her Beauty Bower seemed something like an earthly version of paradise.

A perky, pretty blonde with a passion for all things artistic, Beulah was also a practical person whose hard-scrabble childhood had taught her that life was much easier when there was a little extra hidden under the mattress. She was proud of her earnings from the Bower, which usually amounted to two, sometimes even three dollars a day. But while she was glad she could give Hank a hand with the family expenses, she wasn't in the beauty business for the money. She genuinely wanted to help women make the most of whatever the good Lord had given them, especially when it came to hair.

Now, Beulah went to the basket in the corner, took out the fluffy pink towels (the same pink as the smock she was wearing) and began to fold them. The Sears radio on the shelf beside her hair-cutting station was tuned to WDAR and Tommy Lee Musgrove came on to read a weather bulletin about the dangerous hurricane—the "storm of the century" he called it—that had slammed into the Florida Keys the day before. She paused to listen, remembering that she and Hank and the kids had been enjoying a swim and a picnic while that terrible storm was raging across those little islands.

In fact, the hurricane may have killed as many as five hundred people, Tommy reported, many of them veterans working on the new Overseas Highway. An eleven-car railroad train had been sent to pick them up, but the locomotive and several cars had been blown off the track. "Mountainous waves" had slammed the passenger steamer *Dixie* into a coral reef. A couple of ships were standing by, desperately hoping for the seas to calm enough to launch the lifeboats and rescue the nearly four hundred people on board. The storm was in the Gulf of Mexico now and the Weather Bureau couldn't predict where it was headed. The whole Upper Gulf Coast—from the Florida Panhandle to New Orleans—was on the alert.

*The whole Upper Gulf Coast?* Beulah shivered, remembering a few years back, when a hurricane leveled parts of Miami, crossed Florida into the Gulf, and then smacked into Alabama, flooding poor little Darling. If there was anything to be glad about where big Gulf storms were concerned, she couldn't think what it was.

But she started to smile again when Tommy Lee began playing a recording of Nick Lucas' popular song, "Singing in the Rain." Darling didn't need another flood, but it would be wonderful if the Labor Day hurricane would bring them a little rain. Heaven knows, they could use it. The whole town was tinder-dry, which made the recent grass fires all the more scary. She had just joined Nick Lucas in singing a lusty "Come on with the rain, I've a smile on my face" when Bettina Higgens opened the door and stepped in.

Bettina certainly hadn't been the prettiest blossom in the garden when she applied to become the Bower's first beauty associate. Her brown hair had been lank and greasy, she was round-shouldered and as flat as a board in front, and she (unlike Beulah) had not graduated from beauty school. But Beulah recognized the unspoken desire in Bettina's heart and the untutored talent in her deft fingers and understood that this unlovely young woman possessed the remarkable hidden gift of making the ordinary woman beautiful.

She had been a perfect choice, and as the weeks went by, Bettina had bloomed. Beulah gave her a more becoming hairstyle and permanent wave and saw to it that she had a good lunch every day so that the girl not only blossomed but filled out in all the right places.

What's more, it quickly became clear that the two of them were kindred spirits. They believed that it was not Pollyannaish in the slightest to look on the bright side of things—to play the "glad game," as Pollyanna herself called it. In fact, they both felt that it was especially important to be positive during bad times, like the years they were living through right now, when jobs were scarce and money was scarcer. They also agreed that even a random bit of beauty—a helping hand or a smile, extra zucchini or cucumbers in a basket on a neighbor's doorstep, or even a homemade "I'm thinking of you" card pushed under someone's door—went a long way toward making people happy in this gritty, grimy world.

And if not happy, then perhaps a little easier to get along with, which you have to admit is pretty important when everybody is scrambling just to get by and all people can think is *oh how hard it all is.* Even a little something beautiful might make them a lot more cheerful.

But Bettina hadn't started the morning with a beautiful thought, and she wasn't playing the glad game. Instead, she wore a worried frown as she put on her pink cotton smock, a match to Beulah's. "Have you heard about the house fires yesterday?"

"The *house fires?*" Beulah reached over and turned the radio off. "Oh, my gracious sakes, no! It was so blessed hot that Hank and I took a picnic out to the river so the kids could go swimming. It's far enough away so we wouldn't have heard the siren. What *happened*, Bettina? Whose house?"

For the past year, Bettina had been going steady with Sheriff Buddy Norris, so she usually had the latest news, which definitely wasn't pretty, let alone beautiful. Like last week, when Mr. Clinton imbibed a little too much of Bodeen Pyle's white lightning and drove his old red Ford taxi into the lake. His brother had hitched his team of mules to the Ford and hauled it out, but Rufus Radley said it would take a while to get to the repairs, since he'd just been elected fire chief and had other fish to fry. If you wanted to take the taxi to Monroeville to go shopping, you'd have to wait a week or two.

This morning, the news was even more alarming. "The siren went off twice yesterday," Bettina said. "The first fire was at the Dahlias' clubhouse. The second was the old Popplewell place just down the block from me—the one everybody says is haunted. *Was* haunted," she corrected herself. "It burned down to the ground. If there were any ghosts in it, they've been fried."

"The Dahlias' clubhouse!" Beulah's hand went to her mouth. "Oh, no! It didn't . . . it didn't burn down, did it?"

"Buddy said that Bessie Bloodworth spotted it when she was hanging sheets on the clothesline. She put it out with her rinse water before Big Red and the Hot Dogs got there. Apparently, there's a burned place in the kitchen floor that needs fixing and the walls and ceiling will have to be repainted, but otherwise, the house is okay. And nobody got hurt. So I guess we can be glad of that."

"Amen," Beulah said.

Bettina sighed. "But the Popplewell place sits on the corner behind some trees, so nobody saw the fire until it was too late to save the house. It burned right down to the ground." She began to sort through her combs and scissors, getting ready for the day. "Buddy says it's a bad sign. Whoever is starting these fires has graduated from burning grass to burning buildings." She reached under the counter for a box of pin curl clips. "He's deputized some men to set up lookout posts around town. And Mr. Duffy at the bank is offering a reward. They're hoping that somebody will give them a tip."

Beulah shuddered. It went against her grain to think unpleasant thoughts, but when there were bad people out there setting fire to good people's houses, what else could you think?

"I will be *awfully* glad when they catch him," she said. "Who do you suppose he is? A teenager looking for excitement?"

Bettina set the box of pin curl clips on the counter beside her combs and scissors and went to take a look at the schedule. Over her shoulder, she said, "Maybe it's not a he. Starting a fire doesn't take much more than a match and some tinder. It's the easiest thing in the world. I reckon a woman could do it just as well as a man." She looked down at the schedule and made a face. "Oh, boo-hoo," she muttered. "Leona Ruth."

Beulah felt instantly guilty. "I can take her if you don't want to, Bettina."

"No, I can," Bettina answered. "You did her last time."

Gratefully, Beulah went back to the subject. "A woman could do it, yes. But no woman *would*. I mean, a woman might cause a fire by accident, like letting the grease in her frying pan get too hot. My mama did that once, frying bacon, and caught the tea towels on fire. But no woman would ever burn somebody's house down. Not deliberately, I mean."

"Well, *you* wouldn't." Bettina was thoughtful. "But maybe *she* would. For instance, it could be a case of a woman who's got a grudge against the world. She feels like people are always picking on her or something like that. Lighting fires makes her feel like she's getting revenge. Or maybe—"

Bettina's speculation was interrupted by Ophelia Snow, who came bouncing into the Bower with a bright smile on her pretty face. She was wearing a sunshiny yellow dress, sleeveless, with a swingy skirt bordered with several rows of white rickrack.

"Good morning, ladies!" she sang out. "Isn't it just the most *beautiful* day?"

But Leona Ruth, ten minutes early for her appointment, was right behind Ophelia. "Enjoy the sunshine," she said ominously. She took off her purple hat and checked the bodice of her purple dress to make sure it was buttoned up to the neck. "The radio says it's fixin' to blow up a serious storm. A hurricane, *ack*chually."

"Hurricane?" Bettina's eyes went wide. "Really? We're having a hurricane? How exciting!"

Bettina sounded almost eager, Beulah thought. But then, Bettina hadn't lived in Darling long enough to remember what happened the last time a hurricane had blown in from the Gulf. "Tommy Lee has been reading the bulletins on WDAR this morning. But it's a long way off," she added in a reassuring tone. "We can be glad that the Weather Bureau is watching it for us. They'll let us know if it comes in our direction."

"The Weather Bureau's about as much help as a poke in the eye when it comes to hurricanes," Leona Ruth said sourly. "Last time we had a big storm, my neighbors let the ditch in front of their house get plugged up and a foot and a half of water backed up into my parlor. Ruined my best rug."

Beulah's heart sank. The old lady was in one of her moods, which meant that the next hour would not be as pleasant as she had hoped.

"Oh, that's too bad." She summoned a smile. "Well, now, Ophelia, if you're ready, let's get you shampooed. Leona Ruth, you're getting lucky today. Bettina is going to do you." She patted Bettina's arm in sympathy.

"Yeah," Leona Ruth said darkly. "Like Dish Night at the Palace Theater last week. I was hoping to finish out my Cabbage Rose collection, but Mr. Greer ran out of soup bowls just as he got to me. He *would*, natchurally." She sweetened her tone. "Nothin' personal, Bettina. Just sayin' it's how my luck runs."

A few moments later, Ophelia and Leona Ruth were stretched out in the twin shampoo chairs with their heads in the shampoo sinks, and Beulah and Bettina were at work, washing and rinsing and conditioning. While they worked, they talked, all four of them.

About Rufus Radley, who had bought the fire chief's election and then hadn't shown up at either of yesterday's fires. "I heard he claimed he had a repair job but he really went fishing," Bettina said with disgust.

About Bessie and Roseanne, who had saved the Dahlias' clubhouse from burning down. "We ought to give them an award," Ophelia said. She giggled. "We could call it the Red Hot Mamas Medal."

"Like Sophie Tucker," Beulah replied delightedly. Waggling her hips, she paraphrased a few lines from the song in Sophie's movie, *Honky Tonk*:

> We're the last of the red hot mamas,
> We'll put the other fires out!
> When it comes to fightin' fire, you know where to go—
> And you can always get your hot stuff
> Straight from our volcano!

Beulah couldn't help laughing along with Bettina and Ophelia. Leona Ruth was not amused.

And then they talked about tomorrow's exciting event: Huey P. Long's appearance in Darling, which would likely turn out the largest crowd in the town's history, unless maybe it was back in 1925, when the Coles Brothers circus came to town with a trainload of zebras and elephants and a sideshow of human oddities.

Bettina reported that the sheriff's office was a little nervous about Long's visit. "The senator isn't just real popular with everybody," she said, taking a bottle from the shelf and splashing some of its contents into the rinse water in the shampoo sink. "But Buddy says he's bringing his own security guards. All he and Wayne have to do is direct traffic."

"Hang on just a durn minute, Bettina," Leona Ruth said sharply. She wrinkled her nose. "What's that I smell? What are you putting on my hair?"

Bettina held the bottle where Leona could see it. "I put just a few drops of Mrs. Stewart's Bluing in your rinse, Mrs. Adcock. It tones down the brassy color that folks sometimes get with gray hair." She smiled teasingly. "It might make you look just a little like Jean Harlow."

Everybody knew that actress Jean Harlow, famous for her gorgeous hair in *Platinum Blonde*, used a blue rinse, maybe some of Mrs. Stewart's laundry bluing. But it went much farther than that, Beulah knew. She had read that Miss Harlow's white-blond hair required a weekly application of ammonia, Clorox, and Lux soap flakes, a combination that made her shudder. Sometimes the price of beauty just wasn't worth it, which is what she told anybody who asked her whether they could be as platinum as Jean Harlow.

"I'm sure you don't want all your hair to fall out," she'd tell them. "That's what's going to happen to Miss Harlow, if she's not careful. Even beauty has its limits." But to Leona Ruth, she said, "Bluing isn't going to hurt at all, dear. It's the gentlest thing in the world."

"Well, then, only a few drops," Leona Ruth conceded grudgingly. "I don't want to walk out of here with a head of blue hair."

"Oh, *that's* not going to happen," Beulah assured her. "You'll just be beautiful. Won't she, Bettina?"

"Oh, absolutely," Bettina agreed.

"Hrummph," Leona Ruth said.

A few moments later, as Ophelia was seating herself in Beulah's hair-cutting chair, she went back to the conversation about Huey P. Long. "You don't suppose that Senator Long is *really* afraid that somebody might shoot him, do you? I mean, who would *dare?*"

"Well, there's always a few crazies out there," Bettina replied as she settled Leona Ruth into the neighboring chair. "Don't forget that somebody tried to shoot President Roosevelt just a couple of years ago."

This shocking event had happened not long before FDR's inauguration, when the president-elect was giving a political speech in Miami. The gunman missed Roosevelt and hit four other people, including the mayor of Chicago. The mayor died. The gunman had been executed barely a month later. The story had been front-page news for weeks.

"And lots of people don't like Senator Long, apparently," Bettina went on. "I read that he's been getting a flock of death threats."

Beulah draped a pink cotton cape around Ophelia to keep the clippings off her pretty dress and gave her a bowl of pin curl clips to hold in her lap. "Well, nothing bad is going to happen to him while he's in Darling," she said confidently, picking up her comb and taking the lid off her bottle of setting lotion, which she made herself out of seeds from the quince bush at the back of the yard. "We're a very peaceful little town. Nothing bad ever happens here."

"The fires are happenin'," Leona Ruth objected—to which Beulah had no response. "In fact, somebody could be settin' one right this very minute, for all we know." She winced. "Bettina, you be careful with that comb. You almost got it in my eye."

"Nothing is going to happen to Senator Long because he has all those bodyguards," Bettina said reassuringly, going back to the subject. "Buddy says they're really tough, like those gangster bad guys you see in the movies. They carry blackjacks. And guns. And they stay with him all the time, night and day."

"Mr. Nichols told me that the US Senate is investigating Senator Long," Ophelia chimed in, as Beulah began combing and snipping. "They may even kick him out of office."

At the mention of Mr. Nichols, Leona Ruth gave Ophelia a tight little smile, as if she'd just tasted a lemon. The two women were sitting side by side and they weren't supposed to turn their heads. But they could see one another's faces in the mirrors in front of them.

"I heard that Mr. Nichols is comin' to town this week," Leona Ruth said. "This afternoon, ain't it, *ack*chually?" In an acid tone, she added, "I s'pose you're getting yourself all dressed up for the occasion. And ain't that a new dress? I b'lieve I saw it in the window at Mann's Mercantile just last week. A dollar-ninety-eight is what I remember."

Beulah, winding Ophelia's copper-brown hair around her finger, knew from long acquaintance that Leona Ruth specialized in making hurtful remarks, but this one was more ill-mannered than usual. She winced, and when she glanced at Ophelia in the mirror, she saw the blush rising quickly on her friend's neck.

When Ophelia spoke, her voice was taut. "Thank you, Leona Ruth," she said, handing Beulah a pin curl clip out of the bowl. She was pretending that Leona Ruth had complimented her dress. "I'm so glad you like it. And no, it didn't come out of the Mercantile window. I got it from the Sears and Roebuck catalog. I always think it's a good idea to look your best when you have an important business appointment."

Beulah dipped her comb in setting lotion, then took the pin curl clip and pinned a curl. "A shampoo and set is *always* a good investment," she put in hastily, hoping to smooth things over.

Bettina spoke up, too. "Especially when your business associate comes from out of town," she said, snipping rapidly at Leona Ruth's hair. "My goodness, but that Yankee fellow does make my little Southern heart go pitty-patter. I'm glad you could get such a pretty new dress, Mrs. Snow. If it were me, I'd still be searching through my closet for something to wear." She gave a dramatic sigh. "And of course, I would never have the right dress. Let alone the shoes to go with it."

Ophelia's cheeks were now bright red, but she tried to laugh as she handed Beulah another hair clip. "Well, as I said, I think it's a good idea to look nice—"

"As long as it's just a *business* appointment," Leona Ruth remarked pointedly, lifting her chin. "Didn't I see the two of you havin' supper at the Old Alabama, Ophelia? Let's see . . ." She screwed up her face, pretending to remember. "I believe that must have been the week Mr. Snow was in Mobile."

The remark, so innocent on its face, hung like a threat in the air, stifling all speech. The silence was punctuated only by the sound of Bettina's scissors. In the mirror, Beulah saw that Ophelia's blush had faded to dead-white and her jaw was clenched. It was several moments before she managed to answer Leona Ruth.

"We did have a business supper there," Ophelia said, her voice thin. "Ryan—Mr. Nichols—has an expense account and was kind enough to suggest that we discuss the project over a nice meal." She darted a glance at the mirror. "I sincerely hope you're not suggesting that I—that Mr. Nichols and I—"

"Oh *nothing* like that!" Leona Ruth interrupted, pretending alarm. Her voice turned sweet and syrupy. "Far be it from me to criticize, Ophelia dear, and you know I *never* have a personal opinion. I only *ever* want what is best for all involved." She took a breath. "I was just thinkin' of what our Darling friends could be sayin'. You know what they're like, I'm sure—always tittle-tattlin' about any little thing they happen to see, especially when it's out of the usual. And where there's smoke . . . well, you know. Bound to be fire, even if it's only a little 'un." She paused significantly, both eyebrows arched. "I'm just hopin' that you and your Mr. Nichols will be . . ." Another pause. "Well, careful, that's all."

"He is not 'my' Mr. Nichols." Ophelia's shoulders had now gone rigid and a muscle worked in her jaw. "And I don't know what you're talking about, Mrs. Adcock." Her voice was low and Beulah could tell she was making every effort to keep it from trembling. "I have no reason to be *careful* of anything, especially where my employer is concerned. He is a perfect gentleman."

"Of course he is, dear," Leona Ruth replied, in a tone that said exactly the opposite. "And I'm sure you are a perfect lady."

Bettina wielded her scissors dangerously close to Leona Ruth's left ear. "Well, if it was me, Mrs. Snow, I would jump at the chance for a business dinner at the Old Alabama. A white tablecloth, real china and crystal, and Miz Vaughn playing the piano." Defiantly, she met Leona Ruth's eyes in the mirror. "And if the Darling gossips wanted to talk—well, those old moth-eaten biddies could go ahead and say whatever they want. It wouldn't bother me in the slightest."

"It might if you were *married*," Leona Ruth retorted sweetly. "And if your husband was in a prominent position in this little town. Say, if he were the mayor, as a for-instance." She pulled a long face. "Don't get me wrong, ladies. I am not accusing any-body of anything. I am only thinkin' about what Darling folk might be whisperin' among themselves tomorrow morning."

Ophelia flinched as if she'd been slapped in the face. Beulah, who always tried to look on the sunny side of everything, could no longer escape the creeping realization that in spite of Ophelia's protests, her relationship with the attractive Mr. Ryan might not be as straightforward and aboveboard as she wanted people to think. There were secrets here, unsettling secrets. Something was going on that Beulah knew she did *not* want to know about.

And there was no point at all, ever, in trying to argue with Leona Ruth. The old lady made it her business to put people in the wrong, just for the momentary pleasure of feeling herself in the right. This conversation had to go somewhere else.

Winding another pin curl over Ophelia's ear, Beulah raised her voice a notch. "We're planning to close early tomorrow so Bettina and I can both go to hear Senator Long. I'm sure it'll be as hot as blue blazes out there on the square, so I'm thinking of wearing my pink pongee with the lace collar and angel sleeves. It's the coolest dress I have. What are you wearing, Bettina?"

Bettina took the hint. "My pink plaid shirtwaist, I think," she said quickly. "It'll stay nice and fresh, even in the heat. And it washes, so dust won't do it any harm." She added another pin curl at Leona Ruth's temple. "What will you be wearing, Mrs. Adcock?"

"My green rayon print," Leona Ruth trilled. "And my perky little lime green straw pillbox from two years ago. I've updated it with a couple of green parrot feathers. Oh, speakin' of hats, did you see what Voleen Johnson was wearin' on *hers* on Sunday? I was sitting in the pew right behind her, so I had a front-row seat, so to speak. It was a real bird, dead and stuffed."

And that, thank goodness, was the end of that.

# CHAPTER NINE

# FIRE!

As soon as she got out from under the hair dryer and Beulah had brushed out her curls, Ophelia went directly home, walking fast and hoping she wouldn't encounter anyone she knew. She was still so upset by Leona Ruth's not-so-veiled accusations that she didn't think she could frame a coherent answer if somebody asked her a question.

And if the question was about Mr. Nichols, she would probably burst into tears and spill out her guilty confession—although there wasn't really anything to confess, was there? Of course there wasn't. She hadn't actually *done* anything. But she couldn't prove that.

And Leona Ruth was right about one thing. Gossip was like Reverend Peters' trash fire. He turned his back on it for a minute and the next thing he knew, the whole neighborhood was in flames. What if Jed heard some of the chatter? He was a proud man, and possessive. He would be deeply hurt. And he already had so much else on his mind, with the election coming up. It was all so depressing. And frightening.

The brisk walk did her good, though. By the time she got home, Opie had decided what she had to do to stop the fires before they got going. It was nearly ten, and she had to catch Bessie Bloodworth now, before she made other plans for the day. So she went straight to the telephone and rang up the Magnolia Manor. To her relief, Bessie answered the phone.

"Mr. Nichols will be here for an hour or two this afternoon," Ophelia said, "and maybe an hour or two tomorrow morning. I think it would be lovely if you would be here too, Bessie. You're responsible for a big section of our part of the guidebook and for all of the Darling history. I'm sure he'll want to meet you."

Bessie was obviously thrilled by the invitation. "Why, what a good idea!" she said promptly. "Thanks ever so much for asking me, Opie dear. What time would you like me to come?"

In the pit of her stomach, Ophelia was conscious of a dull emptiness mixed with an unexpected relief—a feeling she recognized immediately for what it was. For several weeks now she had looked forward with an ever-mounting excitement to being alone with Mr. Nichols, just the two of them. She hadn't been *planning* anything, of course. She wouldn't have known what to plan. She was just letting herself be open to whatever might happen. Allowing herself to imagine . . . oh, all kinds of possibilities, some of them interesting, some exciting, and some that she knew she shouldn't allow to pop into her mind for even an instant.

But she hadn't wanted to stop. It was something like "Anything Goes," that jivey new Cole Porter song that was on everybody's lips. The world had gone completely mad today and good could be bad today and black was often white today and even day might be night today. And if you were truly open to scheming new schemes and dreaming new dreams, it was all possible. *Anything* was possible.

Opie sighed. Well, anything might be possible if you were in New York, say, or Hollywood or Miami. But obviously not in Darling, where Leona Ruth Adcock and her friends made sure that everybody walked the straight and narrow and did the things they were supposed to do and nothing else. For Opie, thinking about Mr. Nichols and wondering what was going to happen when they were together *wasn't* walking the straight and narrow. It had offered her something exciting and exhilarating and unpredictable to imagine, in a life that was almost entirely predictable. Pretty darn dull, too.

But now that Bessie would be at their meeting, absolutely nothing unpredictable was going to happen. Opie felt disappointed and deflated, as if somebody had pulled the plug on Christmas after the tree was up and the lights were on and the presents were all made and waiting in the closet.

Bessie cleared her throat and repeated, "What time would you like me to come over, Ophelia?"

Jarred back into the telephone conversation, Opie took a deep breath. "Why don't we say one-thirty? That way, you and I will have a little time to go over a few things together before Mr. Nichols gets here."

"Sounds right to me," Bessie said. "I'll bring my draft of our Darling history—I'm almost up to telephones. See you then. And thanks for including me, Ophelia." She hesitated a moment and added, "I think it's the smart thing to do."

Opie said goodbye, wondering what Bessie meant by that last remark. Had she guessed about Mr. Nichols? How many others suspected—that is, besides Leona Ruth?

For a long moment, she stood at the telephone, thinking how easy it was for a few foolish people to imagine smoke when the fire hadn't even started. Then she took another deep breath and went into the kitchen to brew herself a consoling cup of tea. Christmas wasn't coming and there was nothing to look forward to but humdrum days full of routine sameness.

But balanced against this was that unexpected sense of relief—which, when you got right down to it, was really pretty silly. It wasn't that she had done the right thing or even avoided doing the wrong thing. What she had done was to avoid the *appearance* of doing the wrong thing. There wasn't any fire here, but people like Leona Ruth were never happy unless they were spreading the news about a few little puffs of smoke. Now, however, if anybody wanted to gossip about her and Mr. Nichols being alone together, Bessie Bloodworth was a witness, a highly *credible* witness that nobody would dare to doubt. Bessie could say that she had been here the whole time and there had been absolutely no hanky-panky.

And Jed, who sometimes got all bent out of shape about the least little thing (the way he did about Sarah's two-piece red bathing suit and Opie's trim-fitting slacks, of which he definitely did *not* approve)—Jed wouldn't hear a word of gossip.

Ophelia did feel better. There might've been a fire, but she had put it out. There wouldn't even be a little puff of smoke.

❀

OVER AT THE MAGNOLIA MANOR, BESSIE BLOODWORTH hung up the phone and poked her head into the kitchen, where Roseanne was grating cabbage for coleslaw.

"There's been a last-minute change of plans for this afternoon, Roseanne," she announced. "I'm going to the Snows' to meet with Mrs. Snow and Mr. Nichols about the Darling history project."

Roseanne stuck out her lower lip. "Whut about mahjong? Wasn't us and the ladies fixin' to play this afternoon?" She loved mahjong and was very good at it.

"Oh, drat," Bessie said. "I'm sorry. I forgot. Well, we'll just have to play tomorrow afternoon."

"Not t'morra neither." Roseanne's knife flashed as she sliced off another chunk of cabbage. "Mr. Huey P. Long is comin' to town t'morra. Don' nobody want to miss that, I reckon." She cocked her head. "Less'n his party gets rained on. You heard whether that big ol' hurricane's comin' here or goin' somewhere else?"

"I haven't heard anything about it this morning," Bessie said. "But you're right—tomorrow is out, one way or the other. We'll have to play on Thursday." But the minute she said it, she remembered that Thursday wouldn't work, either. Thursday was the Ladies' Embroidery Club, and she was giving a lesson on french knots. "I suppose it won't hurt us to skip mahjong this week," she said finally. "Or maybe I'll just run upstairs and ask Miss Rogers if she's available to take my place today."

Roseanne heaved a dramatic sigh and scraped the shredded cabbage into a bowl. "It would've been real nice if Miz Snow had let you know about the meetin' a little earlier."

"Yes, it would," Bessie agreed. In fact, as she went upstairs to find Dorothy Rogers, she was remembering the brief exchange with Ophelia on Saturday morning, when they were picking beans for the Hot Dog supper. She had suspected then that Ophelia was trying—not very successfully—to conceal a secret crush on Mr. Nichols, and the more she thought about it, the more uneasy she felt. This kind of thing was like playing with fire. What started with a lighted match could end with a house burning down. Or even worse: a tragic explosion and lives lost, like the time Manley Briggs walked in on his wife and his second cousin in bed together and shot them both dead.

Not that Ophelia would ever let things go that far, of course, and Bessie felt that her faith in her friend's fundamental good sense had been justified. Mr. Nichols might be a fine-looking man and a snappy dresser, but he was Opie's boss and her husband was the jealous type.

And as far as the local gossips were concerned, it didn't matter that nobody ever saw the actual fire—a wisp or two of smoke, or maybe even the *smell* of it—was all they needed. There were strong feelings about Yankees, too. Folks in Darling had been skittish about strangers ever since General James H. Wilson and his boys in blue had burned Selma and then marched south, aiming to burn Darling. They couldn't do much to stop that from happening—the damn Yankees were going to burn whatever they wanted to burn. But folks could at least bury the family silver. Which they did. And they still bore a grudge, especially those who couldn't remember where the family silver was buried.

Pausing before she knocked on Miss Rogers' bedroom door, Bessie sighed. Like Aunt Hetty, she had been hoping for a spark of romance between her friend Liz and the fine-looking Mr. Nichols, but there was no getting around it. The man *was* a Yankee, and when it came to Yankees, it was prudent to be . . . well, careful.

Not that Mr. Nichols wasn't the perfect gentleman he seemed to be, because by all accounts he was. And that business with General Wilson and his Union boys had happened way back in her daddy's day, eighty-some years ago. The times had changed since then. After all, the boys from the South had willingly joined up with the boys from the North to fight the Huns in the War to End All Wars, and they all worked shoulder-to-shoulder in the CCC.

But on reflection, Bessie had to admit that maybe the times hadn't changed all that much. After all, just last year, FDR, that quintessential Yankee, had forced everybody to hand over their gold to the government. Yes, you got dollars in return, but you could count on gold. You always knew what it was worth. The dollar was like one of those new-fangled yo-yos Mr. Dunlap was selling at the dime store. One day it might be worth a dollar, the next day, seventy cents. Or less.

When it came to Yankees, you were smart to be careful. If they didn't find your silver, they might come after your gold.

⚘

ACROSS FROM THE COURTHOUSE AND UPSTAIRS OVER THE DISpatch, Lizzy was answering the candlestick phone on the corner of her desk.

"Good morning, law offices," she said pertly. "Elizabeth Lacy speaking. How may I help you?"

"Good morning, Elizabeth," said a deep male voice. "And you've already helped. Just hearing your voice gives me a lift."

"Oh, such blarney," Lizzy replied with a happy little laugh. "Really, Ryan, you ought to be ashamed."

"Who, me?" he hooted. "Ashamed? Never! Besides, it's true. I could listen to your voice all day." He paused. "But I can't, because I'm calling from a pay phone and I'm short on change. Just checking to be sure we're still on for dinner this evening. At your place." His voice became intimate. "I hope so, anyway. I've been thinking of you while I've been on the road all week. I really want to see you."

A little flame of anticipation raced through her and Lizzy took a deep breath. "Of course we're still on. We're having chicken salad sandwiches on croissants from the bakery, along with cold tomato soup and a fruit and cheese plate. Don't worry about getting here at any certain time. It can all go on the table in a jiffy."

"You are amazing, Elizabeth. You always make everything sound so simple." There was a smile in his voice. "That's one of the reasons I . . . like you so much." There had been a slight hesitation on *like*, and goosebumps prickled on Lizzy's arms. It sounded as if he might have been thinking of saying "I love you."

"It *is* simple," Lizzy told him, although of course it wasn't. Nothing about her life these days was simple. There was her job in Mr. Moseley's office—and Moira Skelton, Bent's lady friend in Montgomery, where he spent a great deal of his time. And Ryan, whom she liked very much—and perhaps more than liked—but who lived far away in Washington and didn't make it down to Darling all that often. And Grady Alexander, her former fiancé, who was now seeing Doc Roberts' daughter Lavinia but who dropped in at least once a week "just to see how you are doing."

And there was her second book to complicate things, which—as Miss Fleming had reminded her this morning on the phone—was due on her editor's desk in just a couple of months. At which Lizzy shuddered, because the book was going absolutely nowhere and she was beginning to doubt whether she was *really* a writer.

"Well, good," he said warmly. "I'm looking forward to hearing all about it tonight. Oh, and I'll bring the wine." His voice became teasing. "I'm hoping we can pick up where we left off last time, when we were so rudely interrupted."

Lizzy's breath came a little faster, but she only said, "Drive carefully."

"Always," he said.

She hung the receiver in its cradle and sat at her desk for a moment, remembering. The last time she had been alone with Ryan—in her living room, on her sofa—she had almost given in to him. In fact, she knew she *would* have, if the telephone hadn't rung at the very moment when, kissing her deeply, he had slipped his hand inside her blouse.

"Let it ring," he had murmured in her ear. "They can call back later." He dropped his lips to her bare shoulder. "Please, Elizabeth."

His electric touch burned her skin and she was eager to yield to whatever might come next. But on the fourth jangling ring, she had managed to pull away and reach for the phone.

The call had been like a bucket of cold water, and she sat up straight, clutching her open blouse. It was Mr. Dunlap, phoning to tell her that her mother was having an appendicitis attack and they were about to leave for the hospital over in Monroeville. Would Lizzy please meet them there just as soon as she could—her mother was *urgent* that she come. And of course, Lizzy did.

It wasn't appendicitis, as things turned out, just a bad case of indigestion. But Lizzy hadn't gotten home from the hospital until four the next morning. Ryan had left early for an appointment down in Mobile, and after that, had driven back to Washington. She hadn't seen him since. But he had sent her several funny little notes and she had thought of him often, especially at night when she was writing in her journal, when—totally without her volition—her pen seemed to want to write his name. At which point she usually slipped into thoughts of how she had felt when he touched her bare skin, thoughts that were too intimate to record. She had thought of him in a different way yesterday, though, when Verna had startled her by saying that she was concerned about their friend Ophelia.

"To be perfectly blunt about it," Verna had said, "I think our Opie has a crush on Mr. Nichols. You must have noticed—haven't you?"

Lizzy had rallied to Ophelia's defense, but Verna's observation had given her plenty to think about. Yes, she supposed it was possible that Opie might have the same feelings she did about Ryan. He was compellingly attractive and in all ways a gentleman. But it *wasn't* possible that Ryan had done anything to encourage her. Lizzy didn't know everything about him, of course, but she felt she knew him well enough to know that he wasn't the kind of man who would make improper advances to a married woman. He himself had been married once, much earlier in his life, and he had said enough about the experience to make her think that he valued the sanctity of marriage.

That didn't mean that Ophelia wasn't *imagining* that he was interested in her, however. And perhaps even hoping that he was. Her Darling life, after all, was as routine and predictable as the three meals a day she put on the table for her family, or the laundry that had to be done at least once a week, before everybody ran out of socks and underwear. Opie often complained that nothing exciting ever happened in Darling, that nothing new ever came her way. It wasn't strictly true, of course. But after being married for nearly twenty years, she couldn't be blamed for craving a little excitement. Romantic excitement—and more, perhaps. The kind of excitement she saw in the movies.

And even if it were true that Ophelia had . . . deeper feelings for her boss, Lizzy knew that there wasn't anything that she herself could—or should—do about it. It was Opie's secret. She couldn't possibly share it with Ryan. She couldn't violate her friend's privacy by trying to discuss it with her. And even Verna, who usually had the unflagging persistence of a bulldog, had dropped the subject.

Lizzy pushed the candlestick phone back to the corner of her desk. Best to let it go. However powerful a crush might be, it usually wore off if you didn't add any fuel to the fire. Opie's sensibleness would keep her from doing something really dangerous. And Ryan . . .

Lizzy's lips curved into a smile, remembering the urgency of Ryan's mouth on hers, the touch of his fingers under her blouse. She had never slept with a man, it was true, but she was no prude. She liked cuddling and petting as well as the next person. The only thing that had held her back with Grady was the realization that if she gave in to him, he would think she was agreeing to marry him, which she had not been ready to do, at least not yet.

And where Mr. Moseley was concerned, the possibility had never come up. One mistletoe-inspired kiss here in the office, a little furtive hand-holding during the picture show, and a few chaste front-porch kisses—that was the extent of their mild flirtation. And even though it might be tantalizing, a flirtation was all it could ever be. For one thing, he was her boss. For another, he was at least ten years older than she. And if that weren't enough, there was Moira Skelton.

But Ryan Nichols was an entirely different kettle of fish. She had known him since the previous October, when he had shown up on her doorstep and announced that she had been recommended for a job with the Federal Writers' Project. Since then, they had grown closer with every visit, and while she had resisted the attraction at first, her defenses had rapidly weakened. Ryan was a powerfully attractive man, not conventionally handsome but with an undeniable magnetism that was unlike any attraction she had ever known. It was spiced, perhaps, with a hint of danger, the peril of going too far, of moving into territory that was completely uncharted and unknown. What was she waiting for? She knew that he wanted her and that she . . .

Well, yes. She felt the pulse beat at her throat. This had been going on long enough. It was time to find out what it was all about. Tonight she would burn her bridges. And then they would . . .

Lizzy was jerked out of that inflammatory thought by the shriek of the fire siren on the courthouse bell tower across the street. She jammed her fingers into her ears, trying to shut it out. But that was sheer futility. She ran to the front window and lowered the sash, but still the sound shrilled through, a pulsating wave that filled the room with a searing wail. All she could do was go back to her desk, stop her ears again, and wait until the siren finally quit, a long ninety seconds later.

Another fire. This was . . . how many? She had almost lost count. Six through the weekend, when the sheriff had announced that five of the fires were being treated as arson. Then two more yesterday, making it seven. The Dahlias' clubhouse had escaped with only minor damage in the kitchen, thanks to the quick work of Bessie and Roseanne. But the Hot Dogs hadn't gotten to the Popplewell place until the fire was out of control, and the empty house and all of its ghosts had burned to the ground.

Lizzy shivered, thinking about it, and the questions began to whirl through her mind. Where was the fire *this* time? Who was the arsonist? Why was he doing this?

And what was next?

❀

IN HIS OFFICE AT THE DARLING SAVINGS AND TRUST, ALVIN Duffy ran the metal tab on his telephone list finder to "C" and the leather top flipped open to the credit reporting agencies. He looked at the alphabetical list distastefully. It bothered him to think that Verna was asking him to do this little job for her. It bothered him even more because she was basically asking him to tell her whether this Yankee she was interested in was a deadbeat or on the up and up.

But Alvin cared about Verna. As one of the two most eligible bachelors in Darling (the other one was Grady Alexander), Alvin had been the object of plenty of female attention, from Voleen Johnson (one of the co-owners of the bank) to the young widow who worked behind the counter at Lester Lima's drugstore. Mostly, the ladies seemed to want to be sure that he was well fed. If he didn't feel like cooking for himself, all he had to do was smile at one of them and she would invite him over for a home-cooked meal.

But it was Verna Tidwell who had won his heart, even though the woman didn't seem to care what she did with it. She was not only attractive in a no-nonsense way, but she was sensible and logical, with an almost uncanny ability to see through people to their intentions—a knack that came in handy in her job at the courthouse. But in this case, Alvin had to suppose that she might be so attracted to Nichols that she couldn't trust her own perceptions. So she was asking him to have a look and tell her what *he* saw.

Well, like it or not, that was what he was going to do. And he was going to be a straight shooter. If Nichols got a clean report and no bad marks against his record, that's what he would tell Verna, even if it meant losing her to the fellow. If he found something he didn't like, he'd tell her that.

He looked again at the list. Dun and Bradstreet wasn't what he wanted for this—they did commercial credit ratings for major companies. Retail Credit—a company that now had over eighty branch offices across the country—was probably his best bet. He'd start with the DC office, since that's where Verna said the guy lived.

Alice Ann Walker, his secretary, was at her desk in the outer office. Alvin picked up the phone and gave her the DC number for Retail Credit, then hung up. Long distance calls could take a while, because they often had to be routed through operators in several cities. He knew from experience that this one would click through exchanges in Montgomery, Atlanta, Charlotte, and Richmond before it finally got to DC.

As he waited, he took a can of Prince Albert out of a drawer and filled his pipe, then reached for one of the bank's new advertising matchbooks. He lit his pipe, leaned back in his chair, and reflected that most people didn't realize what a big business credit reporting had become in the last decade. They had no idea how many details of their personal lives—their employment record, their marital status, their payment histories—were now available through up-and-coming outfits like Retail Credit. Credit reporting had become important in the Roaring Twenties, when the economy was booming and people were racking up debt buying houses, Fords, bedroom sets, Victrolas, and washing machines on the increasingly popular time-payment plans. But it became even more important after the Crash wiped out millions of jobs and people couldn't pay their rent or keep up those monthly installments. Nobody wanted to extend more credit to some poor fellow who was already drowning in debt.

Of course, the reports weren't available to consumers themselves. You couldn't just walk into a Retail Credit office and ask to see your credit score. But as a banker, Alvin knew what to say when Alice Ann told him that the clerk in the DC branch office of Retail Credit was on the line. He put in his query and gave his phone number, for he was asking for the information via telephone, instead of the usual mailed report. He hung up and turned to the three August foreclosures that were waiting for his signature. The economy might be on the upswing, but some people—especially farmers—were still too hard up to make their mortgage payments. He had to decide how long he could afford to carry them.

His request took nearly an hour of lookup time in Retail Credit's voluminous records. But his phone rang at last and Alice Ann put the call through. He reached for a pencil and began jotting details, just as if Mr. Nichols were a new banking client applying for a loan. But when he heard the last set of details, he frowned.

"Hang on a minute," he said. "You're sure this is the right

Ryan Nichols? There's no possibility that his records have gotten mixed up with somebody else's? There's no mistake?"

The clerk confirmed that this was indeed the right Ryan Nichols—the *only* Ryan Nichols, as a matter of fact—and that there was no mistake. "Will there be anything else, sir?" he asked cheerfully.

"No, that's it," Alvin said. "Thanks."

He hung up the phone and sat, scowling. He wasn't sure what he had expected, but it sure as sin wasn't this. What was he going to tell Verna? How would she respond to what he had found out? And he—how did *he* feel about it?

Well, he knew the answer to that. He felt angry, that's how he felt. He was mad enough to throw the telephone across the room, which of course he didn't do. He was still staring out the window, chewing on his lower lip, when the fire siren on the courthouse bell tower began to shriek, so loudly that it nearly startled him out of his chair.

*Oh good Lord*, he thought. *Another arson*. Well, maybe they'd gotten lucky and one of the sheriff's team of lookouts had spotted the guy. He raised his voice. "Alice Ann, call the Exchange and ask Violet what's burning this time."

Two minutes later, he looked up as Alice Ann came to the door. "Well, what is it? Another grass fire, I hope."

"No, sir." Alice Ann's expression was serious. "It's not a grass fire. And Violet says this one is going to be bad."

# CHAPTER TEN

# FIRESTARTER

THE MAN TELLS HIMSELF THAT HE HAS GROWN SMARTER OVER the past several weeks. You might want to stand there and stare at the flame at your feet, watching it, greedy, lick at the grass or the pile of rotten lumber or the corner of a derelict house. You might want to follow the fire as it fuels itself, racing and growing and heaving and cresting and consuming. You might want to—

But you can't. It's not smart to hang around and watch the fire grow. Somebody might be driving along the road or watching from a window or looking on from some hidden spot and see what you're doing and hotfoot it to the nearest telephone and call the Hot Dogs to come and put your fire out. And call Buddy Norris, too, and tell him about seeing you and name you because everybody in Darling knows who you are.

No, not smart, because if the sheriff puts you in jail, you can't start any more fires. And you know that's what you have to do, one more at least, better two, after this one. You have to do it—it's all part of the plan, nine or ten altogether or maybe eleven.

What wasn't in the plan, though, is the unexpected *liking* of it, a liking that has grown stronger and more compelling with each fire. Liking the speed and the ferocity and above all the cleanness of the flame. Liking the power and the attention and the masterful feeling of being the secret agent—the *smart* secret agent—behind the things that are making Darling people anxious and fearful during the day and wakeful at night, wondering whether they will be next. The power, yes. Especially the power.

And since he has to make his escape while his fire is still little bigger than a bright idea, he has come up with a clever doodad that gives him time to get away before the fire attracts attention. A time or two before, he had used a kerosene-soaked cotton rag, wrapped around a short length of loosely-frayed rope, like a fuse, with an open book of matches. This time, instead of the rag, he is using something he swiped from his wife's bureau drawer and soaked in kerosene. He's planting two, to be on the safe side.

Yes, he's smarter now. And even a little pleased with himself, feeling that things are going according to plan. He's always known that this one would be the hard one, the one that has torched his soul ever since he had understood what he had to do. If there had been another way, he would have taken it. But this is it, the only thing he can do. Now, it's just a matter of doing it.

Take a deep breath, light the fuse, plant it. Plant another one and walk away.

Walk away. That's all there is to it.

All there is to it, ever.

# CHAPTER ELEVEN

# YOU ASSUMED WRONG, BUSTER

WHEN TEDDY FOSTER'S GRANDDADDY BUILT THE COTTON GIN out on Pine Mill Creek Road, it was one of five in Cypress County and over five hundred in the state. That was in 1860, when Alabama had a half-million acres in cotton, the same year Abraham Lincoln beat Steven O. Douglas for the presidency. The next year—the year Confederate troops fired on Fort Sumter—more cotton was shipped out of Alabama's Port of Mobile than any other city in the world except New Orleans. Then came the fiery civil conflagration that burned the Confederacy to ashes and ended the South's reign as Cotton King.

And while it may not seem fair to blame a machine and its maker for everything that happened before, during, and after the war, some people believe that the whole blazing catastrophe of it can be laid at the feet of Eli Whitney and his cotton gin.

In the Deep South of the late 1700s, cotton farmers were beginning to realize that acquiring and maintaining enslaved people cost more than the value of the cotton they could produce. It was a troublesome crop anyway. The sticky, embedded seeds could only be separated from their fiber matrix by hand, a grueling and time-consuming process. It took a full day for a single worker to pick the seeds out of a single pound of cotton.

And then came Eli Whitney and his simple little cotton

gin—"gin" is short for "engine." It had a hand-turned rotating drum with ratchet-like teeth that pulled cotton fibers between the teeth of a comb. The seeds fell down and out of one side of the gin while a second drum brushed the fiber from the first, sending it out to the other side. It was truly a labor-saver. Instead of a single slave hand-picking a single pound in a day, two or three slaves using the plantation's gin could produce fifty pounds of ginned cotton lint, it was called, in the same period of time. A larger neighborhood gin, often operated as a co-op, could produce many times that.

Over the early decades of the nineteenth century, Whitney's patented design was pirated and replicated and reengineered. But the basic principle remained the same, and the little engine made an outsized impact on the agriculture of the Deep South. American cotton was now much easier and cheaper to produce, and the mills of the North and of England and Europe wanted it, wanted *lots* of it. The increased demand fueled the need for more cleared land and many more men and women and children to plant and pick it. The gin fueled an explosion in cotton production—and an explosive increase in the number of enslaved people—that transformed this labor-intensive plant into a hugely profitable cash crop. Slave ownership—the only way this whole scheme could work—became the inflammatory issue that fired the War of Secession.

Cotton became even more important as a source of military funding during the war. When the Southern states seceded in 1861, cotton provided the revenue for the Confederacy's government, bought arms for its military, and underpinned the economic and diplomatic strategy of the Confederate nation. As the War Between the States lit up, cotton prices skyrocketed. In 1863–64, it was bringing an incredible $1.89 a pound.

The war and its aftermath brought enormous change. Enslaved Negroes gained their freedom and the plantation economy splintered into sharecropping. Then, just when things started looking up again, the boll weevil began chewing its way into Alabama, reducing cotton production to a dismal ninety pounds an acre and the price to ten cents a pound. By 1914, most farmers in Cypress County had decided that cotton wasn't worth growing, let alone picking and ginning. They gave up and planted peanuts and sweet potatoes. That same year, Teddy Foster's granddaddy gave up, too. But it was time for him— he was 101. He said he had seen the beginning and the end of cotton.

Not quite. The cotton market rallied during the Great War and the early 1920s. With the price at a decent thirty-five cents a pound, farmers went back to planting cotton. Teddy Foster's daddy—still a believer in the future of cotton—decided to replace the ramshackle old wooden barn his father had built with a new two-story frame building, new equipment, and a larger, diesel-powered gin. The gin was equipped with five gin stands, a stick machine, a burr machine, separators, cleaners, a press pump, and pneumatic conveying fans (the latest innovation)—all of it driven by a 125-horsepower Bessemer diesel engine. Now the only gin in Cypress County, the new operation could produce two 250-pound bales of cotton every half hour. It was busy all day and most of the night in picking season, with wagonloads of cotton lined up for a good half mile along Pine Mill Creek Road, mules and Model T Fords patiently waiting their turn.

Teddy Foster's daddy didn't live to enjoy the success of his promising venture. He lost his right arm in a 1928 accident at the gin and Doc Roberts couldn't save him from the gangrene that set in. He died on Thanksgiving Day, leaving Teddy Junior—just a couple of years out of his teens and still pretty wet behind the ears—to manage the gin.

Which he might have done well, in other circumstances.

The gin was a going family concern with seventy-five years of history behind it, a good market, new and updated equipment, and a reliable supply of cotton. Young Teddy had every reason to be optimistic, even to begin thinking about marriage and a flock of strong sons to carry on the family cotton tradition. It wasn't long before he was courting Darling's gorgeous and shapely Miss Cotton of 1929. She was inclined to say yes, too. It seemed perfectly fitting that Miss Cotton should marry the young man at the top of Cypress County's cotton business.

What happened next wasn't Teddy's fault, and Darling folk knew it. He was a likable young man, well-meaning and hard-working, and it was clear that he was putting his whole heart and soul into holding the family business together. The trouble wasn't his fault, no, not his fault at all. The whole world was going to hell in a handbasket and nobody could blame him for that.

It *was* hell, if you were in the cotton business. The 1929 Crash killed the nation's appetite for cotton, and the international market as well. 1930 was a terrible year, with the price bottoming out at a little more than nine cents a pound. 1931 was even worse, at five cents, and the drought in 1932 fried the crop and reduced the yield. And then, just when 1933 was beginning to look like a halfway decent year, the New Deal government began paying farmers to plow under a third of their cotton acreage and keep the fields fallow through 1934 and 1935. Pay farmers *not* to plant? Why, nobody had ever heard of such a crazy thing. The land was meant to be farmed. That's why the good Lord gave it to them—and gave them cotton, too.

What was the world coming to, people wondered.

And now . . . this.

❀

NOBODY HAD BEEN AROUND WHEN THE FIRE STARTED, PROBA-
bly in the ginning shed, but that didn't last long. Within fifteen
minutes, it seemed like the whole town of Darling was gathered
at the gin, watching the flames shoot into the midday sky.

This time, Archie Mann hadn't waited around for the new
chief to show up. When Violet called to tell him the cotton gin
was on fire, he hopped into Big Red, picked up a couple of Hot
Dogs along the way, and gunned it out to the gin as fast as he
could. He arrived at the same time as the sheriff and his deputy,
both of whom grabbed the little gasoline pumper engine off the
truck, pulled it over to the gin pond, and cranked it up so there
would be a goodly supply of water to pour on the fire. With the
sheriff had come Alabama's fire marshal, Harold Dixon, who
that morning had driven down from Montgomery in a state car
with a gold fire marshal's decal on the side. Fire Marshal Dixon
studied the fire with the confident expression of a man who
enjoyed his work and knew what he was looking for.

The Hot Dogs began to arrive, on foot, on bicycles, and by
the carload. An old flivver drove up and disgorged a slew of high
school boys, who paired up and began grabbing bales off the
stack near the back of the gin and dragging them out of reach of
the fire and water. (Wet baled cotton is as unsaleable as burned
baled cotton.) The new chief showed up at the wheel of the
old fire truck, with more Hot Dogs packed into the stakebed.
Charlie Dickens and his young hot-shot reporter arrived, and
the boy began snapping photos. Jed Snow, the mayor, and Mr.
Musgrove, who was running against him in next week's election, drove up together, having recently buried the hatchet over
a late-night poker game at Pete's Pool Parlor. Roger Kilgore,
next to arrive and heedless of his white linen summer suit and
Panama hat, ran over to the gin pond to restart the gasoline
pumper. They had to have more water.

The Darling women came too, among them most of the

Dahlias. But they had to stand back and watch because the men refused to let them help. It was much too dangerous, and anyway, they wouldn't know how to handle the equipment. Before the fire was out, though, several of the Dahlias would go home and come back again, equipped with baloney sandwiches, boxes of home-baked cookies, and jugs of ice-cold lemonade. They knew how to do *that*, Bessie Bloodworth said, with heavy irony.

And then, just when it seemed as if there was nobody left in Darling—they were all at the fire—Teddy Junior arrived, wild-eyed and frantic. He had been over in Monroeville all morning, he said, and had just heard the news. Luckily, the Hot Dogs had managed to keep the fire away from the office. Teddy risked his life by going in to get whatever he could salvage of the gin's important papers, including the ledger, a precious historical document that dated back to his granddaddy's day. He had just gotten out, loaded with boxes, when there was a loud roar and the office roof caved in, sending a fountain of flame into the sky.

"Invoices and bills and records," he said, setting the boxes down where they wouldn't get wet. He wiped the soot off his face and turned to look back over his shoulder. "At least I'll know who I owe money to."

❀

When Alvin Duffy learned that the cotton gin was on fire, he told Alice Ann to hold all his calls and dashed out of the bank, headed for the blaze.

Just two weeks before, he and Teddy had had a serious conversation about the note that was coming due on Mr. Foster's modernization of the gin. Al liked the young man and sympathized with his efforts to keep the family business going, made even more difficult in the current economic and agricultural situation. But things were tough right now, and the bank wasn't in a position to let Foster renew the note. Alvin wasn't the kind of banker who got his jollies foreclosing on people who were trying their damnedest to do what was right, and he knew that the gin was vitally important to the cotton farmers of Cypress County. Still, he had an obligation to the bank, which was also important to the farmers—to everyone in the county, for that matter. He'd been reluctant to tell Foster his decision, but he'd had no choice. The note had come due and Alvin had no idea when or where the young man was going to get the money to clear it.

He was on his way to his blue Plymouth, parked in the alley behind the bank, when he ran into Emmet Piper and told him that the gin was on fire.

Emmet looked dismayed. "The *gin*? Oh, Lord, no! One of my companies holds the fire insurance policy on that place. Can I ride with you? My car's over at Kilgore's for a tune-up." He pulled down his mouth. "I was just this morning congratulating myself on dodging the bullet on these arson cases. But now the gin. The loss could be a doozy."

"Well, that's what we buy insurance for, you know," Alvin said, thinking about the size of the note he had refused to roll over for Junior and hoping that Emmet had sold the boy enough insurance to cover the loss. Otherwise, the bank would be on the hook for yet another uncollateralized note—this time, a whale of a sum. "Come on. Maybe they'll have it out in a hurry."

But that wasn't going to happen. They could see the plume of black smoke and a pillar of flame as they crested the hill on Pine Mill Creek Road. In spite of the best efforts of Big Red, Archie Mann, the Hot Dogs, and even Rufus Radley, the fire had gotten away from them. They didn't have the kind of equipment that could pour enough water on it to do any good. They had turned their attention to keeping the fire from spreading to the surrounding trees and brush, all of it tinder-dry in the summer's drought.

Alvin parked the Plymouth upwind of the flying sparks and he and Emmet joined the crowd of silent onlookers. "This one's gonna burn for a while," he said to Emmet. He pointed toward a large, double-door shed, smoke pouring under the edge of the corrugated metal roof. "I was out here a couple of weeks ago with Junior, talking about his plans. That shed was full to the roof with baled cotton. He was storing it in hopes that the market would look better in a few months." He sniffed the air. "Smell it? Those bales were packed in tight. They'll burn for days."

"Gonna be a sizable claim," Emmet Piper muttered grimly. "The structures, equipment—it was the best that could be had when it was built, six or seven years ago. Plus all those stored bales."

Alvin was still thinking about the size of the note that had already come due. "How much is he covered for?"

"Not enough to cover the loss," Emmet pushed his hands into his pockets. "And definitely not enough to rebuild."

Al shook his head, resigned. "I don't reckon Junior will try," he said. "He took on the business because he had to when his dad died. Things were pretty good back then, but there's not much to rebuild for right now. The government won't let folks plant more than half their cotton acreage, and the price is so low they might as well give it away as pay to get it ginned and baled."

Buddy Norris came up to them, accompanied by a stranger, a mutton-chopped, portly gentleman in a city suit with a big gold badge on his lapel and a white cowboy hat, like the one Roy Rogers wore in the movies, on his mostly bald head.

Buddy introduced him as Harold Dixon, the state fire marshal. He had come down from Montgomery to help with the arson investigations.

Dixon pulled out a notebook and pencil. "Tell me again how many this makes. Six fires? Seven?"

"Eight," the sheriff said. "Five minor fires through the weekend, not counting the trash fire that got away from the reverend. Yesterday, the garden club's house on Camellia and the old Popplewell place. The gin makes eight."

Emmet scuffed the toe of his shoe in the dust. "Two."

"Two?" Marshal Dixon asked, pencil poised. "Two, eight, what is it, boys?"

"I'm counting insurance claims," Emmet said. "No claims on the fires through the weekend. We had a lucky break out at the bottling plant. The Popplewells just walked away from their old place and left it empty, no coverage. The Dahlias' clubhouse is insured, but a neighbor who happens to be a club member was able to put out the fire before it got good and started. The damages are minimal." He paused. "This place is insured. That makes two."

"Two for you," the sheriff said. "Eight for us."

Al turned to the sheriff. "Do you know who called this one in?"

"And when?" the fire marshal asked, making another note.

"Bill Oakley, the mail carrier," the sheriff replied. "This place is on his RFD route. He drove past in his old flivver and saw some smoke coming out of the shed at the back, where the bales are stored. There was nobody around, and he had to drive back to Beauregard Richard's place before he could find a telephone. That old Model T of his is missing high gear, which slows him down some. The gin was a goner well before the Hot Dogs made it out here."

That was the problem with rural fires, Alvin thought. The

whole place could burn and nobody'd know it until the occupants came home to what was left. Aloud, he asked, "Anybody seen Junior?" To the fire marshal, he said, "That would be Ted Foster, Junior. The owner."

"Over there, talking to Wayne," the sheriff said, jerking a thumb over his shoulder. "He's taking it pretty philosophically. If it was me and this was my granddaddy's and daddy's gin, I'd be looking for somebody to shoot. Or arrest."

"That's why you got elected sheriff." Emmet said. "So you could do the shooting." He chuckled. Everybody in Darling knew that Buddy Norris didn't care for guns. If there was any shooting to be done, he'd leave it to his deputy.

"Any clues to our firebug yet?" Al asked the fire marshal.

"Hey, I just got here," Dillon protested. He pocketed his notebook. "We've got eight fires to investigate, including this big one. And arson is one of the hardest crimes to pin down." He turned to the sheriff. "You're thinking it's the same guy that set the others?"

The sheriff nodded. "Wayne looked around and found this, along with a matchbook." He held up a small white cardboard tube, several inches long and a half-inch in diameter. It was stuffed with cotton and heavily charred on one end. You guys got any idea what it is—before it was used as a fuse?"

"Huh," Emmet said. "I know."

"Oh, yeah?" Buddy said. "Well, tell us."

Emmet was blushing furiously. "It's a . . . a thing my wife uses. Something . . . well, modern. You know."

"No, we *don't* know, Emmet," Alvin said, trying to be patient. "Come on, what is it?"

"It's called a . . . a tampon." The red was spreading down Emmet's neck. "Women use it."

"Women?" The sheriff peered at it. "Oh, yeah? Use it for what?"

"For their . . . you know." Emmet's voice was strangled. "Their monthlies. The Curse."

"I thought they wore . . ." the sheriff said, and stopped. He tried again. "So how do they . . ." His voice trailed off.

There was a long silence. The men looked at one another, then down to the ground. Finally, the sheriff cleared his throat. "Does this . . . does this maybe mean that our arsonist is a woman?" He wrapped the cardboard tube in his handkerchief and put it into his shirt pocket.

"We arrested a woman over in Birmingham last week," the fire marshal remarked helpfully. "She set fire to her boyfriend's house. He'd jilted her and she took it amiss. And there was this colored gal down in Mobile who set her beauty parlor on fire for the insurance. Seems like the ladies are getting a little more ambitious. Feelin' their oats, you might say."

"The Dahlias' garden clubhouse was insured," Emmet volunteered. "The claim won't be more than fifty dollars, but it sure could've been more." He cast a troubled look toward the fire. "Nothing like this, of course."

The fire marshal was looking thoughtful. "It's been a bad couple of years for cotton gin fires. This is the fourth one in the state in the last fourteen months. Of course, cotton *is* highly combustible. And folks don't always take the right precautions. The last one was caused by a lit cigarette butt dropped into a cotton wagon parked under the unloading chute. Whole place went up like a torch."

"It's hard for me to think that one of our Darling ladies might have . . ." Emmet's voice trailed away. He was looking at a group of several women standing together.

Al's glance followed Emmet's. The little group included Bessie Bloodworth, Liz Lacy, Ophelia Snow, and Verna, trim and pretty in a light-colored summer dress with a narrow white collar. Her dark hair, bobbed and sleek, gave her a stylish but no-nonsense look.

Alvin turned to Emmet. "Can you get another ride to town?" When Emmet nodded, he excused himself from the group and headed for the women. After hellos, he said, "Verna, do you have a minute to talk?" He tried to ask casually, but he knew his voice betrayed something else.

"Liz is just ready to head back to the office," she said. "I'm riding with her. We took an early lunch hour to have a look at the fire, but both of us have work to do."

"I'm on my way to the bank. How about riding with me?" He leaned closer and lowered his voice. "That job you gave me to do. It's done."

A look he couldn't read crossed her face. She hesitated, then nodded. "Sure. I'll be a minute. Just let me tell Liz."

A few moments later, they were getting into his car. "You found something," she said, the minute the doors were closed. "I can tell by the look on your face." She sounded uneasy, he thought.

"When we get to a place to stop," he said, turning on the ignition. "It's . . . complicated."

She sighed, but didn't object. He drove a mile or so, past the Darling elementary school, where Mrs. Myers was overseeing her noisy gang of first and second graders at recess. School had just opened for the year, and the children wore that starched "first-day" look.

He pulled off the road, switched off the ignition, and turned toward Verna. As a banker, he had never been very good at blunting bad news. Don't beat around the bush—straight from the shoulder was always his motto. No mincing words. If you've got something to say, say it and expect the other person to be adult enough to deal with it. But this was different. He knew it was going to hurt.

She was searching his face with her eyes, clearly eager for what he'd learned. But when she spoke, she sounded more detached than he had expected. "You've found something, I suppose."

*Something.* Yes, he had found something. Something that was going to smash all her pretty little romantic fantasies about Ryan Nichols. But she had asked him to do it, hadn't she? He hadn't wanted to. He had almost said no. He'd rather she do her own dirty work, if she thought it had to be done. But he had agreed because it was Verna who was asking. And because he figured that if Nichols was up to something ugly, they ought to find out what it was.

"I did what I said I'd do, Verna. I ran a credit report, same as I would for a loan applicant at the bank. I got it through the DC office." He made his voice hard, flat. "But it turns out that Nichols doesn't live in DC. He lives in Philadelphia." He paused. Her eyes hadn't left his face. "With his wife. And two children."

"His . . . wife?" She closed her eyes and swallowed, audibly.

Al was suddenly struck with pity. He knew how it felt to be played for a sucker. It had happened to him back in New Orleans. It was the old familiar story: his new wife—they'd been married less than a year—and his best friend, the ultimate betrayal. He remembered how bereft he had felt when Claudia ran off to Reno for that divorce, how forlorn, how *betrayed.* And yet he'd never been able to blame her, somehow. His friend had been a charming con man who knew exactly how to get what he wanted. Claudia had been his victim.

The same with Verna, he thought. It wasn't her fault that she had fallen in love with a phony. She wasn't to blame. It was all Nichols' fault, no question about it. A man like that was every bit as bad as the arsonist who was running loose around Darling. He could set fire to a lot of lives.

He softened his voice. "Her name is Eloise. The children are eight and ten. Both boys."

"Oh, *hell*," Verna whispered. She clenched her hands into fists. "Oh, Al, that's *awful*. How could he? How could he *lie* about something so important?"

"Yes, it is," he said. "It's awful. I don't know how a man—somebody who wants to keep the respect of other people—could behave this way." He took a breath and put a hand on her shoulder, feeling her warmth beneath the thin fabric of her dress. "I'm sorry," he said. "I'm sorry to be the bearer of such bad news. I'm sorry he's hurt you." He knew he was repeating himself, but he did it again. "*Very* sorry."

"Hurt . . . *me*?" She frowned. "But I'm not—" Her dark eyes were large and luminous, questioning. And oddly, half amused. "You mean, you thought I was asking for myself? That I needed to know because I cared—for *him*? Romantically, I mean."

He stared at her. "You don't?"

"No, of course I don't, silly. Whatever gave you that idea?"

"But you said—" He broke off, remembering. "You wouldn't tell me who, so I assumed—"

"You assumed wrong, buster." Her smile flickered and she put a cool finger to his cheek. "How could I feel that way about Ryan Nichols after Clyde has finally decided to tolerate *you*?" She dropped her hand. "I'll say it again, since you apparently didn't hear me the first time. The job I asked you to do . . . it wasn't for me."

"Then who?" He was bemused—and more relieved and pleased and, yes, grateful than he wanted to admit. "Not Liz Lacy, you said. *Who*?"

"None of your beeswax." She looked down at her watch. "Now, let's get back to town, shall we? I've got an errand to do before it gets any later." She paused, her eyes intent, warm. "But first—" She leaned forward and kissed him on the cheek, then turned his face toward her and kissed him full on the lips, lingering. When she pulled back, she was smiling.

"That's a thank you," she said. "But not for me. You idiot."

# CHAPTER TWELVE

## ASHES

VERNA ASKED ALVIN TO LET HER OUT IN FRONT OF THE COURT-house, where she climbed the stairs to her office. But she didn't go back to work. Instead, she sat down at her desk and made a telephone call—a long-distance call that took the best part of a half hour. Then she told her staff she had an errand to run. She'd be back later.

She walked briskly down Rosemont to the Snows' yellow frame cottage, once again admiring its unusual but very attractive purple shutters and bright green roof—a daring combination for Darling and the cause of some talk. She knocked on the front door and, when Ophelia answered, said simply, "Opie, we need to talk."

Fifteen minutes later, she and Opie were sitting together on Opie's rose-colored davenport. Opie hadn't cried, but when Verna told her, she had turned quite pale. She had closed her eyes and clasped her arms around her middle for the longest time, as if she were holding herself together against a splinter-ing pain. But when at last she spoke, in a thin, strained voice, it wasn't about herself, or how she felt, or how much she had been hurt by this unexpected news.

"Oh, his poor wife," she said. "Eloise. I feel so sorry for her. And those boys. How can any man be so *cruel* to his family?"

Verna's first instinct was to say that every man, in her experience, was cruel by his very nature. But the thought of Alvin's gentle concern when he told her about his discovery made her think twice. Maybe it wasn't *every* man.

So she just said, "Well, I don't suppose he's told his wife that he's going around pretending to be a bachelor. She's probably still in the dark."

But Ophelia didn't appear to hear her. "And I feel so ashamed of myself! Lately, I've been having this silly little fantasy about him. My life has seemed awfully dull these past months, I'm afraid. And Ryan—Mr. Nichols . . . well, I'm sorry to say that he brought some spice into it. I began to think . . ." She rolled her eyes. "Oh, I don't know *what* I thought. Some sort of idiocy, I suppose."

Verna murmured something comforting and Ophelia managed a little smile. "I'm glad to say that I kept it a secret from everybody—from you, even." She paused, frowning a little. "Although I'm afraid that maybe Bessie guessed. But nobody else."

Verna only nodded. If it made Opie feel better to think that she had successfully kept her feelings secret, she wasn't going to disillusion her.

"Anyway," Opie went on, "just this morning, when I was getting my hair done at the Bower, I realized how very foolish I was, and how dangerous it might be, especially when it comes to gossipy people like Leona Ruth Adcock. They have a way of making something out of nothing, you know."

"Dangerous?" Verna asked.

"Well, yes." Ophelia nodded earnestly. "Jed would be very hurt if he heard that I . . . that I had given people reason to talk about me and Mr. Nichols. That's why I asked Bessie to come over for our meeting—sort of like a witness. I didn't want to give Leona Ruth and her cronies anything to chatter about."

She smiled a little. "I was trying to fight fire with fire, you might say. Does that fit?"

Verna countered with "Somebody once said 'If you fight fire with fire, you end up with ashes.'"

But Opie's expression had changed. She was thinking of something else.

"What you've found out—it's really serious," she said.

"Yes, of course it is," Verna replied sensibly. "He's your boss. It's going to be difficult for you to work with him, knowing that he has misrepresented himself. But I'm sure you can handle it, now that you know what you're dealing with."

Opie squared her shoulders. "I think it's best not to let him know that I know." She hesitated. "But have you talked this over with Liz? I'm afraid she's going to find it much harder to manage."

"Liz?" Verna frowned. "I know she considered working for him. And that they sometimes go out for dinner when he's in Darling. But she's a big girl, and always so confident, so much in charge. Just look at the way she handled that wretched situation with Grady Alexander."

"Don't be such a goose, Verna." Ophelia rolled her eyes. "Liz only *looks* like she's in charge. Underneath all that confidence, she's every bit as fragile as the rest of us. And she's been seeing Mr. Nichols whenever he's in town, so you need to break it to her gently. She might have more at stake than you think."

"More at stake?" Verna repeated. "How do you know this—and I don't?"

But even as she asked the question, Verna knew the answer. People often said admiring things about the way she got things done, or about her investigative skills—her ability to dig out secret information and figure out what was going on. For her, figuring out what somebody thought was almost an academic exercise, an opportunity to use her brain.

Ophelia, on the other hand, was empathic and deeply in tune with the way other people were feeling. And perhaps it was easy for her to be aware of how Liz felt about Ryan Nichols. After all, she had just confessed to sharing those feelings herself.

"Well, then," Verna said briskly. "I suppose I'd better try to talk to Liz as soon as possible. Do you mind if I use your phone? I'll call and see if she's available."

❀

LIZZY HAD LEFT WORK EARLY THAT AFTERNOON AND GONE home to get things ready for dinner with Ryan. Yesterday, she had traded her neighbor, Mrs. Vader, a signed copy of *Inherit the Flames* for a nice fat hen that had retired from her egg-laying career. (It was Mrs. Vader's rooster who woke her—and the rest of the neighborhood—at dawn every morning, rain or shine.) Last night, she had stewed the chicken so she could bone it for chicken salad today. She had also made a tomato-basil soup the with ruby-red juicy-ripe Scarlet Dawn tomatoes she was trying out in her small backyard garden, and basil from the pot beside the back door. This afternoon, the soup was in the refrigerator. They would have it cold, with dollops of sour cream and basil.

When she got home from work, she had changed into yellow tennis shorts, a blue cotton blouse, and sandals. Looking forward to the evening with goose-bumpy anticipation, she had laid out her prettiest dress—a silky blue rayon print with little flared sleeves that Ryan had admired—and her laciest underthings. She sat down in front of her dressing table mirror and put up her hair in the new metal rollers with alligator clips she'd bought at Lima's Drugs, dipping her comb into the special setting lotion Beulah used at the Bower.

When her hair was rolled up, she went down to the kitchen. She boned and shredded the cold chicken, with a few tasty bites for her orange tabby cat, Daffodil, who sat watching on one of the kitchen chairs. She was dicing a rib of crunchy fresh celery when she heard someone tapping on the screen door. She looked up to see Verna Tidwell.

"Oh, hi, Verna," she said. "Come in." She patted her curlers. "As long as you don't mind my pin-up." She reached over to turn off the radio. She had been listening to "Ma Perkins," a popular soap opera featuring a sixty-something woman who owned a small-town lumberyard but was never too busy with her business to drop what she was doing and listen to a friend's troubles. Ma lived by the Golden Rule but didn't hesitate to go to war if the forces of evil threatened her family or her friends—as they did frequently. This week, Ma's daughter was having more trouble with her rascal of a boyfriend and Ma was giving advice.

"Curlers, no problem," Verna said, stepping inside and closing the screen door behind her. She glanced at the bowl of chicken on the kitchen table and the two places Lizzy had already set in the tiny dining alcove off the small kitchen. She had used her best china and silver on a white damask cloth, with folded white napkins, wine glasses, and a crystal bowl of yellow roses.

"I'm afraid I'm interrupting," Verna said. "Looks like you're getting ready for a party." She nodded at the table. "For two."

"Just making chicken salad," Lizzy said happily, stirring the celery and some diced green onions into the bowl of shredded chicken. She had been thinking—warmly, and with a very real excitement—about what might happen that night, when she finally stopped holding herself back. "Ryan Nichols will be here to meet with Ophelia this week, and he's coming to supper. Chicken salad on fresh croissants from the bakery, cold tomato soup with dill, and a cheese and fruit plate." She nodded at a basket of fruit on the counter. "Cantaloupe from Bessie's garden, raspberries from Aunt Hetty's patch, and figs from my mother's tree."

Her mother lived just across the street—an arrangement that had its pros and cons. Although she was recently married to the owner of Dunlap's Five and Dime, the new Mrs. Dunlap remained passionately interested in every detail of her daughter's life. Lizzy reminded herself that she would have to let her mother know that she was having company tonight. It wouldn't be a good time to pop over for a visit.

Which of course was no guarantee that she wouldn't. Barging in unannounced had been one of her mother's favorite tricks ever since Lizzy could remember. Mrs. Dunlap was also in the habit of sitting beside her parlor window, waiting for Lizzy to come home from the movies or an evening in Monroeville. And once, when Ryan was kissing Lizzy goodnight on her front porch, she had even come out and flapped her handkerchief at them—to Ryan's puzzlement and Lizzy's amused annoyance.

"Looks pretty darned special to me," Verna said, eyeing the dining table. "Anytime you feel like it, you can come over to my house and cook." She paused. "I wonder, Liz—do you have a minute to talk?"

Lizzy had just picked up a hard-boiled brown egg, intending to peel and dice it into the chicken salad. But hearing the tone of her friend's voice, she stopped. "You sound serious, Verna. Is something the matter?"

"I'm afraid so." Verna was rueful. "How about taking a break for a few minutes? There's something I need to talk to you about."

"Well, okay." With a prickle of apprehension, Lizzy put the egg down and opened the fridge. Something was obviously going on, or Verna wouldn't have left her office early. But she kept her voice light when she said, "Ryan is bringing wine for dinner, but I've made both lemonade and iced tea. Which would you like?"

"Lemonade, thank you."

Lizzy took out the frosty pitcher, wishing that she could keep on working while they talked. But Verna had always stood by *her* when things got difficult. In that awful business with Grady, for instance. Perhaps Verna and Mr. Duffy were having a disagreement of some sort. Lizzy had seen the somber look on his face when he pulled Verna aside at the cotton gin fire earlier that day, and Verna had ridden back to town with him. If it was a romantic crisis . . . well, Verna would need her undivided attention.

"We'll go in the parlor where it's cooler," she said, pouring a glass of lemonade and handing it to Verna. "Must be ninety-five or more outside."

"Ninety-eight," Verna said, "according to the thermometer in the hardware store window. Have you heard any word on that hurricane?"

"They're saying on the radio that it's just awful down in Florida—on the Keys, I mean. Everything is flattened—buildings, trees, just everything. There are hundreds of people dead, including a big crew of veterans who were working on the new highway down to Key West." Lizzy poured lemonade for herself and returned the pitcher to the refrigerator. "Yesterday—Labor Day—somebody sent a train to rescue them, but it was too late. The hurricane blew the locomotive and most of the cars right off the track."

Verna pressed her lips together. "Sounds terrible. That storm isn't coming our way, I hope."

"No, thank goodness. It's headed across northern Florida and into the Atlantic, so we're in the clear. A good thing, too," Lizzy added. "People won't have to stand in the rain to hear Huey Long tomorrow."

"He's a hurricane of another sort," Verna said wryly. "Charlie Dickens told me that Roosevelt called him the 'most dangerous man in America.' And Alvin says that Long is like an out-of-control railroad train. The president would be glad to derail him—any way he could."

"I don't doubt that," Lizzy said, leading the way to the parlor with Daffy trailing behind. "Long can certainly stir people up."

Her small cottage wasn't much bigger than a dollhouse, so the postage-stamp parlor was just a few short steps away from the equally tiny kitchen. In the front hall, a flight of polished wooden stairs led up to two small bedrooms, one where Liz slept, the other perfect for her writing studio. Across the front of the house was a porch just wide enough for a white-painted porch swing, a white wicker rocker, and several pots of red geraniums. Behind the kitchen was a screened-in back porch where Liz sometimes ate her suppers. The backyard itself was ten times bigger than the house, with a willow tree and sunflowers against the back fence and pink roses on the trellis, as well as a little kitchen garden beside the back door. As far as Lizzy was concerned, her dollhouse was perfect. And it was even more perfect because it was all *hers*.

The windows on either side of the brick fireplace let in a breeze that puffed the sheer curtains and stirred the air, making it seem a little cooler. The floor was polished oak, the walls painted an antique ivory. Lizzy had chosen small-size furniture that wouldn't dominate the room: a brown Mission-style sofa with throw pillows she had covered with crocheted doilies; a stuffed armchair clad in a summer-white slipcover; a Tiffany-style stained-glass lamp, and a coffee table she had made from a salvaged oak plank.

Verna took the sofa and Lizzy sat down in the chair. Deciding not to beat around the bush, she said, "Mr. Duffy seemed a bit urgent this morning. Is everything all right? With the two of you, I mean."

"With Alvin and me?" Verna looked surprised. "Yes, of course. At least, I think so." She paused, shifting uncomfortably. "But he's learned something you need to know, Liz."

"Learned something?" Lizzy asked in surprise. "Learned what?"

Verna took a deep breath. "Learned that Mr. Nichols—" She swallowed. "That Mr. Nichols is not quite the person he has led people to believe. I had thought that the two of you were just . . . well, casual friends. But maybe I'm wrong. Maybe you're something more. So you should know."

"Know *what*?" Lizzy frowned, now even more puzzled. "Both Ophelia and I have had several letters from the Federal Writers' Project, and she's begun getting her paychecks. There's no doubt that he—"

Verna lifted her hand. "That isn't what I mean, Liz. He *does* work for the Writers' Project. That part is entirely legitimate. But he doesn't live in DC."

"He doesn't? But he said—"

"He doesn't live in DC. And he's . . ." Verna bit her lip. "Oh, *hell*, Liz. There's no easy way to say this. The man is married."

*Married?* Uncomprehending, Lizzy stared at Verna, her heart pounding like a hammer against the cage of her ribs. The word tasted like cold ashes in her mouth.

"Liz?" Anxious, Verna leaned forward and put out her hand. "Liz, dear, are you all right?"

Her friend's question was faint and tinny, as if it came from far away—just one of the blizzard of questions blowing through Lizzy's mind. Ryan was still married? He wasn't divorced, as he had told her? Ryan had a *wife*? She struggled to get her breath, to form words that made some sort of sense, but her lips were cold and stiff.

"What—" she began, intending to say *What in the world are you talking about, Verna? Who is making up such ridiculous nonsense? He's divorced! He told me. He's divorced.*

But the words were frozen in the polar blizzard of her thoughts, and she had to try again: "Where did you hear—" she said, and faltered. Shivering, she finally settled for a choked "How do you know?"

"I had a sneaking suspicion," Verna confessed. "I wasn't thinking of you, actually. I was thinking of Ophelia. I was worried that she might be getting in over her head, so I—" She took a breath. "So I asked Alvin if he could do some checking, the way he does for loan applicants at the bank. He wasn't very eager to do it—moral scruples, I guess, or maybe he thought I wanted to know, for myself." She colored a little. "Anyway, he got the information from the credit check firm he uses. Mr. Nichols' wife is named Eloise. They have two sons, eight and ten. They live in Philadelphia."

*Eloise. Two sons. Philadelphia.* Lizzy clenched her hands in her lap, her nails digging into her palms. The pain was enough to make her cry, but she couldn't. The tears were frozen in an icy block around her heart. If anybody but Verna were sitting here telling her this, she would refuse to believe it. Even so . . .

"You're sure it's true?" she managed at last. "There's no mistake?"

"There's no mistake, Liz," Verna said matter-of-factly. "I thought I ought to double-check Alvin's information. So when I got back to the office after the fire, I telephoned the records clerk at the Philadelphia County courthouse in Pennsylvania. Ryan Nichols and Eloise Benning applied for a marriage license there in 1924. And in the most recent city directory, they're both listed at the same address." Her mouth softened. She looked as if she were going to cry. Her voice broke when she said, "Those are *facts*, Liz. We can't question them. I'm so sorry."

But Lizzy wasn't thinking of questioning the facts. She was thinking that she had been sitting in this same room, in this very same chair the evening—not all that long ago—when Grady had told her he was marrying Sandra Mann. Because he had to. Because Sandra was going to have a baby, and he was the father. Or so Sandra said, and Grady believed it, so Lizzy had to believe it, too. She hadn't been ready to marry Grady when he'd begun asking her, but she had *expected* to, someday. She had counted on it the way people count on having another birthday, had imagined herself as a wife and a mother to the children she and Grady would have together. What he told her that night had turned her world upside down.

Now, tonight, she had been ready—eager, even—to give Ryan what she hadn't given to Grady, what he had gotten instead from Sandra. And Verna's announcement, like Grady's, had changed everything. But not just for her. This information changed a great many things, and she wasn't the only one who needed to know.

"Ophelia." She took a deep breath, steadying herself against the pain. Of course, being married had nothing to do with Ryan's job for the Federal Writers' Project. But since he had lied about this, he might be lying about other things, as well. They couldn't trust him. "Have you told Ophelia?"

"Yes. She was surprised, of course. Shocked, too. She was the one who insisted that I should talk to you, Liz. She wants you to know that she doesn't intend to tell him what we've found out. She doesn't know what to make of it, either, and she can't begin to guess why he didn't tell everybody about his family from the very beginning, instead of pretending he didn't have one. But she's going to act like she doesn't know a thing about this—at least for now."

Lizzy flinched. "Do you . . . do you think *I* should? Should tell him, I mean. If I do, he'll want to know how we found out. How *you* found out. What do you think I should do, Verna?"

Her first thought: How could she confront Ryan with such a thing? In the little time they'd had together, they had become close, had shared all but the ultimate intimacy. He would be terribly hurt that someone, anyone, would believe in him so little or mistrust him so much that they would dig around in his personal affairs. Would invade his privacy. Would *spy* on him, was what it amounted to. He would think it the worst kind of personal affront—and he would be right.

But there was an almost immediate second thought. Ryan had lied to her. That was a fact. Yes, of course he would be offended. He would be hurt. He might even try to provide an explanation, might try to get her to see the situation from his point of view. But he had led her to believe that he was free to create a relationship when he wasn't. He had been the one to reach out to her, not the other way around. And his deception had invited her to do something she would surely regret when she found out the truth, and for a very long time afterward.

And there was more, wasn't there? He hadn't just lied to her, he had lied to others here in Darling—and where else? As a regional director for the Federal Writers' Project, he visited many towns, met and worked with many people. How many other women had been as foolish and easy-hearted as she? How many other . . . liaisons did he have?

And what about his wife? What about Eloise? What did she know about her husband's behavior? She was the mother of his children—she must love him, trust him, have faith in his fidelity. Whether she knew it or not, she was the one who was most fully betrayed. Lizzy could only hope that she didn't know.

And *herself?* Lizzy winced. Yes, of course she was hurt. But at the same time, she was very, very grateful to Verna and Mr. Duffy for doing their detective work. And Ryan wasn't the only one to blame. She had met him not long after the disastrous end of her relationship with Grady. She had been ready for something more, someone different, someone from a world beyond Darling. She had been far *too* ready, she thought now. She had been eager to make room for someone in her life, to trust him, to believe whatever he told her. Ryan was wrong, yes, but she was, too. She had let her guard down. She had allowed herself to be taken in. She was complicit in his deception.

So what should she do? Verna hadn't answered her question. The silence stretched out like a long, long thought. Lizzy said again, "What do you think I should do, Verna? Should I tell him what we know?"

Verna gave her a tender look. "You should do whatever your heart tells you to do, Liz. Whatever that is, I'm sure it will be right."

Shivering, Lizzy pressed her lips together. *Her heart?* That was so unlike Verna, who had a crackerjack mind and the practical ability to make things happen. Verna always said that she worked from her head, not her heart.

But in this case, Lizzy knew, heart and head had to come together.

Ashes.

# CHAPTER THIRTEEN

# FIRE AT WILL

CHARLIE DICKENS HAD BEEN SURPRISED BY THE LABOR DAY telephone call he had received from Virgil McCone. The two of them frequently exchanged letters, but he hadn't seen his former Stars and Stripes colleague since a few months before the Crash, when their paths had crossed in Albany, New York. An old hand on the political beat, Charlie had been working as a stringer for the *Baltimore Sun*, covering FDR's early months as governor. That was Virgil's first year with the Associated Press, and his editor had assigned him to the same beat. Charlie and Virgil had spent a lot of time comparing notes and talking to the natives at Harry's Bar and Grill on Albany's State Street, a couple of blocks from the capitol building.

All of that felt like ancient history, though. Charlie had had to drop what he was doing and go back to Darling to deal with his father's final bout with cancer. And then he'd gotten stuck with the *Dispatch* when the old man died and the Crash became the Depression, a dismal swamp that swallowed all other options. He had hated the faltering *Dispatch* and wished to hell he could unload it and get back to his former life as an itinerant journalist. It had been a thoroughly miserable time, brightened only by the weekends he spent blessedly pickled with Bodeen Pyle's white lightning.

But things had changed for the better when Charlie married Fannie. His attitude had done a complete one-eighty. She brought joy into his days and companionship and more into his nights—to the point where he didn't need to drown himself in Bodeen's finest. Darling was now full of friends (well, mostly), and the *Dispatch* had become a mountain to climb instead of a swamp to wallow in.

His old buddy McCone seemed to be changing, too. In his recent letters, Virgil had hinted that he was thoroughly sick of life on the road—especially the job of trailing Huey P. Long's political circus around the country. In fact, he was only waiting for the right moment to quit his AP job and find a place to settle down and start a new life. If Charlie had any bright ideas, he'd be glad to hear them.

So when Virgil showed up in Darling late Tuesday afternoon, almost twenty-four hours in advance of Huey Long's traveling road show, Charlie was especially glad to see him. When they were both with the *Stars and Stripes* during the war, Virgil had been an energetic, skinny-as-a-rail go-getter with a full head of dark hair and a burning desire to pin down every last detail of a story, the more sensational the better. He had gained thirty pounds, lost 30 percent of his hair, and developed a deep-seated skepticism about the political process, his attitude substantially soured by the years he'd spent following the political misadventures of Senator Long.

Virgil arrived at the newspaper office about four that afternoon, dressed in a wrinkled summer suit, a polka dot bow tie, and tricolor Derby wingtips, with a straw boater jammed on his head. Charlie introduced him to Wilber, Osgood, and Baby and showed him around the press room, giving him a blow-by-blow description of the *Dispatch* operation, both newspaper and job printing. He even described his plan for moving away from ready-print, expanding to twice-a-week publication, and doubling advertising and circulation—a plan that would now have to wait for better times, damn it. Al Duffy had phoned him that morning to tell him that the loan committee had decided to take a six-month rain check on his proposal.

Virgil listened attentively. "My uncle published a newspaper in a small town in Wisconsin when I was a kid," he said, with a reminiscent half smile. "Growing up, I dreamed of working there. Maybe I'm an idealist, but it seems to me that you'd get to do real reporting on stories that matter to real people. Plus, you'd also be involved with the production and business end—advertising, sales, subscriptions and delivery, stuff like that. In the back of my mind, I kept that idea tucked away, something I'd do when I finished seeing the world. But Uncle Steve died five or six years ago and my aunt sold the paper. It's part of Frank Gannett's newspaper chain now. But I still dream about it."

Charlie might have said that whole weeks could go by in Darling without a story that was worth reporting, and that there were too many days when the production and business end of things would eat you alive. But he held his tongue. No point in undercutting his friend's fond memories.

When Virgil saw the old Babcock press, glowering like an evil genie in the back corner, he whistled admiringly between his teeth. "Boy-howdy, Charlie," he said. "I haven't seen one of these Babcocks in years. It's just like my uncle's old press. He let me work on it every summer, growing up. Made me feel like a real newspaper guy."

"Happy to sell you this one if you've got a place to put it," Charlie replied in a practical tone. "I'm planning to replace it with a Country Campbell press—if I can pull off the expansion." He gave a realistic shrug. "That's a big *if*. The bank may not be willing to give me a loan, ever—and I'm not exactly crazy about going that route, either. In the newspaper business, there's always a risk, as I'm sure you know."

"Boy, do I," Virgil muttered, rubbing the bald patch on his head. But they went on to talk about the job printing business and the future of small-town newspapers in a radio age. And then, since Fannie was spending a few days with her son at Warm Springs, Charlie closed the *Dispatch* office and took Virgil next door to the diner.

The usual evening bunch hadn't shown up yet, and Raylene was behind the counter, putting a pair of freshly baked pies— lemon meringue and sweet potato pudding pie—on the pie shelf. She was tall and slim, with heavy dark brows, a full mouth and firm chin, and auburn hair lightly and attractively streaked with gray, snugged into a bun at the back of her neck. She was wearing a blue and white checked uniform with a white collar and white apron, and Charlie thought once again that if he hadn't already handed over his heart to Fannie, he might have tried to strike up a close friendship with Raylene. That could be a little tricky, though. She was said to be clairvoyant, which might or might not hamper the way things developed.

Charlie said hello to Raylene and introduced Virgil. "This is my friend Virgil McCone. He's a reporter, here to cover the Long speech tomorrow afternoon." He grinned at Raylene. "We want Virgil to give our fair town a little plug in his story, so be sure to treat him right."

"We'll make every effort," Raylene said, in her low, husky voice. She gave Virgil a considering look. "Is this your first visit to Darling, Mr. McCone?"

"Yes, ma'am," Virgil said, snatching off his boater. "It sure is a pretty little place."

Raylene arched her brows. "It's pretty when it's not on fire."

"A series of arson fires," Charlie explained to Virgil. "They've been going on for a couple of weeks now. They're generally small enough that our volunteer fire department can handle them. But yesterday's was damned serious. The cotton gin burned."

"Uh-oh," Virgil said. "Bad news for the owner—and for the farmers, I suppose."

"It *is* bad," Charlie said. "Picking season will be starting before long. The growers will have to drive their cotton all the way over to Monroeville." Ruefully, he added, "The fires have been good news for the *Dispatch*, though. Circulation is up. People want to read about what's going on."

"Name of our game," Virgil said. "People aren't much interested in good news. It's bad news that sells papers. Murders, kidnappings, graft, corruption—fires will do if there's nothing else."

Raylene looked at Charlie. "Any developments on the investigation? Everybody's hoping that the reward will help. If somebody knows something, seems like fifty dollars ought to tempt them to spill it."

"Nothing on either front that I've heard," Charlie said. He paused. "What're you and the girls dishing up for supper tonight, Raylene?" To Virgil, he added, "Myra May—Raylene's daughter—owns the diner, with her friend Violet. But the two of them couldn't get along without Raylene in the kitchen. She makes the best meatloaf you'll ever hope to eat, hands down."

With a smile, Raylene nodded at the blackboard on the wall behind the counter. "Menu's on the chalkboard. You boys sit wherever you like and give me a holler when you're ready to order." She put a dry emphasis on "you boys," and Charlie belatedly remembered that Fannie had cautioned him against calling women "girls."

As they sat down, Virgil took off his suitcoat and draped it on the back of his chair. The menu board promised a choice of fried catfish, fried chicken, and meatloaf, with the usual sides: mashed potatoes and gravy, sweet corn, lima beans, okra, collard greens, and coleslaw. After some discussion, Virgil settled on Raylene's meatloaf and Charlie went for the fried chicken.

Raylene brought them a plate of hush puppies, a china tub of butter, and glasses of sweet tea with plenty of ice. While they waited for their supper, they caught up on the latest chapters in each other's lives. Charlie filled Virgil in on his recent marriage to Fannie, along with a quick outline of her millinery business, and Virgil filled Charlie in on his divorce from his second wife, Winona.

"Nobody's fault," he said matter-of-factly. "It's just not fair to saddle a woman with a reporter husband. Especially a reporter who's on the road four or five days a week, three weeks out of the month." He made a face. "To tell the truth, what I miss most about Winona is her cooking. But wives don't like it when you're not home for supper."

"Can't blame 'em," Charlie said, thinking that he wouldn't want a job that took him away from Fannie. And then Raylene brought their plates, heaped and deliciously fragrant.

Virgil leaned over his plate and took a deep breath. "Thank you, ma'am," he said with a smile. "This sure smells wonderful." And for a little while, paying respectful attention to the food, they didn't talk at all.

When they were finished, Raylene arrived to clear their empty plates, pour the coffee, and take their orders for pie (Charlie got Euphoria's sweet potato pudding pie, and Virgil ordered Raylene's lemon meringue). And when the pie arrived, they got down to serious talk about what Virgil had been seeing as he covered Huey Long over the past three or four years, splitting his time between Louisiana and Washington.

"So Long is actually running for president, is he?" Charlie asked, savoring the nutmeg-flavored richness of sweet potato pie lathered with whipped cream.

"He hasn't announced yet. Word on the street says that'll

happen as soon as the Louisiana state senate agrees to give him the legislation he wants. He may be a senator but he still runs the Louisiana statehouse." Virgil dug into his pie. "Truth is, everybody knows he's angling to be a spoiler in the '36 race. But nobody wants to guess how far he intends to go with it. The bookies aren't taking bets, either. Not yet, anyway." He rolled his eyes and forked another bite of lemon meringue. "Mercy, Charlie. That lady bakes a mean pie." He paused. "Nice to look at, too. I didn't see any wedding ring. She married?"

"Not to anybody around here," Charlie said. He went back to their subject. "You've been writing about Huey for a long time, Virg. You must have an idea of what's going on in that head of his." He gestured with his fork. "Is he really as corrupt as you make him look?"

"More," Virgil said. "My editors won't let me tell the half of it." He gave Charlie a twisted grin. "Maybe that'll come in the book."

"Oh-*ho*," Charlie said. "So there's going to be a book?"

"I've already got a good start." Virgil put down his fork and picked up his coffee. "I'm opening with the impeachment. Then I'll pick up the backstory." He looked at Charlie over the rim of his cup. "I'm sure you know the Louisiana House impeached him when he was governor. Eight counts."

"But he wasn't convicted," Charlie said. He added, "On a technicality."

"By the skin of his teeth," Virgil said. "The state senate dithered around until they flat ran out of time—or they ran out the clock, if you want to look at it the other way. They wanted to be rid of him, but he scared them all to death. They're still scared, every man Jack of them. He's seduced the voters in their districts, so the politicians are afraid that if they don't toe Huey's line and show up to kiss his ring whenever he calls, he'll have them booted out at the next primary. He even campaigns against them himself." He shook his head. "Talk about the consolidation of power."

"Like Tammany Hall," Charlie offered, thinking of the New York Democratic political machine he had written about in years past.

"Not really," Virgil said. "Tammany is a cohort of political bosses all working together in support of the party. And it's decentralized. Ward leaders, even ward heelers—they all have a role to play—and they all get a piece of the action. In Huey's universe, forget the ward leaders, forget the bosses, forget the damn *party*, even." Virgil's voice was becoming more insistent, more emphatic. "In Louisiana, the party's dead. It's a personality cult. Long's the man, the Kingfish, start to finish, top to bottom, nobody else. He buys loyalty in the usual way—through jobs, money, real estate, even pardons. He buys voters with his grandiose campaign promises, things that *only he* can fix, fixes that *only he* can engineer. Of course, it's all a swindle, a big lie. But people believe him." He shook his head. "Tomorrow, you'll get a chance to see him work your crowd. When it comes to voters, he's the best con man in the country, hands down."

"FDR calls him one of the most dangerous men in America," Charlie said.

"I've heard that." Virgil grinned. "And I've heard that MacArthur is the other one. Well, FDR got rid of MacArthur by deporting him to the Philippines. Short of shooting Huey, it won't be that easy to get rid of *him*. He says he ain't goin' nowhere, and I believe him." He cleaned the last bite of pie off his plate. "And yesterday, in a radio talk, he called President Roosevelt a 'faker' that he wouldn't believe under oath. So I'm guessing that you'll be hearing Huey's opinion of the president tomorrow, too."

"Then what's to be done?" Charlie asked seriously. "The way I read it, Long figures he doesn't have a much of a shot at upsetting FDR and grabbing next year's party nomination. But he's only forty-two. He can play the long game. He'll be just forty-six in 1940. About the right age to run a winning presidential campaign."

"Yes." Virgil cocked his head. "The odds are that he won't win next year, but he could siphon off enough Democratic votes to allow the GOP candidate—Herbert Hoover, maybe, or Alf Landon, whoever it is—to waltz into the White House." He sighed. "And even if Roosevelt manages to pull off a win, you're right about the long game. Huey is looking ahead to 1940. By that time, folks will be sick of the New Deal and skittish about what FDR wants to do about the Supreme Court."

"The court?"

"Yeah. You won't hear much about it until after the election, but he's talking about increasing the size of the court. It's old, decrepit, and backward looking, he says. He wants to add one new justice for every justice who is over seventy."

Charlie knew this was serious business. Just a couple of months before, the court had virtually destroyed FDR's popular plan for industrial recovery when—in a unanimous decision involving a kosher poultry business in Brooklyn—it shot down the NRA, the National Recovery Administration.

"Every justice over seventy?" Charlie mused. "Isn't that *all* of them?"

"Six of the seven," Virgil said. "So FDR would add six new justices, making the court fifteen. People will be afraid of change on that scale, and Huey will be out there on the stump, preaching against it." He leaned back in his chair. "If he lives that long, that is."

"Lives that long?" Charlie was surprised. "You're not suggesting—"

Virgil raised a hand. "Not suggesting anything, my friend. But there have been plenty of death threats, and Long is getting more paranoid by the day. He eats conspiracy theories for breakfast, lunch, and dinner. A couple of weeks ago, he told Senator Byrd that his Louisiana enemies had hired gunmen to ambush him the next time he drove through a rural area. 'I'm not going to live much longer,' he said. 'You just watch. Some damned fool is going to shoot me.'"

"I reckon that's why he has so many bodyguards," Charlie remarked.

Virgil nodded. "He just added another one, I heard, which makes eight. He keeps a couple with him twenty-four hours a day, and a team of four or five always travels with him. When he's in DC, the three toughest ones actually live in his suite at the Broadmoor. They're the butt of everybody's jokes. When Long came to Tennessee to make a speech, the *Nashville Banner* joked that the state had to make Huey's boys deputy game wardens, so they could carry their guns out in public."

"Appropriate, I suppose," Charlie said. "Since they're guarding the Kingfish." He paused. "They'll be with him tomorrow?"

Virgil chuckled. "You bet your life." More soberly, he added, "Keep an eye on George McQuiston. That's Huey's top man. He carries his sawed-off shotgun in a paper bag, with a hole for his trigger finger. Huey's told him, 'If there's trouble, fire at will.'"

"Fire at will?" Charlie stared at him. "Come on, Virg. You're jerking my chain."

"Not a bit of it," Virgil said. "I heard him myself. 'If there's trouble, boys,' he said, 'You fire at will. You shoot somebody by accident, I'll fix it for you later.'" He paused. "If there's trouble, Charlie, be sure to get out of George's way. That guy is trigger happy. If he decides to shoot, he'll fire right through the bag."

"You don't really think there'll be trouble, do you?" Charlie asked, frowning, and then answered his own question. "Darling people aren't activists, but Long may attract some from elsewhere. Some might come with the intention of raising a ruckus."

"Could be," Virgil said. "There were protestors at the train station in St. Louis last week, and Huey's bodyguards roughed them up a little when they escorted them out. The senator doesn't take kindly to hecklers, so let's hope your crowd is friendly."

"And if there's trouble," Charlie added, "we'll be there to get the story."

Virgil's smile was lopsided. "Yes, but our boy Huey likes to control the story. He doesn't take kindly to reporters, either. I always stay in the background as much as I can. And I especially try to stay out of the way of his bodyguards. McQuiston always carries that gun. And Joe Messina—the hulk who looks like a B-movie thug—is plenty free with his fists. I saw him beat up a reporter in Baton Rouge a few weeks ago." He shuddered. "Made mincemeat out of him."

"That's bad," Charlie said soberly. "That kind of threat can make even good reporters think twice before they write a critical story."

While they talked, the diner had been filling up with people. Now, Raylene came to the table with a coffee pot in her hand. "You boys want some more coffee? And how about seconds on that pie? Glad to cut you another slice."

Charlie and Virgil exchanged glances, then shook their heads. "That does it for us, Raylene." Charlie pulled out his wallet and handed her a bill. "Come on, Virg," he said, pushing back his chair. "Let's take a walk around the square, so you can see the layout before it fills up with Long's friends and fans tomorrow. I know you're a big-city guy, but Darling is a pretty fine small town."

"With some pretty fine Southern cooking," Virgil stood,

giving Raylene an appreciative grin. "What time is breakfast tomorrow?"

"Aren't you staying at the Old Alabama?" Charlie asked. "You can get a good breakfast there."

"I'd rather eat here," Virgil said. "What time?"

Raylene cocked her head at him. "Coffee's fresh by seven. That's when the biscuits come out of the oven." She smiled. "See you then?"

"Yes, *ma'am*," Virgil said. "Nice lady," he added under his breath as they went to the door. "Makes a superior meatloaf, too. Even better than Winona's."

Charlie and Virgil were stepping out onto the street just as the sheriff and Harold Dixon, the state fire marshal, pulled up in the marshal's car in front of the diner. The two men got out, hot and sweaty in their shirtsleeves, and Charlie introduced Virgil.

After a round of handshakes, Charlie said to Buddy, "Raylene Riggs was asking if there were any new developments in the investigation—like maybe a response to the reward."

Crossing his arms and leaning against the hood of the state car, Buddy exchanged glances with Dixon. With an uncomfortable frown, Dixon gave a slight shake of his head, and Buddy said, "Not for publication, yet."

"Yet?" Charlie raised an eyebrow. "Well, that sounds promising." He paused. "Tomorrow's Wednesday. The paper goes to bed Thursday afternoon and onto the press Thursday night. Of course, we'll be running a full story. But if you think you might have a public statement, I can save an extra half-column until about three o'clock Thursday. More if you need it."

Another exchange of glances. This time, it was Dixon who spoke up. "No problem coming up with a statement," he said cautiously. "But I seriously doubt that we'll have the case wrapped by then. These investigations are complicated, you know. And it's not just the cotton gin fire. There are several crime scenes to consider."

Buddy grinned. "Haven't you got enough news in that rag of yours for one week, anyway, Dickens? Huey Long's appearance tomorrow ought to fill up a whole page, maybe two, all by itself. He'll probably draw a couple of hundred people."

"Long's a big story, that's for sure," Charlie said. "But the local firebug is bigger—especially now that he's burned down the only cotton gin in the county."

Virgil spoke up. "If I were you, Sheriff, I'd up that estimate by another couple of hundred people. Long draws a big crowd—sometimes an unruly one. And if you're having the event on the square, you're making some extra problems for yourself." He gestured. "Traffic control, for instance. Has his security team contacted you yet?"

It was the sheriff's turn to frown uncomfortably. "His *security* team?"

"He'll have four or five bodyguards," Virgil said. He glanced up at the windows in the Dispatch building next door and down the street to Mann's Mercantile, also two stories. "They may want to clear out the upper floors in the buildings around the square. The courthouse, too." His mouth twitched. "Snipers, you know. The senator takes the threat seriously. He's not going to be too happy with these windows looking down on him."

The sheriff rolled his eyes. "That is just *swell*," he muttered. "Just what we need."

Charlie frowned. "Virgil will have to tell you about George McQuiston and his paper bag—and Huey's orders to fire at will."

"Fire at will?" the sheriff asked, and Marshal Dixon echoed incredulously, "*Fire* at will?"

Virgil told them.

Charlie looked at Buddy. "You don't suppose it's too late to move Long to the baseball field, do you? Out there, people could sit in the bleachers and Long could have a microphone and loudspeakers. You'd have better crowd control."

Buddy straightened. "Sounds like the right thing to do," he said decidedly. "I can tell Mrs. Biddle—she's the head of the local Share Our Wealth Club—that we have to move it for security reasons. Tommy Lee can announce it on the radio a couple of times every hour, and the club can put up a few signs around town."

"You've got your own radio station?" Virgil asked. When the others nodded, he said, "Then you're way ahead of most towns. You'll be glad you moved the event, Sheriff Norris. Save yourself a lot of grief."

Charlie sighed. This was one of those occasions—it struck him that there were more of them all the time—when WDAR was a heckuva lot better than the *Dispatch* at getting the word out in a hurry. If he couldn't get his expansion plans underway pretty soon, radio might just make his newspaper irrelevant.

# CHAPTER FOURTEEN

# SMOKE GETS IN YOUR EYES

RYAN WAS LATE. THE EVENING DARK HAD ALREADY FALLEN BUT the temperature was still in the upper eighties when Lizzy decided to wait for him outside, on the porch swing. She had changed into the blue dress and brushed out the pin curls so that her hair fell loosely onto her shoulders. But the lacy underthings were back in her dresser drawer. And she hadn't finished setting the table or making the chicken salad or done anything more about the supper she had planned.

The scent of honeysuckle was heavy on the night air. She took a deep breath of the steadying fragrance, willing it to cool the anger that had been simmering inside her ever since Verna had told her the news. Daffodil was on her lap, purring as she ran her fingers through his thick fur. Next door, she could see Mr. and Mrs. Graham sitting in their parlor. Mr. Graham was reading a newspaper and Mrs. Graham was knitting as they listened to the *Fred Waring Show*. Their parlor windows were open and the music—a popular Jerome Kern favorite, "Smoke Gets in Your Eyes"—spilled out into the darkness.

As the chorus sang about hearts on fire and tears blinding your eyes, Lizzy thought how oddly apt the song was. Once, she supposed that the smoke in her eyes was kindled by passion. But right now, it was produced by a smoldering anger.

She hoped she would be able to keep it under control when she talked to Ryan. She didn't want to make a fool of herself by yelling. Or worse, crying.

It was almost nine when he pulled his blue roadster to a stop in front of her house. Carrying a bottle of wine, he walked jauntily to the porch where she was sitting on the swing. "Oh, there you are," he said in surprise as he came up the steps. "I didn't notice you. Why are you sitting in the dark?"

"It's cooler out here," she said. "And more pleasant." She had turned off the lamp in the parlor window, welcoming the outdoor dark. She hoped it masked her face. "Come and sit." She pointed to the wicker rocking chair.

"Sorry to be late," he said, putting the wine bottle beside the chair. "It took a while to go through Mrs. Snow's projects with her and Miss Bloodworth. And then there was the 'America Eats' project to discuss. It's not ready to go yet—we're still looking for ideas. Anyway, when I got to the hotel, I thought I had time to catch forty winks. Slept longer than I intended. Sorry."

He was wearing a plaid sport shirt, the collar unbuttoned, and pressed khaki trousers. In his thirties, well-built and tall, he moved with the easy confidence of an athlete. Somehow, Lizzy was always aware of his commanding *maleness*. But the sun-bleached blond hair that fell across his forehead gave him a boyish look—that, and his quick, disarming grin. He wasn't quite handsome, she thought; his features—a firm jaw, high cheekbones, pale eyes—were too craggy for that. But he was striking. When they were out together, people noticed him.

"It's no matter," she said, accepting his apology for being late. She made a quick mental note to ask Ophelia about the "America Eats" project, but she didn't want to get into that now. There was too much on her mind—and in her heart. She stroked Daffy, glad for his substantial reality under her fingers.

He took out a cigarette. "It's what, now—nearly nine? And

still hot enough to fry an egg on the sidewalk." He scraped a match with his thumbnail, the flame briefly illuminating his face. "Swear to God, Liz. I don't know how you Alabamians tolerate the summers." He pulled on his cigarette. "It gets warm in Washington, but nothing like this. The heat is exhausting."

"We've learned to live with it," she said quietly, willing her voice not to shake. "We take things slow. We don't get . . . all fired up."

That was a lie. *We don't get all fired up?* She was so angry now that she knew that if she allowed it, if she gave in to it, the explosion would be volcanic. On her lap, Daffy stirred and yawned, stretched out a paw, then fell asleep again. The tree frogs sang in the magnolia next to the porch. Somewhere down the block, an owl hooted eerily. The smoke from Ryan's cigarette drifted toward her.

Ryan leaned back in the chair, relaxing, stretching out his long legs. "Well, at least we won't have to worry about that hurricane—the one that made such a mess of the Florida Keys yesterday. I heard on your little radio station that it's heading across Florida this evening. It'll end up in the Atlantic tomorrow." He pulled on his cigarette again. "I also heard that Huey Long will be here in Darling tomorrow." He blew out a stream of smoke. "At the baseball field. Good place for Long's wild pitches." He chuckled at his joke.

"At the baseball field?" She was surprised. "That's a switch."

"Security reasons, the radio said. I gather that it was originally scheduled for the courthouse square." He paused, peering at her. "You're looking very pretty tonight, Liz. I can't quite see what you're wearing, it's so dark. But that's your blue dress, isn't it? My favorite."

He spoke in a brisk Yankee accent, hard-edged and clipped and very different from the slow Southern drawl Lizzy was used to. It was strong, definite, confident. It had always intrigued her. It didn't tonight. And she didn't respond to his compliment. Or linger for more small talk. It was time to get this over with.

"I think there's something you've forgotten to tell me," she said. His face was a pale blur in the dark. She kept her voice determinedly even and conversational. Daffy stirred beneath her fingers, and she felt the comforting rumble of his throaty purr.

"Oh, yeah?" Lazily, he propped his feet on the railing. She heard the smile in his voice. "What did I forget to tell you? That you're the prettiest thing I've seen all day—all week, for that matter? That I spent almost every minute of the long drive here just thinking about you?"

His voice was lightly teasing, the way he might speak to a little girl. It suddenly struck her that he had used that patronizing tone to her before. Why hadn't she recognized it then?

The anger flared, a hot, sour taste at the back of her throat. "You forgot Eloise," she said, glad for the dark. "The boys," she added in the same controlled tone. "Back home in Philadelphia. Where you and Eloise live."

He turned his head swiftly, as though she had slapped him. He was silent for a long moment. When he spoke, his voice was rueful. "Be sure your sins will find you out."

"A wife and children aren't sins," Lizzy objected mildly. Her heart was beating hard, and it took an effort to keep it from altering her breath. "For most of the men I know, they're something to brag about, something to share." She forced herself to smile into the dark. "You know—family photos in the wallet. The boys' accomplishments, Eloise's cooking, or perhaps her piano playing. That sort of thing." In spite of her efforts, her voice tightened. "Or maybe that's just what we do here in the South. Maybe up north, folks are different."

The tip of his cigarette glowed bright as he inhaled. He swung his feet off the railing. The air seemed to be charged now with tension and his voice was edgy when he replied. "You're right, Liz. You're right. Of course, you're right. I should have told you. I meant to, when the time came. But the time never seemed to come. And I just—"

She heard the squeak of the rocker as he leaned forward again, elbows on his knees. His hands were clasped. He dropped his head. "I just . . . needed some space, that's all. A little time. And to tell the truth, I wanted to know you better." A quick glance up at her, then back down. "You're pretty damned special, you know. There's nobody like you. Such a talented writer, yet so modest about it, hidden away down here in this dowdy little town. You're so . . . so *Southern*. So soft, but you've got a spine like a steel spike. And so beautiful, although you never seem to know it."

He paused, and in the silence, the Grahams' radio next door began playing "Stars Fell on Alabama." They listened, saying nothing. At the end, he cleared his throat.

"Yeah, that's just how it's been for me," he said. "The way it is in that song. Just the two of us, stars falling all around. That's how it's been for me, anyway. I like to think you felt it, too." His voice broke. "Honest, Liz, I didn't *plan* this. It just happened." His sigh was regretful. "I'm making excuses for myself, when there aren't any, not really. But I just wanted to . . . well, enjoy you—and our own private fairyland—for as long as I could. I knew it wasn't going to last."

She sucked in her breath, refusing to allow herself to be taken in. She didn't doubt that he was being honest, but it only revealed his selfishness. "And you were never concerned about how *I* might feel?" she asked. "That is, when you finally got around to telling me that you're married."

The flaring anger prodded her to ask him how many other *special* women he had found in his travels around the coun-try—and what he would do if one of them wanted to turn their friendship into an affair, or even a marriage. Would he go so far as bigamy, like the man she'd read about recently, who had one wife in Chicago and another in Denver—and children by both? In these days when men could be gone for weeks at a time, traveling for work, anybody might have more than one family and keep both of them in the dark. But what kind of man was it who would do such a thing?

"Of course I was concerned about you." His voice rose. "I've been trying to think what to do. It's been on my mind for—"

She couldn't let him finish. "What about Eloise? Were you concerned about her? And the boys. Were you going to tell *them* about all the new friends you've been making down South?"

His voice grew gruff. "My family is a whole other story, Liz. I'd rather not get into it right now. All I can say is that I didn't mean it to go this far—you and me, I mean. I knew that I had to tell you, but I kept . . . well, putting it off. I enjoyed the time we had together. I always looked forward to seeing you, to hearing about your writing, about the funny episodes in that law office where you work, about all the things you and your friends do to keep busy here in this little town. There was always a reason not to tell you." Rubbing his jaw, he added, half reluctantly, "If it means anything, I'm sorry. I apologize."

Finally. *I'm sorry. I apologize.* The words she'd been waiting for. She could end it now. Her fingers tightened involuntarily in Daffy's fur. Annoyed, he stopped purring and jumped off her lap.

"I'm sorry, too, Ryan," she said. "Very sorry. Now, if you'll excuse me, I'm not especially hungry. I'm afraid the diner is closed, but I'm sure you can find something to eat at the hotel." She stood.

He put out a hand. "No, wait, Liz, please. I need to ask what you're going to do. I mean, who have you told? Who knows about . . . this?"

Lizzy had thought about this and decided that it was better to keep Ophelia out of it, since she had to continue to work with him. But he ought to hear the rest.

"Verna Tidwell," she said. "I believe you've met her occasionally. And Mr. Duffy, at the Darling Savings and Trust. They know."

"Duffy?" he asked sharply. "What's he got to do with this?"

"Mr. Duffy is my friend," she said simply. "As a banker, he's in the business of assessing people's honesty. He didn't want to see anybody . . . tricked."

"Tricked?" Ryan sounded startled. "But that's not what I—"

"Verna and Mr. Duffy," she repeated firmly, not wanting to hear any more protests. "And me, of course." When she had thanked Verna for her investigative work and asked her to thank Mr. Duffy, too, Verna had said that it would be their secret. The story wouldn't go any further. With a crooked smile, she added. "It isn't exactly the sort of thing that my friends and I are eager to spread around our dowdy little Southern town, you know. Even if it is the most sensational bit of gossip in a very long time. We don't often get to hear about men keeping their families a secret."

If he heard the sarcasm, he didn't let on. He stood too. "And my wife? You're not going to tell her, I hope." He sounded as if he was almost begging. "It would only make things difficult for me. At home, I mean."

Lizzy sighed. There it was again. The selfishness. "Of course not," she said. "What's between you and your wife is your business."

"Well, I guess I can be grateful for that." He hesitated. "I suppose this is quits, then? I won't be seeing you again?" He spoke tentatively, as though he might be hoping for a hint that she might reconsider.

Lizzy thought about the supper she had planned, the

anticipation she had felt about the evening, the hopes she had nurtured—innocently, naively romantic, but hopes just the same. She was swept by a wave of fierce disappointment. And buoyed by an equally fierce resolve.

"Yes," she said emphatically. "We won't be seeing each other again."

Her last few words were underlined by the shrill shrieking of the fire siren on the courthouse bell tower.

Startled, Ryan looked around. "Good Lord, what's that? What's that noise? What's going on?"

"That?" Lizzy squared her shoulders. "Oh, that's our town fire siren—just our firebug providing us with a little local excitement. I'm afraid we've heard it so often lately that we're getting used to it. Goodnight, Ryan."

# CHAPTER FIFTEEN

# FIRESTARTER

Now that the hardest one is safely behind him, the man is feeling a little easier in his spirit. He's got a couple more on his list, and tonight, he's going to settle a score that goes back to when he was a boy. Marvin Musgrove might be a solid Darling citizen and important enough to run for mayor, but the fact of the matter is that he's a shady character. He cheated the man's daddy out of twenty-four dollars, back when it mattered, when his daddy didn't *have* twenty-four dollars and finding it meant some hard scrabbling. That may have been thirty years ago, and the man might have been just a kid. But he has a long memory. It's payback time.

And this one isn't just about an old score that needs settling. Now that the man has learned what fires can do—or to put it a little more accurately, what he can do with fire—he's discovered that he *loves* it.

He admires the way it grows from the flick of a match to a roaring blaze, a live thing fed by its own greedy energies.

The way the new fire siren on top of the courthouse tower gets everybody's attention.

The way the Hot Dogs have to rush to undo what he's done while the Darling citizens stand watching, their mouths stupidly open, awestruck and frightened.

The way it's the hot topic in the diner the next day or over at Mann's Mercantile or the post office or when people are standing around chatting after the Wednesday night prayer meeting.

He especially likes the way Darling people talk about *him* even when they don't know who he is and have no idea that he's standing right there beside them, listening and putting in his two cents from time to time.

And the more often he does this—plants his little doodads in the right place, flicks a match and stands back to watch the flame—the more he likes being the secret, sinister agent of all their fears. It gives him the kind of power he's never had until today. Until tonight. Until right *now*.

But he has decided, after a great deal of thought, that torching Musgrove's Hardware might not be a very good idea. Marvin knows the man has a grudge against him and he might just begin to suspect him. Of course, Marvin couldn't *prove* anything, but the accusations could be a nuisance. And anyway, he has come up with another plan, which when it comes to settling that old twenty-four-dollar score is every bit as good as burning down the hardware store.

And who knows? Maybe he'll even get around to burning the hardware store. Later.

Tonight, he's going to burn *this*.

# CHAPTER SIXTEEN

# MILK IS JUST AS WET AS WATER

EARLYNNE BIDDLE WAS NOT AT HER BEST, HAVING SPENT THE better part of the evening at The Flour Shop making bread—*not* her favorite thing to do.

Her hand on the light switch, she took one last look around the bakery kitchen. The counters were clean, the pine-topped baking table was scrubbed, the dishes were washed, the supplies were returned to the pantry, the electric refrigerator was humming contentedly, and the linoleum floor was swept. It was almost nine and time to go home—finally.

Earlynne was working late tonight because Zelda Clemens was home sick with the flu that was making the rounds in Darling. Which meant that Earlynne herself would have to be back in this kitchen at five-thirty tomorrow morning, in order to bake the twenty loaves needed to fill the glass display case out front, as well as prepare those wonderful French pastries that were her specialty: croissants, beignets, éclairs, macaroons, madeleines, crepes, and petit fours. Which, along with sticky buns and tarts and cookies and pocket pies, brought customers flocking to The Flour Shop.

Now, this was all well and good. Very good, in fact, except for the unfortunate fact that Earlynne hated making bread. It was the croissants that were her favorites, and she made them with the dedication of a zealot: mixing the dough with a devout attention, reverently rolling it out, then rolling the chilled butter to just the right size and layering the butter and the dough, turning it tenderly, folding it into something that resembled a book. And then doing it again and then again, until at last she cut the layered dough into lovely little triangles, shaped the triangles into gorgeous croissants, and popped them into the oven. For Earlynne, the baking of croissants was an art, and she was Leonardo.

Bread, on the other hand, was boring start to finish. Consequently, Earlynne had never quite managed to master the craft. (She did not consider it an art.) Somehow, over the many years she had fantasized about opening her very own bakery, it had never occurred to her that a bakery was expected to sell bread. And that to pull the loaves of hot bread out of the oven first thing in the morning, the sponge would have to be set the night before. And that baking twenty or thirty loaves of bread at a time might not be any sort of fun. It would forever and always be a *job*—a boring job that she really did not want to do.

As it turned out, her partner, Mildred Kilgore, didn't want to do it either. Aunt Hetty Little and the Dahlias had pitched in to help during the rocky few weeks after The Flour Shop opened, contributing loaves of bread they baked in their own kitchen ovens. Under Aunt Hetty's energetic tutelage, Earlynne finally got the hang of it, more or less. But while she improved to where she could make a passable loaf, she never found it anything but boring. Many times, as she told her husband Henry, she had thought about throwing in the sponge (to make an unfunny joke). What good was owning a bakery (well, half of it) if you had to bake bread when you wanted to be making croissants?*

Who knows what might have happened if Liz Lacy hadn't

---

* For the full story of Earlynne and Mildred's bread-baking misadventure: *The Darling Dahlias and the Poinsettia Puzzle.*

introduced them to Zelda Clemens, a Darling girl who had gone to Chicago to seek her fortune but was now back home, empty handed and looking for work. As Earlynne and Mildred learned, Zelda had been one of the regular bakers at Roeser's Bakery in Humboldt Park, on the west side of Chicago. Roeser's was famous for its bread, and Zelda demonstrated what she had learned there by producing six amazingly symmetrical sample loaves, beautifully browned and divinely fragrant. Earlynne and Mildred gobbled down half a loaf between them, the warm slices drenched with butter. They had held a brief two-minute executive meeting and hired Zelda on the spot.

Now, as Earlynne switched off the light, locked the deadbolt on the kitchen door, and started for her car in the alley behind the bakery, she found herself wishing Zelda a swift and complete recovery. In fact, they had just talked on the telephone and Zelda thought she might be back tomorrow, if she could come later, around noon. Earlynne had agreed. Zelda could keep the bakery open while Earlynne and Mildred went to hear Senator Long's speech, which was now scheduled for the baseball field.

When she thought about this, Earlynne felt a stab of justifiable pride mixed with an understandable nervous apprehension, for she was the president of Darling's Share Our Wealth Club and responsible for introducing the senator tomorrow. She was going home right now, to write out her speech. Not much of a writer, she only hoped she'd be able to come up with something worthy of the great man.

She also had to talk with her son, Benny, who was one-half of Darling's new radio station WDAR (Benny's friend Tommy Lee Musgrove was the other half). Benny was responsible for what the boys called "remote broadcasting." He would be setting up the equipment that allowed the senator's speech to be heard, via telephone and the air waves, as far away as eight or ten miles—all the way out to Miss Tallulah LaBelle's plantation, they hoped. This seemed like a miracle to Earlynne, who had never understood air waves and was pretty sure she never would. She still couldn't quite get her mind around the fact that it was her boy Benny—that freckled kid with the buck teeth and the fire-engine red cowlick that wouldn't stay down no matter how many little dabs of Brylcreem he slicked on it—who was making this miracle happen. While Benny certainly had his faults (and no mother would ever overlook a son's faults), the fact that he could command the airwaves was little short of amazing.

Benny's father was of the opposite opinion. He would shake his head and grouse that the boy was never going to amount to a hill of beans if he didn't get busy and find something more productive to do than messing around with that dad-blamed radio station, which only broadcast foolishness and would never amount to a hill of beans. If you wanted news, it was the *Dispatch* you turned to. If it was music you were after, there was the First Methodist choir, and if it was good enough for Jesus, it was good enough for everybody else. So when Benny asked his father if the Coca-Cola bottling plant (which was under Mr. Biddle's management) would pony up for a commercial, it was a hard sell.

"Radio?" his father snorted. "Think anybody's going to buy anything they hear on that little radio station of yours?" But he paid for a commercial because . . . well, because Benny was his son. And because it was Coca-Cola's advertising money he was spending, not cash dollars out of his own pocket.

Earlynne, on the other hand, was convinced that there was great economic potential in what Benny was doing. She was confident that, in a few years, WDAR would be as big and important as WALA down in Mobile or WSFA up in Montgomery. Why, the boy might even end up in Atlanta or New York with one of the big broadcasting companies, NBC or CBS or somebody like that. Earlynne was of the opinion that, given Benny's outstanding brain, all things were possible.

And anyway, it was better than drinking beer with those rowdies at Pete's Pool Parlor, wasn't it? Or mooning after Rowena Rose Wilson, that flirty little girl who worked at the telephone exchange and whose highest ambition had already been achieved when she was crowned as Darling's Junior Miss Sweet Potato of 1934.

Tomorrow would be a big day for WDAR, with Benny managing the remote broadcast of the senator's speech and Tommy Lee back in the studio, doing the announcing. Earlynne had her fingers crossed that there wouldn't be a lot of static, the way there'd been when Benny tried to do a remote broadcast from the bakery just last Thursday. They'd had Bessie Bloodworth and Ophelia Snow come in to tell everybody about the Darling history Bessie was writing for Ophelia Snow's Federal Writer's Project. It had been a dark and stormy morning and the airwaves apparently didn't like lightning when it happened in the neighborhood. Earlynne was hoping for clear weather tomorrow. Senator Long was bound to be impressed that their little town had a radio station of its very own. He might even recommend the boys to bigwigs he knew in the radio business over there in Louisiana, which he practically ran single-handed from Washington DC, according to the newspapers.

Still thinking about static and airwaves and Benny's promising future, Earlynne arrived at her car—a pretty little 1928 Nash, light blue, bought just before the Crash turned everybody's world upside down. She put a hand into her pocketbook for her car key, which was on Henry's stamped leather Fraternal Order of Odd Fellows key fob, along with the key to the bakery. But she couldn't find it in the jumble of coins, comb, hairbrush, lipstick, face powder, pencil, notebook, aspirin bottle, a slightly used handkerchief, and a paper sack containing a half-dozen eggs. She was short on eggs for Henry's and Benny's breakfasts this week so she had borrowed the eggs from the bakery's refrigerator. She left a note saying she would pay them back from the next dozen she bought at Mrs. Hancock's, with an extra egg for interest.

*Well, bother*, she thought, putting her pocketbook on the hood of her car and beginning a serious search among the loose coins. She hoped she hadn't locked those keys in the cash register, the way she'd done a couple of weeks ago. If she had, she'd either have to walk the eight blocks home, or walk over to the Exchange and call Henry to come and get her. Neither offered an inviting prospect, especially since by now it was very nearly full dark.

Earlynne had pulled just about everything out of her purse and strewn it across the hood when she became aware of a strange odor. The sack of eggs in her hand, she lifted her head, sniffing the air. It was an odd time of the night to be burning trash, wasn't it? The only businesses on this side of the courthouse square—the Darling Savings and Loan, The Flour Shop, and Fannie Champaign's hat shop—were all closed, and everybody was home in their parlors, listening to *Lum and Abner* (straight from the hills of Pine Ridge, Arkansas). Or *Major Bowes Amateur Hour*, which was said to be getting ten thousand applications a week from country musicians desperately hoping to hit the big time in New York City or get the Major's nod to go on the road with one of his Amateur Hour troupes.

There were only two buildings on the other side of the alley. One was Mrs. Cooper's old barn. The other was the garage that Benny and Tommy Lee rented from Mr. Barton for the WDAR studio and office. Mr. Barton had sold his beloved 1928 DeSoto when he couldn't make the payments on it, so he'd agreed to rent the garage to the boys for only four dollars a month. The place had a dirt floor, but it was wired for electricity, had a small wood stove, and the roof only leaked a little. Most importantly, it was less than a block from the Darling water tower, on top of which—forty-some feet from the ground—the boys had installed one end of their long T-wire antenna. They hoped that the tower would provide enough height to allow WDAR's signal to reach as far as Miss Tallulah's Atwater-Kent cathedral-model radio in the sitting room at the LaBelle plantation. That was important because the lady had made a sizeable investment in the radio station's equipment and might make another, if she could hear WDAR when she turned on her radio. Of course, if Earlynne had known that Benny was up there risking his life on the top of that tower, she would have been a nervous wreck until he was safely on the ground. And then she would have given him a piece of her mind for scaring her to death, and another piece on general principles.

Now, she took a deep sniff. Smoke. Yes, this was definitely smoke. But where in the world—

And then she saw it, a bright tongue of flame licking hungrily at the far corner of the back wall of Mr. Barton's garage—the home of WDAR. The Darling firebug had been at it again! And if the Hot Dogs didn't get there quickly, the ramshackle old garage, dry as a bone and easy to burn, would go up like a tinderbox, and with it all of Benny's and Tommy Lee's hard work and Miss Tallulah's investment and the money the boys had borrowed from Mr. Duffy at the bank and the little bit their parents had contributed.

Earlynne's first impulse was to yell for help, which she did, at the top of her lungs. "Fire!" she screamed. "Help! Fire! Somebody, please—fire! Fire!"

Her second thought was to grab the key to the bakery and dash back inside and use the telephone to call the Exchange and report the fire. She whirled toward the bakery. But as she turned, she heard a car engine start—very close to her, just a few yards away, probably—and she whirled. A black Model T Ford, its headlamps off, pulled out of the dark space behind Mrs. Cooper's barn, right in front of her. As it made the ninety-degree left turn onto the alley, it was almost close enough for her to touch, and she could see that there was what looked like an Every Man a King poster in the back window. If only it hadn't been so dark, she would have been able to read the license plate.

With a sudden, sharp conviction, Earlynne knew that the driver, whoever he was, had to have set the radio station on fire. If she only had a rock, she could throw it through his back window and maybe hit him in the head. There wasn't a rock anywhere in sight. But she did have the paper bag containing Henry's and Benny's breakfast eggs. She snatched it up and hurled it at the car as hard as she could.

But by that time, the Ford was speeding away from her, tires spinning in the loose gravel of the alley. The bag hit the spare tire mounted on the car's rear end. It split open, the eggs smashed, and the raw yellow yolks dripped messily down through the tire's wire spokes.

Less than a minute later, Earlynne was fumbling the key into the lock on the back door of the bakery. Two minutes later, in the kitchen, she had that flirty little Rowena Rose Wilson on the line, telling her that she needed to turn on the courthouse fire siren and telephone Archie Mann, or whoever was fire chief this week.

"It's Mr. Barton's garage that's on fire," she said, stumbling over the words. "Tell Mr. Mann to bring the fire engine to Mr. Barton's garage."

"Where?" Rowena Rose asked, sounding confused. "Whose garage? I don't—"

"It's WDAR!" Earlynne yelled into the phone. "It's the *radio* station, you silly girl!" In desperation, she added, "Where Benny Biddle works."

"Oh, Benny's place," Rowena Rose trilled. "Sure. I know where that is, over behind the bakery. I've *been* there." And in another breath, she was adding, "Hey, Benny, some lady says your radio station is on fire. Do you know which fire chief I'm supposed to call? And maybe you can tell me which button to push to make that siren thing work."

Wincing, Earlynne put down the phone. Benny was at the Exchange right now, mooning after Rowena Rose? But he was a Hot Dog, so he would have an idea of what to do, even if that foolish girl didn't. Twenty seconds later, when the fire siren began to split Darling's quiet night with its fierce shrieks, Earlynne was glad he'd been where he was when she called, although she didn't like to think what he and Rowena Rose might have been up to.

Anyway, there wasn't time to think about that now. She looked around. The galvanized scrub bucket sat in the corner, together with the mop. But the tap in the kitchen sink was slow as molasses in January, and by the time she filled that bucket, the garage could be gone. Then she thought of something else. She opened the refrigerator and grabbed the two big pitchers of milk from the top shelf.

When it came to putting out a fire, milk was just as wet as water, wasn't it?

# CHAPTER SEVENTEEN

# FLAME OUT

Buddy Norris frowned. "*Milk?*"

"Well," said the woman, "it was handy. And every bit as wet as water," she added, a little defensively. "It didn't put the flames out, Sheriff, but it was better than nothing."

"I'm sure it was," Buddy agreed, trying not to smile. "Good thinking, Mrs. Biddle."

Chief Mann had told him that, while the lady's two large pitchers of milk hadn't extinguished the fire, they had slowed the advance of the flames just long enough to save Mr. Barton's garage from destruction and WDAR from the loss of its equipment. Buddy shone his flashlight on the back wall of the building. It appeared to be charred up to about waist height, but the structure itself was barely damaged. The Hot Dogs and the lady with the milk had done good work.

"Is the fire out?" Mrs. Biddle asked anxiously, peering through the darkness.

"Looks like it," Buddy replied. This had been a much simpler fire than the cotton gin, but it had been set by the same arsonist. He knew this for a fact, because he had possession of the evidence, a delay device identical to the one found at the cotton gin fire: a book of matches and a cardboard tube stuffed with cotton, designed to be used in a way that made Buddy blush, when he thought about it. This would be added to their collection of clues, and when the state fire marshal got back to Darling, they could continue their investigation. It was a shame that he'd been unexpectedly called back to Montgomery. He'd missed tonight's excitement.

"I hope none of the boys' radio equipment got damaged," Mrs. Biddle said nervously. "Benny and Tommy Lee Musgrove have put months of hard work into that station."

"Doesn't appear to be," Buddy said. He was watching Archie Mann leave a conversation with Charlie Dickens and the young reporter from the *Dispatch* and climb into Big Red, which was parked on the street at the far end of the alley. The Hot Dogs had already packed up their hoses and loaded the rest of their gear.

"Everything's been checked out," he added reassuringly, thinking that Mrs. Biddle was probably worried about her son's investment. "There was no serious water damage."

That was important, he knew. Water would be every bit as destructive as fire, when it came to broadcasting equipment. "But it was darned lucky you noticed the flames before they got a good start," he went on. "A few minutes more, and that garage would be nothing but ashes."

"I'm just sorry I didn't get out here in time to see him actually doing his dirty work," Mrs. Biddle said regretfully. "I might have caught him. As it was . . ." Her voice trailed off.

"As it was," Buddy prompted after a moment.

But by this time, he wasn't paying much attention. He was watching Big Red drive off, its lights flashing but without the siren. He was thinking how glad he was that Rufus Radley had realized he didn't know the first thing about firefighting and that he'd better turn the chief's job back over to Archie Mann. Archie had sent his Hot Dogs home as soon as they got the WDAR fire out, telling them to get some rest so they'd be ready to jump and run the *next* time the fire siren went off. Which it would, until the sheriff caught that gol-darned pyromaniac.

"As it was," Mrs. Biddle said, "I only saw the back of his head."

"Whose head?" Buddy asked, thinking that if he didn't catch that gol-darned pyromaniac pretty fast, his chance of being reelected would go up in smoke.

"Why, the man who started the fire. I'm sure that's who it was," Mrs. Biddle added reasonably. "Poor Mrs. Cooper is having so much trouble with her eyes that she can't see to drive anymore. And anyway, she hasn't had a car since Mr. Cooper died. Which had to have been three years ago January, because that's when the cemetery got flooded on New Year's Eve and it was too wet to bury anybody until almost Valentine's Day." She put her head on one side. "I'm sure it was the arsonist I saw. Who else would be parked there in the dark at this hour of the night?"

Who else indeed? Belatedly startled into attention, Buddy turned back to the woman beside him. "You actually *saw* him?"

"Only the back of his head." She frowned. "As I was *telling* you."

Buddy felt as if he had come in when the movie was already ten minutes old and was stumbling over people's feet, trying to find his seat. "How about if we go back to the beginning," he said apologetically. "Tell me what you saw."

She straightened her shoulders. "Well, it was almost nine when I finished up in the bakery. I had to do the bread myself, you see, because Zelda is home sick—that's Zelda Clemens, our bread baker—and Mildred Kilgore doesn't like doing bread any more than I do. And after I set the sponge, there was the cleanup and the dishes to wash. I was hurrying because I was later than usual and Mr. Biddle was probably wondering what had happened to me. But when I got out here to my car"—she put a proprietary hand on the hood of the Nash—"I couldn't find my keys. I was half afraid I had locked them in the cash register again, but I was hoping they were somewhere in my pocketbook. It was dark, of course, so I had to dump everything out to look. I was standing right here, looking for my keys, when I smelled the smoke." She paused. "That's when I heard the car start up."

"Where?" Buddy asked. "Where was the car?"

"There." Mrs. Biddle took three steps and pointed off to her left, to the space beside Mrs. Cooper's barn. "It was parked right there, in the dark. Then it pulled out in front of me and sped off down the alley. That's when I—"

"Whoa." Buddy frowned. "What kind of car was it?"

She considered. "I'm not much on cars, but I'm pretty sure it was a Ford. A Model T. I couldn't see the color, but it was probably—"

"Black," said Buddy, with a sinking heart. Henry Ford had been quoted as saying that a customer could have his Model T painted any color, so long as it was black. Which wasn't strictly true, because Mr. Clinton's taxi was as red as a beet and Buddy had heard that the young doctor over in Monroeville had a green one. But there must be a hundred black Model T Fords in Cypress County. At least.

"I don't suppose you were able to make out the number on the license plate," he added hopefully.

Mrs. Biddle shook her head. "It was just too dark. I could see that he had an EVERY MAN A KING poster in his back window. And if I'd had a big rock I could have thrown it through the window and maybe knocked him in the head. But I didn't have a big rock. Not even a little one."

"Oh, too bad," Buddy said, although he knew from experience that the Ford's back window was practically indestructible. A rock would bounce right off.

"I did have a bag of eggs, though," Mrs. Biddle said thoughtfully. "Half a dozen. I'm sure they made quite a splash. Once they dry, it'll take some elbow grease to scrub them off."

"Eggs?" Buddy stared at her, not quite connecting. "Quite a splash?"

"Isn't that what I said? On the back of the car. On the spare tire. You know, on the wires." She was getting impatient. "I think they're called spokes."

"Oh," Buddy said, and a little spark of hope flamed up inside him.

# CHAPTER EIGHTEEN

# HOTTER'N HADES

*Wednesday, September 4, 1935*

BUDDY TIPPED THE PEACH CRATE UPSIDE DOWN. "HERE," HE said. "We'll just sit right here and watch the cars as they drive through the gate."

Deputy Wayne Springer took off his blue baseball cap and wiped the sweat out of his eyes with his sleeve. The air was boiling hot, the sun was a blast furnace, and there was no shade where the two men were stationing themselves, just inside the gate to the baseball field, home of the Darling Boll Weevils.

"Hotter'n Hades," Wayne remarked emphatically, slapping his cap back on. He sat down on his crate. "Just right for old Huey, if you ask me." He chuckled shortly. "The senator had better get used to it, see'n as how that's where he's headed."

Buddy tipped the bottle and swigged the last of his orange Nehi soda, which was disagreeably warm from sitting too long in the hot squad car. "Kinda hard on the feller, aren't you?"

"Not on your life," Wayne said emphatically. "But I'm not somebody the Kingfish has to worry about. There are plenty in Louisiana who would like to see him turned on a spit, or better yet, deep fried in a kettle of boiling lard. And maybe a few in Washington, the way I hear it—even at the very top. He's running scared. That's why he's got all those thugs trailing along behind him, armed to the teeth." He shook his head. "If you ask me, those bodyguards of his are as much of a danger as the people Huey is afraid of."

Buddy didn't like the sound of that, but since there wasn't much he could do about Huey Long's bodyguards, he kept his opinion to himself. Anyway, there was work to do. The senator and his entourage weren't expected to arrive until just before two in the afternoon. But given what Mrs. Biddle had told him last night, he had decided it would be a good idea if he and Wayne stationed themselves at the gate to the baseball field— *before* the rest of Darling got there.

When they had arrived just after noon, however, they discovered that the Share Our Wealth Club was already making a day of it. A couple of dozen cars along with the usual patient mules and farm wagons were parked along the edge of the outfield. The Boll Weevils were playing the Anniston Invincibles on Saturday afternoon (with a box supper after the game), so Clyde Perkins had mown the infield and outfield grass. The speaker's stand was set up just inside the first-base line, emblazoned with red, white, and blue bunting. Draped across the back of the platform was a white bedsheet, with "Darling Loves Huey P. Long!" freshly lettered in bright red paint, which had dripped a little more than the painter probably intended.

In the bleachers in front of the speaker's stand, some fifty folks had already staked out their seats, the ladies deploying brightly colored umbrellas to ward off the sun, the men shading their heads with newspaper tents. Under the live oaks at the corner of the field, families were relaxing on quilts, enjoying sandwiches and lemonade and watching their kids pretending to be Dizzy Dean and Lou Gehrig and Pepper Martin, while dogs chased the loose balls, barking and generally making happy nuisances of themselves.

Down by third base, Sammy Ray Turnbuckle had set up his popcorn and soft drink stand, which was pulled by his horse,

Kernal. He was already serving the younger kids crowding around with nickels clutched in their hot little fists. Out past second base, members of the Darling Academy Band, impressively togged out in their blue and white uniforms, were tuning their instruments and lining up for their first formation. Three trombones, trumpet, tuba, and snare drum were already warming up with a thumping rendition of "The Liberty Bell March."

Seeing that a number of vehicles had already arrived, Buddy had changed his plan. He and Wayne had gone from one Model T to the next, all twelve of them black, of course. A close inspection of each had failed to reveal what they were looking for. If the target of their search was coming, he hadn't arrived yet, Buddy decided. And he was pretty sure the fellow was coming, since Mrs. Biddle had spotted a Share Our Wealth poster in the car's back window. The driver surely wouldn't want to miss seeing the senator in person. That's why the sheriff and his deputy had stationed themselves at the gate, where they could give every Model T a good once-over.

In quick succession, they waved through an older Plymouth, a 1923 green Chevrolet, and Bailey Beauchamp's lemon-yellow Cadillac touring car, with Bailey and his big Cuban cigar in the back seat and his uniformed colored man, Lightning McFall, at the wheel. The Caddy was followed by two Ford Model Ts, the second of which was driven by a smiling Beulah Trivette, with Buddy's steady girlfriend, Bettina Higgens, in the passenger seat. Wayne stepped out and put up his hand to stop both Fords, ambled slowly around each car, then waved them on.

Beulah and Bettina had just driven through when Buddy saw Benton Moseley climbing down from his seat in the bleachers and strolling over to the gate, hands in the pockets of his rumpled white summer suit, a straw boater shading his eyes. Mr. Moseley was currently serving as the Cypress County attorney (a job that was taken in rotation by the local lawyers), which meant that Buddy got to work with him on cases where there were criminal charges. In his couple of years as sheriff, Buddy had become acquainted with all the other lawyers in town. He preferred Mr. Moseley, who seemed to keep an eye on everything that was going on in Darling and was always glad to answer his questions.

Now, Mr. Moseley had a question for him. "What I want to know, Sheriff," he said, "is what in the devil you and Wayne have been doing the past half hour. I have watched you prowl around all those parked cars, and here you are, giving some of the folks who drive in a good going-over. But not *all* of them." He tipped his boater to the back of his head. "Just what in the devil are you looking for?"

"A Ford Model T," Buddy said. "Black."

"You didn't find one you liked?" Mr. Moseley inquired iron-ically, gesturing toward the parked cars. "You and Wayne must have inspected at least a dozen while I was watching."

Wayne chuckled ironically and Buddy cleared his throat. He knew this wasn't going to sound like . . . well, like evidence. But it was.

"We're looking for a specific Ford," he said. "With a Huey Long poster in the rear window and raw eggs on the spokes of the spare tire."

"Eggs?" Mr. Moseley took off his hat and used it to fan himself. "I knew that Thomas Edison was looking for a rubber substitute for Mr. Ford's tires. Last I heard, though, he'd landed on goldenrod, not *eggs*."

A little stiffly (it was sometimes hard to tell if Mr. Moseley was cracking a joke), Buddy filled in the details of Mrs. Biddle's adventure in the alley the night before. "She thinks the driver was the arsonist, and I believe her. If we're lucky," he added, "the fellow has no idea that he was egged. He may not have noticed that he's driving around with the evidence on his spare tire."

"And even if he tries to scrub it off," Wayne volunteered, "he might leave a few traces. Dried eggs are pretty hard to remove completely." He shrugged. "Anyway, it's the best lead we've got."

Buddy turned down his mouth. "It's our *only* lead. We've got some physical evidence—the delay devices we've picked up at the fires. The one we found last night has a pretty good fingerprint on it, too. But that's the only thing that could point us directly to the arsonist." He paused. "It's about time we got a lucky break."

Out on the field, the Academy band had formed itself into a giant letter D and was playing the first few bars of "When Johnny Comes Marching Home Again," with Wilma Pearl Franklin soloing on the piccolo and a pair of pretty baton twirlers in short white skirts and tall white boots strutting their stuff in front of the band. There was appreciative applause from the bleachers and a couple of wolf whistles.

"Say you spot the egg on the tire and feel like you've got your man. Then what?" Mr. Moseley wanted to know. He raised his voice over the music. "Kinda good to think these things out ahead of time."

"Take him in for questioning, I guess," Buddy replied—slowly, because he hadn't thought much further than finding the Ford and identifying the driver. "Impound the car, someplace where it won't get rained on," he added. "And search it. We might find one of those delay devices the arsonist is using to set the fires. We might oughtta get a search warrant for his house, too. Could maybe find something there. Oh, and get his fingerprints," he added.

"Sounds like that pretty much covers the bases," Mr. Moseley remarked approvingly. "At least for now. If you want that warrant, you'll find Judge McHenry in his chambers. He said he didn't intend to waste five minutes listening to Long's campaign speech." He put his hat back on. "You reckon your man will give you any trouble?"

Buddy frowned. "Kinda hard to answer that, since we don't know who he is yet." He didn't like trouble, which was why he'd hired Wayne. The more trouble there was, the better the deputy seemed to like it.

Mr. Moseley nodded. "Well, if he does, you just put up a holler. There're several folks up there in the stands who are pretty riled up about these fires, especially the cotton gin. Picking season is coming up and the farmers don't like the idea of hauling their cotton all the way over to Monroeville." He grinned mirthlessly. "They'd jump at the chance to help you collar this fellow and give him a piece of their minds."

The Academy band swung into a rousing rendition of "Dixie" and the twirlers began a new routine with a complicated series of vertical and horizontal twirls and coordinated aerials. The spectators in the bleachers stood up to sing along, and somebody unfurled a flag.

"They might even prefer it if the sheriff and I would just step back and let them thump on him," Wayne drawled. There was a hint of amusement in his voice.

"I don't disagree," Mr. Moseley said. "But I doubt he'll give them the chance. Arsonists are a cowardly lot, by and large. That's why they do what they do, the way they do it. I don't think he'll make any trouble for you. Just lay out the evidence, clear and simple. He should be able to see that you've got the goods on him." He turned to go. "With luck, he'll give up and we'll get a plea. Save everybody the trouble of a trial."

It didn't exactly happen that way, though.

# CHAPTER NINETEEN

# EXTINGUISHED

WHEN LIZZY LEARNED THAT SENATOR LONG'S WEDNESDAY afternoon speech had been moved from the courthouse square to the Boll Weevils' baseball field, she had decided she wouldn't go. The day promised to be cloudless and hotter than blazes, the field offered no shade, and she wasn't that interested in the senator's message. In fact, she had the distinct impression that Long was more of a sideshow than a serious candidate, and probably not worth listening to.

Mr. Moseley (who had just gotten back from a few days in Montgomery) had a different idea. When he heard that Huey Long would be making a campaign speech in Darling that afternoon, he insisted that they go—not because he thought the senator was *worth* hearing, but because he felt obliged to hear what Long had to say.

"I hope Roosevelt is taking that man seriously," Mr. Moseley said in an ominous tone. "Long is as corrupt as a dead skunk crawling with maggots. But where voters are concerned, those catchy slogans of his have a strong populist appeal—strong enough to fire up a third-party challenge and knock FDR out of the White House in '36. If Huey does that, he can put himself into the presidency in '40, and then it's Katy bar the door." His face was dark. "I'd hate to think what would happen with

Long in the Oval Office and Hitler and Mussolini threatening to gobble up Europe and Africa."

Lizzy shivered. "You don't *really* think that's going to happen, do you? Long in the Oval Office, I mean."

She wasn't sure about the "gobble" part, either. Hitler was frightening, and the Nuremberg rallies she had seen in the newsreels made her anxious. It certainly looked like a storm was brewing. Surely the Nazis couldn't wield enough power to threaten all of Europe, though. Could they?

But Mr. Moseley was still talking about Senator Long. "I don't think he's likely to get elected in '36. But he has a lot of support out there, especially across the South and the Midwest. That's why we ought to listen to what the man has to say. Hear what he's promising people."

When she was still slow to say yes, he added, "Well, *I'm* going, Liz, and I wish you'd go with me. We can hear Long out, then drive over to Monroeville and sample that new Cajun-Creole eatery. The Jambalaya Shack, it's called." He gave her an appreciative glance. "You look pretty in that yellow dress, like you're ready for an evening out with an old friend. And I'm told that the Shack gets three or four sacks of oysters every Wednesday afternoon, fresh from Mobile Bay. If we leave right after Long's talk, we might get a dozen before they're gone."

Lizzy had the feeling that there was something behind this invitation. Had Mr. Moseley somehow heard about Ryan Nichols and wanted to make sure she didn't mope around, feeling sorry for herself? But that didn't seem likely. He had come back from Montgomery late the night before and appeared in the office by nine that morning. *She* hadn't mentioned it, of course. Who else might have told him? Verna? Ophelia? Mr. Duffy?

There wasn't any answer to that question, of course. It wouldn't matter, anyway—he would find out sooner or later. That's just how Darling was. No matter how hard you might try to keep a secret, it was bound to get out. Mr. Moseley made it a point to know everything that happened in town. He would certainly hear that Ryan had lied about being single, probably from Alvin Duffy himself.

"Well, I can't say no to fresh oysters." She managed a laugh and handed him the stack of invoices she had typed the day before. He always reviewed them, in case he wanted to make adjustments for deserving people who couldn't pay their bills. That was one of the things she had always admired about Bent Moseley. He cared about his clients' welfare.

"That's terrific," Mr. Moseley said with satisfaction, taking the invoices. "It'll be something to look forward to, while we bake our brains in the sun and listen to Long firing up the crowd." He grinned. "Inside of fifteen minutes, he'll have them all convinced that he's the only one who can fix what ails America. Unless they vote for him, they'll be chewing on their old boots for beef jerky and begging the Red Cross for a sack of cornmeal and a bushel of sweet potatoes. That's one of his favorite lines, you know. It shows up in every speech. We'll probably hear it this afternoon."

⊛

THAT WAS WHY LIZZY FOUND HERSELF SITTING ON THE FOURTH (and next to the top) row of the bleachers under her yellow umbrella, watching Mr. Moseley make his way across the field to talk with Sheriff Norris and Deputy Springer at the gate. Tall, lean, and athletic, he wasn't especially good-looking. But he had an air of confident command and personal authority that inspired respect in most people—and in Lizzy, admiration.

Around her, the bleachers were filling up. In the rows below, Lizzy could see quite a few Dahlias. There was Bessie Bloodworth, sitting between Aunt Hetty Little and Miss Rogers,

Darling's librarian. Miss Rogers was wearing that funny little feathered hat that she always wore to revival meetings, while Aunt Hetty wore a wide-brimmed purple straw hat and Bessie was bareheaded. Farther down, on the front row, she could see Earlynne Biddle and Mildred Kilgore, with Violet Sims and her little girl, Cupcake, and Uncle Hiram Bond and his big accordion, part of the entertainment for today's event. Beulah Trivette and Bettina Higgens sat right behind them, chatting with Alice Ann Walker. Verna wasn't far away, with Mr. Duffy. And just behind them sat Charlie Dickens, with a man Lizzy had never seen before. He was probably Charlie's newspaper-reporter friend, the one Lizzy had heard about—Virgil somebody, who covered Senator Long for one of the wire services. Doc Roberts, Darling's family doctor, was sitting with them, eating a hot dog.

Everybody in the bleachers seemed to be keeping an eye on the gate beyond left field, where the senator was expected to drive in. Lizzy wondered whether they were all fervent Long supporters. Or maybe they had come (as she had) because somebody else insisted. Or because Long was always making the news and they wanted to see for themselves. Or because they didn't have anything better to do and were looking for entertainment.

On the speaker's platform, Benny Biddle was crouching behind the podium, fiddling with a microphone and some wires—the hookup to WDAR, Lizzy guessed. Behind him, on the field, the band was now playing the opening bars of "The Stars and Stripes Forever," her favorite Sousa march. It was upbeat and stirring and as she listened, she smiled—and then found herself smiling because . . . well, because she was smiling.

She had gone to bed the night before feeling disillusioned and deceived. Angry, too, and not just at Ryan. Almost as much as he had used her, she had allowed herself to be used. She would never let that happen again, she vowed.

But when she got up this morning and looked at herself in her dressing table mirror, she promised her reflection that she wasn't going to let bitterness poison her life. She had put Ryan Nichols behind her. She had been foolish, but luckily, her heart wasn't broken, only a little dented. She had escaped his deceit and her mistake without serious damage to her sense of self-worth or her personal integrity. She would go on with her work for Mr. Moseley. She would spend more time on her new book. There might be something missing in her life, but it was full enough.

So while Daffy watched from the foot of her bed, Lizzy had brushed her hair until it shone, put on some bright lipstick and a little rouge, and buttoned herself into a sunny yellow cotton dress with a white portrait collar, white-cuffed short sleeves, and a white belt. Today, she would *make* herself smile.

But now she realized that smiling didn't take any real effort. She had lots to smile about, even if she had to sit through an hour of Huey Long's political bombast. She and her friend Bent—*not* Mr. Moseley, since they were out of the office—were going to enjoy a plate of fresh oysters and some different and tasty food at the new restaurant in Monroeville. And when Verna put up a hand and waved at her, she waved back with a big smile.

A few moments later, Bent had finished his conversation with the sheriff and was climbing the bleachers to resume his seat beside her. He had stopped at Mr. Turnbuckle's refreshment stand and was carrying a white paper bag full of hot buttered popcorn and a couple of bottles of cold Dr Pepper. He sat down beside her and handed her one of the bottles.

"Since we've come to watch the circus," he said, "I thought we should have some popcorn and soda pop."

The two of them munched in silent appreciation for a while, listening to the band, now playing the Alabama state song that had been adopted a few years ago. Everybody stood up and some tried to sing along. But since the song had seven verses and almost nobody knew the words, all but a few had to stop singing. Most people managed to join the last line of the verses, though: *Alabama, Alabama, we will aye be true to thee . . .*

Lizzy and Bent sat down again. The band finished "Alabama" and the players began shuffling through their music, looking for the next song. Bent ate another handful of popcorn. And then, his eyes on the field, he spoke into the silence.

"I've closed the Montgomery office, Liz."

"Closed—" Startled, Lizzy turned to stare at him. "But . . . but *why?*" She handled the billing, so she knew the office hadn't been losing money.

He ate another kernel of popcorn, then another. "Judge McHenry and the Cypress County commissioners have decided to make the county attorney's position full time and elective. They've asked me to serve until the next election. I've agreed."

Lizzy blinked, still trying to process this unexpected news. "But that question has come up before and you've said no. Why are you saying yes now?"

"Because I don't like what I'm doing in Montgomery," he said finally. "I don't like what everybody has to do, when they work in a city where every single decision is fueled by political ambition." Another kernel. "I don't like the way I feel when I'm working on a case that isn't as . . . as clean as I wish it were. There's nothing I can do to change things. So I've decided to get out."

*As clean as I wish it were?* Lizzy couldn't see his face, but she knew him well enough to know that there was more here, and she needed to know what it was. She took a deep breath. "Does Mr. Jackman's indictment have anything to do with this?"

Surprised, he slid a sidelong look at her. "You know about that?"

"I read about it," she said. "In the newspaper." A few weeks before, she had picked up a copy of the *Montgomery Advertiser* from Mr. Moseley's desk. On the front page, below a black banner headline, was a story about a power company executive and two attorneys who had been indicted on criminal charges of mail fraud, wire fraud, and bribery. The charges related to land that the Tennessee Valley Authority was acquiring for a dam on the Tennessee River in northern Alabama. If the three men went to trial and were found guilty, they would face heavy fines and lengthy prison terms. One of the attorneys was Jeremy Jackman, a close friend from Mr. Moseley's law-school days and an associate in the Montgomery office.

And of course Lizzy knew Mr. Jackman. He was the attorney for whom she had worked immediately after Grady's marriage to Sandra. He had been kind enough to hire her for a few months so she could escape from Darling and its inevitable gossip. And it was Mrs. Jackman who had introduced her to Nadine Fleming, now her literary agent. Whether Mr. Jackman was found guilty or innocent, the scandal was likely to end his legal career. Lizzy knew it must be difficult for both of them.

Bent leaned forward, propping his elbows on his knees, eyes on the field. "I've agreed to help with Jeremy's defense, of course. But I've been considering this decision for nearly a year. I stopped taking new clients a couple of months ago and the ones who are left are being transferred to another lawyer." He turned toward her. "I'm coming back to Darling, Liz. I'm going to practice the kind of law I *really* want to practice, in a place where I can be who I am. Who I want to be. It's as simple as that, really."

He spoke with controlled passion, and Lizzy didn't doubt him. He had often spoken about his unhappiness with what he called "big-city law," which was heavily influenced by the cut-and-slash politicking that went on in the state's capital—as opposed to "country law," which was what he practiced in rural Cypress County.

But there was something in Bent's voice that made her suspect that perhaps this wasn't the whole truth, or the only truth. Was there something about the Jackman indictment—about the bribery scandal itself—that had made Bent decide to pull out of Montgomery? Was he implicated? He had business dealings across the state, and it wouldn't be a surprise if the sale of land to the TVA was one of them. Was he involved in the scandal in some way or another? He held out the bag of popcorn and she took a few kernels. If he was, she didn't think she wanted to know about it.

Or maybe his decision had something to do with Moira Skelton, who (from everything that Liz had heard about her) was an adroit political animal. Perhaps Moira had decided to end their relationship, and Bent had chosen this way to deal with his disappointment. Perhaps he had asked her to marry him and move to Darling and she had laughed and said that was ridiculous.

In the years Liz had worked in the law office, she had learned that decisions could be a lot like onions: made up of tightly wrapped layers, some so deeply hidden that they were impossible to reach and even more impossible to fully understand. She had the feeling that there was more to closing the Montgomery office than Bent wanted her to know just now. More, perhaps, than he knew. And certainly more than *she* wanted to know.

So she asked a different question—an easier one, on the face of it, but one that also had to be answered. It was a worrisome question, since it concerned her paycheck. But she made her voice as casual as she could.

"If you close the Montgomery office, can we afford to keep the Darling office open?"

While Mr. Moseley's Montgomery clients generally paid their legal bills on time and in real dollars, the Darling clients were more likely to pay late and in kind. A client might bring a half-dozen laying hens to the office, for instance, or a fat pig. They had received a bushel of peaches in June, sweet corn and watermelons in July, potatoes and pumpkins at Thanksgiving, a half-cord of firewood at Christmas. The Montgomery office had always brought in more money—and in lean times, it had actually kept the Darling office afloat.

Bent gave a careless shrug, as if this was the last thing on his mind. "The county attorney's job will be a paid position. Anyway, it doesn't matter, Liz. We make more money in the capital city, it's true. But money isn't what I need. What I need *most* is to get out of the political rat race, not get dragged deeper into it." His voice was gruff. "And out of Montgomery. There, it's hard to say no, especially to . . . certain people."

He fell silent, and Lizzy understood that, while he wanted her to think that money wasn't important, the question was simply one he wasn't prepared to answer right now. And saying no to certain people . . . was he thinking of Moira Skelton? She had met the woman only a few times, but she had the feeling that absence might make Miss Skelton's heart grow fonder—and then what? Would she make an effort to reclaim the man who got away? Lizzy thought briefly of what Edna Fay had said about Miss Skelton's "duplicity" being a hazard for Bent but then pushed the thought away. She was never one to invent trouble where trouble didn't exist. Moira Skelton—past, present, or future—was Bent's business, not hers.

He cleared his throat. "I made the announcement at the end of last week. There's the Jackman case and one or two others that I'll be handling from here. There'll be a few court appearances in the city, but aside from those, I'll be in Darling full time." His chuckle was slightly rueful. "There'll be two of us in the office, five days a week, from now on. Are you ready for that, Liz?"

Lizzy didn't have to give her answer any thought at all. The words came easily, quickly. "You know I'm with you, whatever you choose to do."

His eyes met and held hers. "Yes," he said. "I know that. I've even been hoping that we might—"

He didn't get to finish his sentence. There was a stir in the crowd around them. A man shouted "Hey, here comes Huey!"

Somebody else cried, "Lookee over there, folks—it's the Kingfish! He's here!"

Everyone turned to look out past left field, toward the gate. Cheering and whistling, people began to wave the little American and rebel flags they had brought. Signs went up: DARLING FOR HUEY. WE LOVE SENATOR LONG! TAKE THE LONG WAY TO THE WHITE HOUSE! The band struck up a bouncy, energetic "Hail, Hail, the Gang's All Here" as a gleaming blue Cadillac sedan with white sidewall tires and a US flag fluttering from its hood ornament drove through the gate, closely flanked by two sleek black Chevys.

There was more cheering as the entourage sped across the field and stopped beside the speaker's platform. The Chevrolets' doors popped open and six very large men in dark suits and fedora hats jumped out, forming a protective pod around the Cadillac. Several wore their jackets conspicuously open to reveal guns on their hips. One was holding a large paper bag, which looked to Lizzy as if it might conceal a weapon. All of them kept their eyes on the crowd, which had begun a rhythmic foot-stamping, accompanied by a loud chant, "Huey, Huey, Huey!"

Lizzy felt a chill. "Those men," she said, under the noise. "They're his bodyguards?"

"That's right," Bent replied tersely. "Long has at least six around him at all times—the bigger the better, all of them armed. The man may be paranoid, but he has reason to be." He glanced at the crowd in the bleachers. "Yes, plenty of people love him. But just as many hate him. And for all anybody knows, there could be a hater right here."

The Academy band marched around the right end of the platform and sat down in the folding chairs lined up on the field. Darling Mayor Jed Snow, Share Our Wealth Club president Earlynne Biddle, Reverend Peters, little Cupcake, and Uncle Hiram Bond (carrying his accordion) got up from their front-row bleacher seats and filed up the platform steps to take chairs behind the speaker's podium. Benny Biddle handed Cupcake a microphone and—Shirley Temple style—she performed a spirited song-and-tap-dance version of the senator's campaign song, with Uncle Hiram accompanying her on his accordion. She was cute as a button, Lizzy thought, in a perky red and white pinafore over a blue dress, and her tap dancing was flawless.

When Cupcake had finished her song and while everybody was applauding, the Cadillac's door burst open and the senator popped out like a genie out of a bottle. He was of average height, but because he was inches shorter than his oversized bodyguards around him, he looked like a dwarf. His white suit was rumpled, his red bow tie was crooked, and his bulbous nose made him look like a W. C. Fields cartoon. As the crowd roared, he grinned toothily and flung both hands high over his head, fingers in the classic V-for-victory sign. He stood for a moment, grinning and gesturing, then dashed up the platform stairs while the crowd rose to its collective feet and began to stamp and shout.

The six men in dark suits who had jumped out of the two black Chevys now stationed themselves at attention at either end of the speaker's platform, alertly scanning the crowd. Senator Long took the only empty seat on the platform as Jed Snow got up to introduce Reverend Peters. The reverend offered a lengthy seven-paragraph prayer, calling down blessings on those on the platform and in the bleachers, as well as on shut-ins who couldn't come out today, and especially on their good brother Huey P. Long, may the Lord continue to smile on him. Then Earlynne Biddle got up and said that the Darling Share Our Wealth Club was astonishingly proud to welcome the amazing Senator Long to their humble little town, and without further ado, here was Senator Long!

And then Huey Long went up to the microphone and told them that he wasn't going to make a speech. He had just dropped in to say hello to all the fine Darlin' friends who had gone to the trouble of gatherin' in the blazin' sunshine to hear him today. No speech, just a few words off the top of his head and from the bottom—indeed, the *very bottom*—of his heart. With great earnestness, he clasped both hands over the left side of his chest, to show where his heart was.

But he was afraid his few words weren't very happy words, and for that, he sincerely apologized in advance. What had to be said *had to be said, howsomever, and he was a-goin' to say it.*

And then, in a twangy, slangy, folksy, booming voice that could be heard in the top row of the bleachers and beyond, the senator began his speech—the same speech-that-wasn't-a-speech that he had given in Birmingham and Atlanta and St. Louis and points west.

"Now I know you folks have heard it said many a time that the saddest words of tongue or pen are these, 'It might have been.' But I have to tell you Darlin' people that the saddest words I have for you are '*I told you so*,' which I say and have said and will go on sayin' as long as the good Lord gives me breath." He chuckled, and as a kind of aside, said, "I used to get things done by addin' please when I asked folks to do something. Now, I don't bother with that. I just dynamite the naysayers outta my path and get on with the bidness."

He paused for the laughter, then pulled himself up on his tiptoes, leaned forward, and whispered into the microphone. "Yes, you heard me right a minute ago, folks. I told you so. I *told* you—'"

He straightened up and slapped the podium hard with the flat of his hand. It sounded like a gunshot and everybody jumped. "I *told* you folks that the government of the US of A was out to take ever' penny of what little you've got and give it to the rich folks and the bankers and the big corporations on Wall Street. And I *told* you that if we're a-gonna make America great again, we have got to put a stop to the dastardly, low-down, double-dealing that comes out of the White House and the halls of Congress and gets parroted and praised in the newspapers, which are full of nothin' but *fake news*." Another pause, this time for a murmur of agreement. "And today I aim to tell you just how we're a-gonna do this—how we are a-gonna make every man a king, and all you wimmin and childern too!"

"AMEN, brother!" a man shouted from the bleachers. "We're a-gonna be kings! Hear that, folks? We are all a-gonna be KINGS! Praise the Lord!"

And with that, the crowd jumped to its feet, erupting into another roar, and kept on roaring until Huey raised his arms and made them sit down again. When they were almost quiet, he swung into a rambling story about a poor Alabama dirt farmer who was trying his gol-darndest best to grow cotton on his measly little fifty-some acres.

"Which he farms," Huey said, "with the help of his five strappin' boys and his faithful mule, Petunia. Yes, that was her name, Petunia, and she was a beauty, she was. One hundred percent mule and stubborn as God made her.

"But come last year, Mr. Roosevelt's New Deal gov'ment wouldn't let that farmer plant but a third of his usual crop— and how is he goin' to make any money a-doin' *that*?" (Another loud slap on the podium.) "I *ask* you now, people, how in the sweet name of Jesus is our poor farmer a-gonna earn enough to feed his family over the winter and buy seed for the next spring's plantin'? You know the answer, yes, you do. You know down deep in your heart that by the end of the year this poor fella and his five fine boys and his sweet little wife will be chewin' their old leather boots for beef jerky and beggin' the Red Cross for—"

The senator was interrupted by several loud shouts and the slam of a car door at the left-field gate. He broke off and turned apprehensively, his attention caught by the unexpected clamor. Lizzy, who had been totally mesmerized by his speech, followed his glance. She saw a man sprinting across the outfield in the direction of the speaker's stand, the sheriff and his deputy in hot pursuit. The sheriff was shouting "Police! Stop! Stop where you are, or we'll fire!"

But the man didn't stop. The deputy raised the gun in his hand and fired a couple of warning shots into the air, the sounds crashing like clenched fists against the people in the bleachers. The man was still running, zigzagging now. In the stands, boys shouted. Dogs barked. Women screamed. Men yelled. Somebody cried, "He's a-comin' for Huey! Look out, Huey! Duck!"

Bent put his arm out and yanked Lizzy close against him, shielding her. "Stay down, Liz," he commanded roughly. But she pulled away from him and sat up straight to see what was happening.

"Stop!" the sheriff shouted again. "Stop!"

But the man only ran harder. Now, they could see that he had something in his hand. Lizzy gasped. "He's got a gun, Bent! Isn't that a *gun?*"

Was it a gun? Was it? Yes, she was sure it *was* a gun, or a knife or something, and the man was running toward the platform, clearly intent on reaching Long and—

And then, from the left end of the speaker's platform came the brutal blast of a shotgun punctuated by a volley of loud, fast pop-pop-pops. The man staggered, stumbled, and fell face down on the field, arms flung wide. The sheriff ran up and dropped to his knees beside the motionless figure. In the stands where he was sitting with Charlie Dickens, Doc Roberts scrambled to his feet, snatched up the medical bag he always had with him, and charged down the bleachers on his way to the field.

Bent got up too. "You stay here," he commanded Lizzy, and followed the doctor. This time, she obeyed.

At the same moment, one of Long's burly bodyguards rushed to the senator, wrapped his arms around him, and bundled him off the platform, down the steps, and into the blue Cadillac. The guard dove into the car behind the senator and slammed the door. The motor started with a backfire that sounded like another gunshot, then the car spun its wheels and took off in the direction of the gate. The other bodyguards piled into their two Chevys and raced after the Cadillac. A few moments later, the entire entourage was speeding across the outfield, through the gate, and down the road, throwing up a cloud of dust behind them.

In the stands, there was a stunned silence. Then: "Where's he a-goin'?" somebody cried. "Where is Huey a-goin'?"

"To the devil," came the wry answer. "Where he come from."

"Oh, he'll come back," another man said, but he didn't

seem very certain. "You wait. You'll see. He'll turn around and come back."

"Like heck he will," a woman replied, sounding disgusted. "He's up'n left for good. He didn't even finish his *sentence*."

"Well, this a fine how-do-you-do," groused a gray-haired farmer in bib overalls and a blue work shirt. "I come all the way here from Piney Grove and missed a good day's plowin' just to hear the Kingfish, and now he's jumped in his Caddy and drove off."

"You'd run off, too, I reckon," somebody remarked defensively, "if'n a feller came at you with a gun."

"Was that a gun?" a woman asked. "It looked to me like a soda pop bottle he was wavin' around."

"Is he dead?" a boy cried excitedly. "The deputy shot that man *dead*, didn't he?"

"Not the deputy," his mother corrected him. "Them others, son. Huey's guards."

"Way I saw it," a young man ventured helpfully, "that feller was runnin' away from the sheriff, not runnin' at Huey. But the guards, from where they was, they couldn't tell the diff'rence. They was just doin' their job."

"Coulda told if they'd bothered to look," someone put in grimly. "And that warn't no gun in that feller's hand, it was a soda pop bottle. Saw it myself. He couldn't of done much harm with a soda pop bottle."

"They sure poured a bucketful of lead into him," a man said somberly. "If he ain't dead, he will be soon. They didn't need to of done it." This prompted a chorus of disgruntled agreement.

"Them guards'ud druther shoot than anything else."

"Trigger happy, is whut they are."

"Who is that guy on the ground? Anybody know is he *really* dead?"

"Cain't see who he is, but he looks dead to me. Deader'n a door nail."

"Well, maybe he ain't, after all. Lookee there. Doc's got him movin' around a bit."

The crowd peered resentfully at the little clutch of men gathered around the figure sprawled on the field—who was indeed, Lizzy saw, beginning to stir. Doc Roberts, who had been kneeling beside the sheriff, now stood and said something to the deputy, who turned and ran for the sheriff's squad car. In a few moments, the man on the ground had been transferred to the back seat of the automobile and the deputy and the doctor were driving off, fast.

"Well, at least he ain't entirely dead," somebody said. "Doc's prob'ly takin' him to the hospital over in Monroeville." Lizzy couldn't be sure whether he was relieved or disappointed.

The man who had left his plowing, however, was clearly irritated. "No reason why Huey couldn't just of gone on with his speech, 'stead of leaving us lookin' at one another like idjuts. I'll be gol-*darned* if I vote for him now."

The crowd in the bleachers, feeling deeply discontented, continued to mutter. But out on the field, the Academy band's director sprang out of his chair, waved his baton smartly, and the band swung into a jaunty rendition of "Alexander's Ragtime Band." On the platform, the Darling dignitaries were leaving. Benny Biddle unplugged the microphone and gathered up the wires he had laid. In the stands, people began to pick up their things and head for their vehicles, still muttering.

Lizzy joined Bent and Sheriff Norris on the field. "Afraid we'll have to take a rain check on those oysters, Liz," Bent told her regretfully. "The sheriff and I are headed for the hospital. Doc says Foster will probably make it, so Buddy's going to try to get a statement from him as soon as he's in any shape to talk. I want to be there."

"A statement from . . . *Foster*?" Lizzy repeated. "You're saying that was *Teddy Foster* who got shot? The owner of the cotton gin?"

"Yeah," the deputy said, sounding satisfied. "The arsonist got doused with a shower of lead. Huey's boys put out his fire for sure."

Lizzy could scarcely believe her ears. "Ted Foster set fire to his own family's business? But why in the world—" And then she understood. "For the insurance, I suppose. And he set the other fires to—"

"Confuse us," the sheriff said.

"Cover his tracks," Bent said. "I'll fill in the details after I've heard Foster's story." He put a hand on her arm. "Over craw-dads, if those oysters are already gone." His fingers tightened. "Okay?"

"Okay," Lizzy said.

And it was.

# CHAPTER TWENTY

# HOT STUFF

*Thursday, September 5, 1935*

As they had expected, the oysters were gone when Lizzy and Bent got to the Jambalaya Shack on Thursday evening. Lizzy had grown up eating crawdads (also called crawfish, crawdaddies, and Alabama mudbugs) and knew that it was a messy business. So she wore a washable cotton plaid blouse and a denim skirt and planned to tuck a napkin into the collar of her blouse, bib-style.

The Jambalaya Shack turned out to be just that—a small cooking shack perched uneasily on the bank of a slow-moving creek, under a heavy overhang of dark trees. The shack was surrounded on three sides by a screened-in porch veiled in vines, with fans turning slowly in the ceiling and roll-down brown canvas curtains (in place of walls) to protect diners from the rain. The porch was crowded with sawhorse tables and benches of various sizes, the tables spread with red plaid oilcloth and centered with tin cans filled with cheerful bouquets of local wildflowers and weeds. Inside the shack, a Victrola was playing dance music, snatches of song audible above the sound of voices, occasional loud laughter, and the rattle of dishes.

Jimmy Ray Ricketts, another Darling lawyer, had ridden to Monroeville with them to pick up his newly repaired car, so Lizzy had to wait to hear the latest news from the hospital about Teddy Foster, now thought to be the arsonist who had terrorized Darling. She had her first question ready when Bent came back to the table after putting in their crawdad order. He brought Mason pint jars filled with sweetened iced tea, a basket of crispy hushpuppies, a bowl of Cajun dipping sauce, and a couple of plates.

"How *is* he?" she asked, as he put the food down. "Teddy Foster, I mean. Is he going to be all right?"

She knew Foster, of course. Everybody knew him. He came from a leading Darling family, all of whom were active in the community. His father—dead for several years—had been a member of the local Lions Club, his mother was active in the Methodist Ladies Guild, one sister was a schoolteacher, the other was a nurse at the Monroeville Hospital, and his wife—a former Miss Cotton—did the gin's bookkeeping. If Teddy really *was* the arsonist, Lizzy knew that the whole family would share in the tragedy.

"He's lucky, that's how he is," Bent said, tasting his tea and adding more sugar. "Both pistol shooters missed—not surprising, given the range and the moving target. And it was lucky that Teddy was thirty-some yards away from McQuiston's sawed-off shotgun. A dozen paces closer and Doc Rogers says he'd be a dead man." He nodded at the basket. "Hushpuppies, please."

Lizzy handed it to him. "I suppose the bodyguards opened fire because they thought he was aiming to attack Senator Long."

"That seems to be the general assumption," Bent said. "Foster claims that he had no such intention. He was running because he was panicked. And because two lawmen had him pegged as the arsonist and were hotfooting it after him." He dipped a hushpuppy into the spicy Cajun sauce. "He was trying to get away. His bad luck to run into enemy fire."

Lizzy broke a hushpuppy apart, and dipped half of it. "Long's guards—the men who did the shooting. Will you charge them?" The warm sauce was bold and spicy, a just-right accompaniment to the hushpuppies.

Bent grunted. "I would if we could make it stick. But we have a weak case. McQuiston would claim he thought Foster had a gun in his hand and plead self-defense. We'd have to seek extradition from Louisiana, and Long would almost certainly order the state's attorney general to fight it. Anyway, the sheriff and Judge McHenry and I talked it over. Like it or not, we're letting it go. No charges."

Reluctantly, Lizzy could see the wisdom in that. "What about the arsons?"

Bent's grin was crooked. "An entirely different matter. There, we have *evidence*. In fact, the evidence is so good, I don't think we'll have to go to trial. It may take a while, but Foster will plead."

The Victrola was playing a jazzy version of "I Wanna Be Loved by You." A boy came up with a lard pail full of steaming-hot crawfish. He spread several layers of newspapers on the table between them and upended the lard pail. The bright red crawdads, redolent with sauce, spilled out onto the newspaper. He put the lard pail on the table. "For the shells," he said, before he left. "Don't throw 'em on the floor."

"Evidence?" Lizzy asked. "What kind of evidence? I haven't heard of any witnesses—unless you count Earlynne, and she only saw the back of the arsonist's head."

"True. But she socked his vehicle with a sack of eggs." Bent said. "The sheriff has impounded the spare tire. There's dried egg all over it. I'm sure that Mrs. Biddle would be glad to tell a jury how it got there. She felt she was defending her son's radio station, you know." He picked up another crawdad. "But there's more. The tampons we found in his car, for instance."

Lizzy stared at him. "*Tampons?*"

"Yep." Bent grasped the crawdad in one hand and the tail in

the other. He pinched the tail, twisted, and pulled out a chunk of tail meat.

"Yes. You know." He kept his eyes on his crawdad. "Those things that women use for—"

"I *know* what tampons are, Bent," Lizzy said. She could feel herself flushing. "I brought a box back from New York so my mother could order them for the dime store. She's keeping them under the counter. Mr. Lima isn't carrying them at the drug store," she added. "I heard that he doesn't approve of them." It had something to do, Ophelia had told her, with the fear that girls who used them might no longer be virgins. Which seemed pretty ridiculous to both of them, since you were a virgin until you had sex. With a man. Tampons were not the same thing at all.

Bent dipped the tail meat in the sauce and popped it into his mouth. "Another mystery solved. I was wondering where they came from." His eyes were twinkling. "I might have guessed you were somehow involved. They did seem a little . . . avant-garde for Darling."

Trying not to smile, Lizzy picked up a crawdad. "But what I *don't* understand is why tampons are evidence in an arson case."

"Because," Bent said, "Foster used them to start his fires. He dipped the ends in kerosene and planted them with a match-book where they were likely to start a fire. In fact, we have a fingerprint."

Somebody had changed the record, and a band began playing "Blue Is the Night." Lizzy looked up. "A fingerprint?" she asked doubtfully. "On *cotton*?"

"No. On the cardboard tube. The sheriff found one, only partially burned, at the cotton gin fire. It's Foster's fingerprint."

"That sounds pretty conclusive," Lizzy said, working on her crawdad.

"It is." Bent licked sauce off his fingers. "Jimmy Ray has

agreed to represent him. When I told him about the fingerprint, he said he'll advise Foster to plead to whatever charges
we come up with. Thankfully, nobody's been hurt in any of the
fires, so we have some room to negotiate."

"I'm glad to hear that," Lizzy said, thinking of the family.
"This is so hard for everybody. I saw his mother today. She looked
just awful. And his sisters and his wife—" She shook her head.
"I suppose he burned the cotton gin for the insurance money."

"That's right. A note was coming due at the bank, a very large
loan that he had inherited from his father, along with the gin.
Alvin Duffy told him that the bank couldn't renew it, so he
knew he'd have to come up with the money from somewhere.
The insurance was the only thing he could think of. The other
fires, before and after, were set to cover up the *real* motive. He
says he didn't mean for any of them to be very serious." Bent
took a sip of tea. "Except for the radio station. That one, he set
because he had a longtime grudge against Marvin Musgrove,
the father of one of the WDAR boys. Says Marvin cheated his
father out of some money. So he thought he'd take the opportunity to get even."

Lucy shook her head. "The only saving grace is that nobody
was hurt in any of the fires. What if somebody had *died?*"

"Then he'd be facing a murder charge," Bent said. "Foster
says he filched the tampons from his wife's supply. Which
she bought at the dime store. And your mother ordered them
because *you—*"

"But I had absolutely nothing to do with arson," Lizzy protested. "Anyway, it sounds like Teddy Foster was determined to
set those fires. If he hadn't used . . . what he used, he would've
used something else."

"Of course." Bent reached for another crawdad. "I was just
thinking that actions have consequences. And that sometimes
we don't know what those consequences are until it's too late."

He was silent for a moment, intent on the crawdad in his fingers. "Speaking of consequences, Al Duffy told me about Ryan Nichols, Liz. What he found out when he ran that credit check, I mean."

"Oh." Lizzy sighed. "Oh, dear. I wish . . . I wish Mr. Duffy hadn't told you. It's really not—"

"Look, Liz." He met her eyes. "You may not want to talk about this, but I have to say that I'm sorry for what happened. I know that you and Nichols . . . that you had something going between you for a while. I even . . ." He looked down again. "I even envied the two of you."

"Envied?" That surprised her.

"Well, envied him, anyway." He smiled crookedly. "I know how good it feels to have somebody you can count on. To tell the truth, I figured him for a lucky guy. So, yes. I'm sorry for the hurt this must have caused you."

She was surprised—and touched, too. Bent had been so busy and out of town so often this spring and summer. She didn't think he had noticed that she and Ryan were seeing one another when he was in Darling.

"You don't need to be sorry," she said honestly. "It's over and done. Ryan isn't really a bad person. And I was too ready to—"

"Don't make excuses for him, Liz," Bent said emphatically. "That jerk lied to you about something really important. Which makes him a bad person, in my book. *Evil*, in fact."

Lizzy attacked her crawdad, glad to have something to do with her fingers. "What I was saying when you interrupted me," she went on quietly, "is that I was too ready to believe him. To let myself be taken in."

Bent started to say something else, but she put up her hand to stop him.

"I can't blame Ryan for everything. There's enough blame to go around, and some of it is mine. And while I can't say that

I'm grateful for being taught a lesson, I can say that I'm glad it wasn't worse." She picked up another crawdad and twisted its tail.

Bent sighed. "Well, you're way ahead of me, then. And way more generous than I am. How do you do it?"

"Generous?" She tilted her head. "What do you mean?"

"Since we're sharing confidences—" He paused. "I let myself be taken in, too. By somebody who wasn't . . . everything she pretended to be." His mouth tightened and his voice took on a bitter edge. "But I doubt that I'll ever be able to say I'm glad it wasn't worse. Because I don't think it could be."

Lizzy wanted to ask if he was talking about Moira Skelton— but what if he wasn't? What if there was somebody else? She had known this man for so long. She knew a great deal about the work he did—the politics, the legal work, both in Darling and in Montgomery. And yet she knew so little about him, who he *really* was.

But there was a good reason for that, wasn't there? In the time she'd worked in his law office, he had been married and divorced. After that, an attractive and eligible and sought-after bachelor, he had become rapidly involved with first one woman and then another and another, all of them in Montgomery, where he did most of his work. And then Moira Skelton, longest of all. He might be talking about somebody entirely new, as far as Lizzy knew.

She couldn't think what to say, so she only murmured something and reached for another crawdad. The shellfish might be messy eating, but they kept her hands busy—and gave her a good reason not to look at his face.

There was a long silence as they both concentrated on their food. At last, in a more neutral voice, he said, "Moira and I stopped seeing one another a couple of months ago."

Well, that dispelled that little mystery. She looked up. She didn't say she was sorry. Instead, she said, "That must have been . . . painful."

"Under the circumstances, it was," he said. "Very painful. It's taken me a while to put it behind me. I'm still working on that." He dropped a shell into the pail. "It looks like both of us—you and me, I mean—are . . . well, temporarily disconnected, if not free. So I was wondering if we might . . . well, if we might see one another. Outside of work, I mean."

"But we *have* been seeing one another," she said, confused. "We've been to the movies together. We—"

"I know. But what I'm thinking of would be more like . . . well, like a date. Like seeing how we feel about one another." His crooked grin came back and his voice lightened. "What do you think, Liz? Want to take a chance with me?"

*A chance?* Taken completely aback, Lizzy couldn't think what to say.

Seeing her hesitancy, he raised his hand. "Oh, hey, that's okay. Really. I'm sorry. I shouldn't be putting any pressure on you. I know that you probably need to take some time after . . . well, after that situation with Ryan Nichols. That's perfectly understandable. You must be thinking that it could be awkward, working together all day and going out together, after work. Understandable, too." He made a face. "And of course, I'm an old guy. That is, older than the other men you've dated."

"Older?" She was startled into speech. "I've never thought our ages had anything to do with it."

Which was true, actually. She knew that he was nine or ten years older, but she had never given their age difference a great deal of thought. There were so many other differences. Experience, education, the women he knew. He had always been so . . . inaccessible. Not remote, exactly. And close enough to reach out and touch—but very far away.

"Mmm." She looked at him curiously, then asked what

seemed to her to be the next logical question. "Do I seem too young to you?"

He laughed. "Too *young*? No, of course not." His laugh became a chuckle, then he sobered. "To be honest, I haven't thought of *your* age at all. Just of mine, and of the difference. I'm forty-four. And you must be—"

"Thirty-five," Lizzy said. "Old enough, as Verna says, to know better—but young enough to learn." Stoutly, she added, "Since you brought it up, no, I don't think of nine years as a terribly important difference. And as far as awkwardness in the office—well, I suppose we'd just have to wait and see."

She stopped, momentarily surprised by her boldness. Was this really *her*, talking like this to Mr. Moseley?

But at this moment, he was Bent, not Mr. Moseley, and what she had said felt right. So she went on. "We've worked together so long that I doubt it would be a serious problem."

His expression brightened. "Then you're saying we might . . ."

"Wait." She raised a finger. She had come this far, she might as well go the whole distance. "If there's one thing I've learned from the episode with Ryan Nichols, it's about the need for honesty. So I am going to be completely honest with you, Benton Moseley." She took a deep breath. "When I first came to work for you, and for years after, I had a silly schoolgirl crush on you."

"A *crush*?" he exclaimed, his eyes widening. "You're kidding. Really? I never had any idea. I—"

"Hush," she said firmly. "I managed to get over my crush a while back. I no longer suffer from it. But after what happened with Grady and then Ryan, I am not ready for *anything* other than friendship for a while. Maybe for a *long* while. So if you're looking for a hot and steamy romance to replace whatever you had with Moira Skelton or somebody else, don't look at me. I'm not your girl." She paused. "I'm not saying that's out of the picture forever. I'm just saying not now. And I don't know when. If ever." She narrowed her eyes at him. "Is that understood?"

"Understood?" He stared at her as if he were seeing her for the first time. After a moment, he muttered, "Understood. But about the crush, I have to say—"

"Hush," she said again. "I'm not finished. There's something else that this Ryan episode taught me. If I ever allow myself to get involved with a man again, it's going to be with someone who has no secrets from me. I don't mean that his past has to be an open book and he has to invite me to read every paragraph on every page. I just mean that there has to be no significant bit of hidden history that has the potential to pop up like a genie out of a bottle and change everything. Something like a wife and kids or a girlfriend with a child out of wedlock or—"

He was looking startled and she took pity on him. "I'm not suggesting that you have any big secrets tucked away, Bent. I'm just laying down some ground rules for myself and that man with no secrets in his pockets. I may not have met him yet. I may never meet him. He may not even exist. But if he happens to be you, please consider yourself on notice."

"A crush," he said softly, shaking his head. "If I may point out, *you* kept that secret all these years."

"Well, it's not a secret now, is it? And anyway, it's over." She smiled sweetly at him. "Now, if you don't mind, I'd love to dig into these delicious crawdads while they're still hot."

Looking bemused, Bent nodded. "Yes, ma'am," he said softly. "Yes, *ma'am*."

# CHAPTER TWENTY-ONE

# FIRE'S OUT

*Sunday, September 8–Wednesday September 11, 1935*

Sunday nights are "radio nights" in the Dickenses' flat above Fannie's hat shop on the Darling courthouse square. Around six, Charlie ties on an apron and makes something to eat, usually an easy soup-and-sandwich supper. Tonight it was grilled cheese sandwiches and chicken noodle soup out of a Campbell's can, which he and Fannie ate at the little table in front of the kitchen window.

Fannie was full of the news from Warm Springs, where she had been visiting her son. Yes, she thought Jason was stronger; he wasn't able to walk yet, but he maneuvered his little wheel-chair so expertly that he zipped around with very little trouble. No, he wouldn't be coming for a visit anytime soon. Warm Springs had its own educational program and his school was just about to start. But his rehabilitation supervisor thought he might come to Darling for a visit over the Thanksgiving holiday, so that was something to look forward to.

No, the president hadn't been at Warm Springs while she was there, but Mrs. Roosevelt and her friend Lorena Hickok had stopped in for dinner one night. They were on a driving tour, visiting CCC camps in the Southeast. Fannie had had a pleasant conversation with both of them and had learned that Mrs. Roosevelt—at the urging of Miss Hickok, an experienced journalist—was planning to start a daily newspaper column. She was calling it "My Day," which would be syndicated in dozens of newspapers.

"She says it will be a women's column," Fannie told Charlie, "but she'll also write about politics and current affairs."

"A *daily* column?" Charlie raised both eyebrows. "That's an enormous undertaking, on top of everything else she does. My guess: she won't last the year."

"I don't agree," Fannie said firmly. "She's committed. And she has plenty of grit. She'll keep it going, and Lorena will help. I've invited both of them to Darling," she went on. "They can visit Camp Briarwood and Mrs. Roosevelt can give a talk here in Darling on her pet topic, whatever it is at the time." She sniffed. "And don't roll your eyes at me, Charles Dickens. If Bessie Bloodworth and Earlynne Biddle can invite Huey Long, *I* can invite Mrs. Roosevelt. And Miss Hickok, too."

"Oh, I agree, I agree," Charlie said hastily. "Far be it from me to tell Lorena Hickok or the First Lady where to go." He had never met Eleanor Roosevelt, but he knew Lorena from his time on the East Coast, before FDR's election as governor of New York. She was a fierce journalist with an eye for a good story. She didn't suffer fools gladly. And she never took no for an answer.*

After supper, the two of them took glasses of wine into the living room, where Charlie turned on the RCA console radio—a Christmas present to both of them last year, bought with some of the extra money Fannie had earned from her latest Lilly Daché collection. Outside, the shadows lengthened. The window was open wide and a soft breeze blew through the screen, stirring the sheer curtains. Fannie was tired from

---

* You can read about Lorena Hickok and Mrs. Roosevelt in *Loving Eleanor*, Susan Wittig Albert's standalone biographical novel.

her long drive, so she kicked off her shoes and pulled her feet up under herself on the sofa with her needlework as Charlie settled in his favorite chair with *Jonah's Gourd Vine*, a first novel by Zora Neal Hurston, a black folklorist and anthropologist. There had been talk of Miss Hurston making a trip through the South and Charlie wanted a look at her work. He enjoyed what he was reading while the radio played softly in the background.

First in tonight's programming was the *Eddie Cantor Show*, sponsored by Pebeco Toothpaste on CBS—a musical variety show with comedy skits, ending with Eddie crooning his closing theme: "I love to spend / Each Sunday with you / As friend to friend / I'm sorry it's through . . ."

After that came the *Manhattan Merry-Go-Round* on NBC, which was built on the concept of a wining-and-dining tour of New York nightclubs. The show was filled with currently popular music and a few comic acts by people like Bert Lahr and Jimmy Durante. It featured a catchy theme song: "We're serving music, songs and laughter / Your happy heart will follow after."

The *Merry-Go-Round* was followed by Fannie's favorite, *The Ford Sunday Evening Hour* on CBS. The program featured a musical mix of popular ballads, classical favorites, hymns, and even the occasional show tune, played by the Detroit Symphony Orchestra before a live audience in the very grand Orchestra Hall. The Ford commercials were low-key, and it was said that Henry Ford himself chose the music.

For Fannie and Charlie, the evening ended with *Walter Winchell's Jergens Journal*, on the Blue Network, ABC. Winchell was a syndicated journalist famous for turning the news into entertainment. His news and commentary program always began with the loud, rapid-fire tapping of a telegraph key, followed by Winchell, in his harsh, staccato voice: "Good evening, Mr. and Mrs. North America and all the ships at sea, let's go to press!"

Charlie liked Winchell, so he dropped *Jonah* onto the floor beside his chair and leaned back to listen. Tonight, the journalist began with a colorful description of the speed trials at Bonneville Salt Flats in Utah, where Malcolm Campbell had just become the first man to drive an automobile over three hundred miles per hour. Then he swung into a more somber story about the four hundred or so veterans who had been lost in the Labor Day hurricane that had devastated the Florida Keys—and about Ernest Hemingway sailing his boat, *Pilar*, in a futile rescue attempt. Then he was about to go lighter, with a story about Saturday's Miss America contest, where the new talent show requirement had—

But he broke off in mid-sentence, was silent for a couple of beats, and then fired up his telegraph key again. "FLASH!" he cried excitedly. "FLASH, Baton Rouge, Louisiana. Senator Huey P. Long has just been shot by a would-be assassin in the Louisiana state capitol building."

There was a brief pause, as if Winchell himself didn't quite believe what he was saying. Then, breathlessly, "I repeat, Mr. and Mrs. North America! Senator Huey Long has been shot by a man in a white suit, just outside the governor's office in the state capitol building in Baton Rouge! Details are still coming in. You've heard it from Walter Winchell first. The Kingfish has been shot!"

❀

THE KINGFISH HAS BEEN SHOT!

As Sunday turned into Monday, the news swept through Darling. People glued their ears to their radios and listened, spellbound, as the shocking details began to emerge. Long wasn't dead yet, but he was gravely wounded and it was doubtful that he would survive. He had been shot by Dr. Carl Austin Weiss, a young eye, ear, nose, and throat physician, the son of another physician and the son-in-law of a prominent judge whom the senator had personally targeted for his political views. It was whispered that Long was attempting to discredit his opponent by spreading the rumor that the judge's family—one of the oldest and most influential in St. Landry Parish—had "coffee blood." Among the bills Long was attempting to push through was one intended to gerrymander the judge's district in a way that would make his reelection unlikely.

On both Saturday and Sunday evenings, the senator had gone to the capitol building in Baton Rouge to make sure that the legislature, which was in special session, was going to pass the bills he favored. He took his bodyguards with him, one of whom created quite a ruckus by slapping an elderly congressman.

Dr. Weiss, whose wife Yvonne had recently given birth to a son, was by all accounts a mild-mannered professional man with a strong sense of obligation to his family, his patients, and his city. He had taken Yvonne and the baby to early mass at St. Joseph's on Sunday morning, then to his in-laws, where they spent the rest of the day. That evening, after the baby was in bed, he took a shower and put on the white suit he'd worn to mass, telling his wife that he "had to go out on a sick call."

Instead, he drove his Buick to the capitol, parked it in the drive in front of the building, and walked inside. He encountered Senator Long in the hallway outside the governor's office. It wasn't clear what happened next, but in the space of a few seconds, the senator had been wounded and Dr. Weiss had died in a hail of bullets fired by Long's bodyguards. A little later, the doctor's .32 pistol was found on the floor nearby. Still later, it was reported that there were sixty-one bullet holes in his body, which meant that he was shot at least thirty times.

The senator had fled to his waiting automobile and was driven to Our Lady of the Lake Hospital. At first, his injuries did not appear serious, but his condition worsened by morning. His doctors informed his family and political associates that the surgery performed on him after the shooting had failed to stop his internal hemorrhaging, and that he could not survive additional surgery.

There was nothing more to be done. At 4:06 a.m. on Tuesday, September 10, thirty hours after the shooting, the Kingfish was dead.

When Charlie heard, he just shook his head. "Well," he said, "at least FDR won't have to send him to Timbuktu."

And then he wondered.

❀

THE KINGFISH HAS BEEN SHOT!

All day Tuesday, all over Darling, people were talking about what had happened over in Baton Rouge. They paused to chat at the post office, stopped one another on the street to ask about the latest news, huddled together in little groups at the courthouse, and dropped in at the *Dispatch* to share their conclusions with the editor.

All of them had the same thing to say: that they had seen those bodyguards in action out at the baseball field. It was no surprise that several of the senator's defenders had whipped out their guns and killed the man who shot their boss. In fact, it was argued, they might even have been compelled to that action by what happened right here in Darling just four days before the fatal shooting.

And as far as blame was concerned, yes, the guards had taken the law into their own hands, which they probably shouldn't have done. By law, the attacker should have been cuffed and hustled off to jail. But no jury in the state of Louisiana would have acquitted him, no matter how family-and-civic-minded his defense lawyer tried to make him appear. He would have been found guilty. He would have faced the hangman. Better that they shot him, Darling folks said. Saved Louisiana the expense and the Weiss family the agony of a trial. Now everybody could get on with their lives.

On the order of Alabama's Governor Graves, both the US and state flags were lowered to half-staff through the weekend. All of the members of the Darling Share Our Wealth Club, inconsolable, chipped in whatever they could afford and sent a large wreath of calla lilies to Baton Rouge. Huey was a martyr and for the next week, black was the color of the day.

But to many in Louisiana (and to some in Darling), Carl Austin Weiss was a hero, not a murderer. The good doctor had stood up for the rights of the people against a dangerous man who was undermining the principles of democracy. He had the courage to do what many others wanted to do but were too afraid to try.

On Tuesday, Dr. Weiss' funeral was conducted at St. Joseph's by Monsignor Gassler, who had said early mass at the same church just the Sunday before. Among the hundreds of mourners were the dean emeritus of the Louisiana State University law school, the district attorney for East Baton Rouge Parish, Congressman J. Y. Sanders Jr., every member of the Baton Rouge Kiwanis Club, and all of the doctor's patients and the family's many, many friends. It was, one observer remarked, "the largest funeral of an assassin in American history."

On Thursday, Huey Long was buried on the capitol grounds, where an estimated 175,000 people crowded onto the lawns, perched in live oak trees, or stood on nearby roofs. They watched silently as the heavy bronze casket was carried down forty-eight steps into a sunken garden. There, Long would lie inside a copper vault inside a concrete crypt.

The LSU band accompanied the coffin, marching in slow-step and playing "Every Man a King"—as a dirge.

❀

IT WAS ON THURSDAY, ABOUT THE TIME THE SENATOR WAS going into that concrete-and-copper crypt, that Virgil McCone called, long distance from Baton Rouge. His voice was high-pitched, thin and reedy. He sounded as if he was barely holding himself together. But he wouldn't say what was the matter.

"Gotta see you, Charlie," was all he would say. "I'll be there quick as I can."

He must have driven like the very devil, because he was walking into the *Dispatch* office just as Charlie's little team was calling it quits for the day. He hadn't shaved recently, and he looked like he'd been sleeping in his clothes. Charlie took one look at him, opened the bottom drawer of his desk, and pulled out a bottle of Bodeen Pyle's white lightning. Charlie no longer drank, but he kept it for emergencies.

"Here," he said, pushing the bottle across the desk. "You look like you need this."

"You bet I do," Virgil said. "Thanks." He closed his eyes and took a healthy swig, then another. He handed the bottle back. "Better take it, before I drown myself."

"Well, maybe you should," Charlie said. "Unless you gotta be sober for the next leg of your trip."

"That's what I came to talk to you about," Virgil said.

He reached into the side pocket of his wrinkled suit jacket and held up a fat envelope. "There's three thousand dollars here, cash. I want to buy into your newspaper, as a partner. You can use the money to get that Campbell Country press you were talking about last week or whatever else you want. Me, all I want is to stay here in Darling and write and do good newspaper work. Maybe get better acquainted with the lady who makes the meatloaf." He slapped the envelope onto the desk. "Right here, where nobody knows who I am."

Charlie stared at him. "Hold on a minute, Virgil. I'm not saying no to a partnership, but what about that book you're working on? The book that starts with Huey Long's impeachment. Now that he's dead, it's going to be a hot property. You need to get it finished and find yourself an agent and—"

Virgil shook his head violently. "Not gonna happen. The book is as dead as Huey. And I can't do anything under my name. So far as the rest of the world is concerned, I'm somebody else. Haven't picked out a new name yet, but I will. Soon as I can pull myself together."

He pushed the envelope across the desk to Charlie. "Take it. I wrote up a simple partnership agreement. It's in there, with the money. If you want to negotiate on terms, that's fine. Or if you want your lawyer to draw up the paper, that's fine, too. I'll be easy. I just want to get it *done*."

Charlie looked down at the envelope. Three thousand dollars. It was close to the amount of the loan he'd hoped to get from Alvin Duffy. Together with Fannie's investment, it would enable him to turn the *Dispatch* into the finest little newspaper in Alabama, maybe even in all of the South. And Virgil would bring exactly the kind of journalistic talent he needed to make this happen. But first—

"What the hell is going on here, Virgil? I gotta know what you're running from."

Virgil looked over his shoulder. "You don't want to know." His voice was taut as a bowstring. "It's dangerous. It nearly got me *killed*, I tell you. It could get you killed, too."

"Virgil," Charlie said patiently, "I remember the two of us

digging into a foxhole in France. *That* was where we could've been killed." He pushed the envelope back in Virgil's direction. "Now you tell me what's going on with you, or I'm booting you and your money out the damn door. You got that, friend?"

It took a few more moments and a few more strong words, but Virgil finally got it. And then, stopping and starting and refueling with a few more pulls at Bodeen's bottle, he managed to get the story out.

He had been with the rest of the press pool at the Louisiana state capitol on Sunday evening. Since it was the weekend and Huey wasn't expected to make any news, the group was small, only three or four. Most of the evening, they'd hung out in the gallery of the House chambers, watching Huey twist arms and talk tough down on the floor, telling people what he was going to do to them if they didn't vote his way. Finally, close to nine o'clock, the senator left, along with a couple of staff and four or five of his bodyguards. The reporters and a camera man trooped wearily behind, Virgil, as it happened, in the front of the pack.

Huey stopped at the governor's office, which took only a few minutes. He came out and started down the hall, knotted into a tight little group with his bodyguards and a couple of state troopers close around, followed by the reporters. The hall was about twelve feet wide, with marble walls and a marble floor. The group was moving along at a pretty fast clip, with Virgil close behind Joe Messina, who was behind and to the right of Long.

After a dozen paces, the group came face to face with a slender, thin-shouldered man in a white suit. He was wearing round gold-rimmed glasses that gave him the look of an earnest school teacher. The man stepped up to Long and said something to him. Virgil was behind Joe Messina, one of the bodyguards, who was immediately behind and to the right of

Long. He couldn't hear what the man was saying, although he didn't sound angry.

But all of a sudden, Long put a hand to the guy's chest to shove him out of the way. As he did, Virgil saw Messina pull his sidearm out of its holster. It hung up, and when he jerked it free, it cocked and fired and hit Long in the back, in the kidney area.

When Messina's gun went off, the other bodyguards immediately yanked out their guns and began firing at the man in the white suit. Virgil said there were some thirty or forty rounds fired, with bullets whizzing around fast, ricocheting off the walls and the floor. One of them hit Long in the groin.

"Wait a minute," Charlie said. "I saw the wires. They were reporting that the doctors said he was shot *once*, in the upper right side, with the bullet exiting in the back."

"Yeah. That's what they said, all right," Virgil replied bleakly. "But it's not true. That wasn't an exit wound in the back, it was an entrance wound. He was shot in the back first, then the front."

And what was more, the man in the white suit was unarmed, Virgil said. When that uncomfortable fact was discovered, one of the state troopers supplied a throw-down weapon, a .25 caliber handgun he had picked up when he helped raid a gambling parlor that afternoon. That gun was replaced with Weiss' own .32 caliber pistol, which the troopers took from the glove compartment of his automobile, found parked outside the capitol building after the shooting.

"Took from Weiss' automobile?" Charlie asked, frowning. "How did you learn that?"

"From one of the troopers," Virgil said. "A guy I've known for a while—a poker buddy. He didn't feel right about what was being done. Blaming Dr. Weiss, I mean, for an accident caused by one of Long's own bodyguards. He's the one who told me I'd better make myself scarce."

"But I don't—"

"Of course you do," Virgil said impatiently. "What happened after the shootings was a law-enforcement conspiracy to cover up the accidental death of the senator and the killing of Dr. Weiss. A *conspiracy*. And anybody who tries to tell the true story is going to be silenced." He gave Charlie a hard look. "You got that, Charlie?"

"I got it," Charlie said slowly. "It doesn't sound . . . safe. To report the true story, I mean. At least, not now." He paused. "But what about later? Don't you think it could be told—later?"

"Maybe," Virgil said. "But that's not the only story, you know. There's plenty of other stories out there, waiting to be told." He nodded at the envelope. "Have I got a job? You gonna take that or not?"

"I'm taking it," Charlie said, picking up the envelope. "You and I are going to build us a real newspaper, Virgil. And maybe someday you'll feel like writing the *true* story about the way the Kingfish died."

# RECIPES AND RESOURCES

You can find recipes for this book on Susan's website: **www.susanalbert.com**, on the Mysteries tab. (Look for the book title and scroll down to the link near the bottom of the page.)

There, too, you will find Elizabeth Lacy's Garden Gate column, featuring the red hot poker lily, as well as the Dahlias' suggestions for other red flowers you're sure to enjoy.

# ABOUT SUSAN WITTIG ALBERT

GROWING UP ON A FARM ON THE ILLINOIS PRAIRIE, SUSAN learned that books could take her anywhere, and reading and writing became passions that have accompanied her throughout her life. She earned an undergraduate degree in English from the University of Illinois at Urbana and a PhD in medieval studies from the University of California at Berkeley. After fifteen years of faculty and administrative appointments at the University of Texas, Tulane University, and Texas State University, she left her academic career to write full time.

Now, there are over four million copies of Susan's books in print. Her best-selling mystery fiction includes the Darling Dahlias Depression-era mysteries, the China Bayles Herbal Mysteries, the Cottage Tales of Beatrix Potter, and (under the pseudonym of Robin Paige) a series of Victorian-Edwardian mysteries with her husband, Bill Albert.

Susan's biographical historical novels feature remarkable women—hidden figures who have not been recognized because they stand in the shadows of more widely known people. This series includes *A Wilder Rose*, the story of Rose Wilder Lane and the writing of the Little House books; *Loving Eleanor*, a fictional account of the friendship of Lorena Hickok and Eleanor Roosevelt; and *The General's Women*, a novel about the World War II romantic triangle of Dwight Eisenhower, his wife Mamie, and his driver and secretary Kay Summersby. Planned for late 2022: *Maria and Georgia*, a novel about the friendship of Maria Chabot and artist Georgia O'Keeffe.

Susan is also the author of two memoirs: *An Extraordinary Year of Ordinary Days* and *Together, Alone: A Memoir of Marriage and Place.* Other nonfiction titles include *What Wildness Is This: Women Write about the Southwest* (winner of the 2009 Willa Award for Creative Nonfiction); *Writing from Life: Telling the Soul's Story*; and *Work of Her Own: A Woman's Guide to Success off the Career Track.*

An active participant in the literary community, Susan is the founder of the Story Circle Network, a nonprofit organization for women writers, and a member of Sisters in Crime, Women Writing the West, Mystery Writers of America, and the Texas Institute of Letters. She and her husband Bill live on thirty-one acres in the Texas Hill Country, where she gardens, tends chickens and geese, and indulges her passions for needlework and (of course) reading.